Sexy Beast III

Also by Kate Douglas:

Wolf Tales

"Chanku Rising" in *Sexy Beast*

Wolf Tales II

"Camille's Dawn" in *Wild Nights*

Wolf Tales III

"Chanku Fallen" in *Sexy Beast II*

Wolf Tales IV

Also by Lacy Danes:

What She Craves

Also by Morgan Hawke:

Kiss of the Wolf

Sexy Beast III

KATE DOUGLAS
LACY DANES
MORGAN HAWKE

APHRODISIA

KENSINGTON PUBLISHING CORP.

http://www.kensingtonbooks.com

KENSINGTON BOOKS are published by

Kensington Publishing Corp.
850 Third Avenue
New York, NY 10022

All Kensington Titles, Imprints, and Distributed Lines are available at special quantity discounts for bulk purchases for sales promotions, premiums, fund-raising, and educational or institutional use.

Special book excerpts or customized printings can also be created to fit specific needs. For details, write or phone the office of the Kensington special sales manager: Kensington Publishing Corp., 850 Third Avenue, New York, NY 10022, attn: Special Sales Department, Phone: 1-800-221-2647.

Aphrodisia and the A logo Reg. U.S. Pat. & TM Off.

ISBN-13: 978-0-7582-1987-9
ISBN-10: 0-7582-1987-3

First Trade Paperback Printing: September 2007

10 9 8 7 6 5 4 3 2 1

Printed in the United States of America

CONTENTS

Chanku Journey

Kate Douglas

1

Tia Mason stared, transfixed by the creamy white box covering her lap. After a long, silent moment, she slowly raised her head, glanced to her right, and caught her new packmate, Lisa Quinn, smiling at her. Tia took a deep breath. Let it out. Took another. With trembling hands, she slipped her fingers beneath the white satin ribbon and pushed it down the length of the box and over the end. She looked at Lisa once more, then stared at the box again.

"What's the matter? You act like you're afraid it'll bite." Lisa's teasing laughter was followed by a soft, supportive hand on Tia's forearm. "Open it, hon. It's okay."

Tia nodded as she slipped her fingers beneath the edges of the stiff cardboard lid and lifted it. A dusty hint of rose-scented sachet wafted into the air. Her first thought was how much the sweet perfume reminded her of her mother.

Then she promptly burst into tears.

She was so not ready for this. She forced the lid back on the box. The scent of the rose sachet lingered. "I can't do it, Lisa. I really can't do it."

"Can't do what? Marry your bonded mate, the man you've been in love with since the first time you saw him? Wear your mother's wedding gown? Say 'I do' in front of the people who love you? C'mon, hon. You should be happy, not sitting here in a puddle of tears. What's the matter?"

Tia tried to talk, couldn't, and took the tissue Lisa shoved into her hand. She blew her nose and wiped her eyes. "I have panic attacks just thinking about the wedding. What does that tell you? Putting on my mother's dress ..." She brushed the top of the box with her fingers. "Having Dad walk me down the aisle. I mean, it all sounds perfectly normal, but everything's going to change and it's scaring the crap out of me."

Lisa snorted. Tia swung her head around and glared. "You're not taking me very seriously, are you?"

Holding up both hands, Lisa said, "Yes. Yes, I am, but it's just so funny to hear you complaining about something normal. You're a shapeshifter, for crying out loud. A fucking wolf, Tia, just like the rest of the pack. There's not anything remotely normal about any of us."

Tia glared at Lisa and then realized she suddenly felt like giggling, not crying. With a dramatic sigh, she held out her hand for another tissue, which Lisa dropped into her palm. Tia wiped her eyes again, patted the top of the box for good measure, and settled back against the arm of the couch. "Okay," she said, fighting the lingering urge to laugh hysterically, "panic attack averted. For now. I've got it under control. Dad may have to carry me down the aisle kicking and screaming, but ..."

"You'll be fine. We'll check out the dress later if you want. Concentrate on who's coming." Lisa poured a glass of wine and handed it to Tia, obviously prepared for some heavy-duty girl talk. "It's more important, don't you think, to focus on the people who love you, not on whether you're going to make it down the aisle without tripping over your toes?"

Tia laughed. "Gee, thanks. Now you've given me a whole

new set of worries." She sipped at the chilled Pinot Grigio and began to relax. Thank goodness for Lisa. Like her mate, Tinker, she was loving and warm and so wonderfully practical. Though she hadn't known Lisa all that long, Tia felt unbelievably comfortable with her.

Just as she felt comfortable with all the others who were coming here to celebrate. Every one of them, including the often mysterious Anton Cheval. Would she and Luc have the same kind of loving relationship as Keisha and Anton? Sometimes Tia found it hard to believe Luc loved her as much as he did, as much as she loved him.

Then she'd remember their mating bond, the fact there were no secrets between them. Yes, he definitely loved her. In every way possible, at every opportunity.

She glanced at Lisa and realized that, in their own way, all of her pack members loved her, and Tia loved every one of them. The bond of Chanku was more than mere membership in a particular pack; it was a blood link among all of them, a tie that could not be broken.

She thought of Shannon, her longtime friend who was also coming west to be her maid of honor. They'd been like sisters growing up, long before either one of them suspected they were connected by more than friendship but also by their Chanku blood.

Shannon was coming out from Maine with her mate, Jacob Trent, along with Lisa's brother, Baylor. Tia took Lisa's hand and squeezed her fingers. "I just thought of Bay and it reminded me, I got a call last night from Mik Fuentes. He said they've completed their assignment in Alabama in plenty of time to get here for the wedding, so not only will Baylor be here, you'll finally get to see your sister Tala."

A huge smile spread across Lisa's face. "I can't wait to see Mary Ellen . . . er, Tala, and Bay. It's been over ten years. I still can't believe she's bonded with two men."

Tia squeezed Lisa's hand again. "Makes my bout of nerves look pretty dumb. You must be a basket case, waiting to reunite with your brother and sister."

Lisa nodded. "Excited, scared. Anxious . . . We were such a dysfunctional family."

Typical of Chanku, Tia thought. So confusing, to live as a human with the heart and mind of a wolf buried away, hidden deep in your soul. She was one of the lucky ones. She'd found the answers to all her questions in the love of one man, in the love of the pack.

Like Lisa, she'd been given the gift of an amazing birthright. Lisa was right. What was she so nervous about? Tia leaned close and kissed Lisa on the lips. "You're not dysfunctional anymore . . . and that brother of yours . . . wow! When Bay was here for those two months working while Luc got his resignation from the Secret Service all straightened out . . ." Tia fanned herself with her palm. "He is very, very hot."

"If you say so." Lisa laughed.

Lisa's dry comment and burst of laughter wiped away all of Tia's lingering nerves. For now. She slipped the lid off the box in her lap and gently shook her mother's wedding dress out of the tissue. "I can't imagine this will fit. Mom was such a tiny little thing." She held it up, barely controlling the sudden sting of tears behind her eyes. If only Camille had lived to see this day.

"Well, you're skinny all around. Just taller, I'll bet." Lisa took the white satin gown with its tiny seed pearls and held it up to Tia. "It probably touched the ground on your mom. Try it on. I think it's going to be gorgeous. I'm a decent seamstress. Trust me. I'll make it work."

Tia stood up and slipped her shirt over her head. It had better work. She'd put this off much too long—the wedding was barely two weeks away.

* * *

Shannon Murphy rolled over in bed and snuggled close against her packmate's backside. The Maine morning was crisp and cold, and Baylor Quinn radiated heat like a furnace. He slept soundly, but when she wrapped her fingers around his partially tumescent cock, he rolled his hips closer to her belly.

Even in sleep the man was more than a handful. Her fingertips barely met where they circled his girth. Still half asleep herself, Shannon rubbed her thumb lazily over the smooth flesh of the crown, touching the sensitive tip usually covered by Bay's foreskin.

Bay moaned in his sleep. The thrusting movement of his hips took on a slow but steady rhythm as Shannon rubbed lazy circles over his silky skin.

Where was Jake? She nuzzled her chin along Bay's spine and cast her thoughts for her mate. He'd been gone since long before dawn. She imagined him even now, racing along the dark trails beneath the heavy canopy of leaves with a big wolven grin on his face.

There was no answer to Shannon's questing thoughts. Instead, the mattress dipped behind her and her mate slipped beneath the covers. Jake smelled of forest and golden grass. His skin felt icy from the morning chill.

Shannon shivered when he stretched full-length along her spine. His nipples were hard little points pressing into her back. His cock, as hot as his body was cold, slipped naturally between her legs from behind and rested hard and thick against her sex.

"Were you starting without me?" he whispered.

Shannon felt the warm tickle of Jake's breath against her ear. "Thought about it. I was getting worried. I didn't expect you to be gone for so long."

"I needed the run. I've had a lot on my mind."

"I forgot to ask. Did you get the plane tickets yet for San

Francisco?" Shannon tilted her hips just enough to bring his cock into perfect contact with her clit. "The wedding is just two weeks away."

That's part of what's on my mind.

Jake's switch to mindtalking hinted at more concern than mere tickets from Maine to San Francisco. *What's up?* Shannon asked.

I plan to tell Luc we're staying here permanently. Is that okay with you? He knows I've been thinking of my own pack, but . . .

You know it's okay with me, though I do want to go to the wedding. I hardly know the guys, but Tia's been my best friend for most of my life.

Wanna go on the back of my bike?

"What?" Shannon whispered fiercely as she swung her head around to look over her shoulder at Jake. He was grinning like a damned fool, even as his cock began riding slick and fast along the crease of her butt and down between her thighs. "That's got to be at least three thousand miles. I don't think so."

"Think of all that power between your legs." His voice dropped to a deeper level as he whispered the words against her neck. His lips tickled her nape. He tilted his hips and angled his cock higher until the silky crown kissed her swollen clit. Shannon moaned when he nuzzled the side of her neck and whispered in her ear. His rough, sexy voice affirmed the images filling her mind and heating her sex.

"Think of it, sweetheart . . . the rumble of that big engine throbbing, hot and solid and almost alive, the way it vibrates the warm leather over your sweet little pussy. The smells of forest and plains and the wind in your face . . ." Jake emphasized his words with the smooth glide of his cock over her suddenly very wet sex and almost took the breath from Shannon's lungs.

Almost.

She took a deep breath and reached for a bit of common sense and control. "Right. The wind in my face and my hair tied in knots. You forget, Bay doesn't have a bike and he's going with us." Shannon let go of Bay's now fully erect cock, slipped away from Jake's, and rolled over completely. Now that she could glare directly at Jake, Shannon realized he didn't seem the least perturbed.

Bay raised up and flopped over on his left side, obviously wide awake. At least, his cock was awake. Shannon felt the thick slide of it against her buttocks and couldn't help but angle her hips just enough for him to take over Jake's smooth glide.

Bay nipped her shoulder and chuckled softly in Shannon's ear. "Sorry, sweetie. Bay does have a bike. Jake talked me into buying one yesterday. I pick it up Monday."

"I don't believe you two." She really should put her foot down, but all the time Shannon was fuming, Bay was rubbing his cock between her cheeks and Jake was meeting him in the middle, rubbing slowly between her legs.

It was hard to argue with two guys when they double teamed a girl. She knew they got off on the sensation of their sizeable penises sliding one against the other as much as they did the creamy heat between her legs. Shannon tilted her hips back against Bay's belly as his arms came around her waist and his hands found both her breasts. Crossing his arms over her chest, Bay plucked at her nipples, pinching them none too gently between callused fingers.

Not to be outdone, Jake hugged Shannon, grabbing her buttocks with his fingers, slipping them between her butt and Bay's flat belly to press against her anus. She wriggled closer, realizing Jake had managed not only to sandwich her even tighter between the two men, but that he also stroked Bay's cock with his fingertips on each thrust.

Shannon closed her eyes and absorbed the sensations, the myriad nerves tingling with each perfect sweep of Jake's fingers. She heard the rustle of crisp sheets, the steady breathing of both men, and the squishy, wet sounds of their cocks sliding against each other between her legs. When she listened very carefully, she caught the rapid beat of their hearts and the wet little click of two swollen cock heads rubbing, one past the other.

She pictured the flared crowns, wet and distended now, glistening with fluids from her well-lubricated sex blended with the uncontrollable flow of pre-cum seeping from the tips. Both men were uncut. Their foreskins would be stretched back behind the swollen heads now, the skin flushed dark red, the sensitive tips exposed.

Shannon's pussy clenched as Jake's cock slipped between her slick labia with the lightest of touches. She bit back a moan. Every part of her body reacted, teased by the passage, by the smooth heat and perfect friction against her ass and her clit. Jake had found a rhythm now, pressing against her sphincter with his fingers as he thrust his cock slowly between her legs. Bay's tight grasp on her nipples made them ache, but the pain sent a constant pulse of pleasure directly to her clit.

She tightened the muscles in her sex against the hollow, needy sensation growing in the pit of her belly. Jake's fingers pressed tighter against her ass, Bay twisted her nipples, and their cocks slipped one over the other against her swollen sex.

The tension grew. She needed penetration, anything to take her over the edge. Shannon's breathing turned choppy; her eyes closed as she absorbed the pleasure. Her whole body shivered with growing arousal.

Jake's fingers penetrated her ass just as Bay pinched her nipples. Shannon jerked and screamed, her back arching as she spasmed through her first climax, shuddering and shivering, her pussy awash in a liquid orgasmic release.

Without even breaking rhythm, Jake entered her with his next stroke, burying himself all the way to the hilt on a single thrust. Shannon's muscles clenched around his cock. Her sex still rippled with aftershocks as Jake rolled over to his back and took her with him.

Bay quickly knelt between their legs and pressed the broad crown of his cock against her bottom. Still relaxed from Jake's fingers, Shannon tilted her hips to make Bay's access easier. He circled the puckered entrance with his fingers first, relaxing her even more, then pressed harder with his cock. Shannon pushed out as Bay moved forward. He was so damned big and it burned when he stretched her, slowly pressing in and out, a little farther each time as he worked beyond her tight sphincter. Once his broad crown passed beyond the loop of muscle, the pain disappeared, melding swiftly into a dark slide of pleasure. Shannon groaned as Bay entered her slowly, carefully, deeply.

Jake sighed as well. Sex-drugged, drifting in waves of sensation, Shannon opened her eyes and stared into his, into the deep amber eyes shaded in inky lashes so much like Bay's. Jake took her hands in his and stretched her arms over his head, pulling her down until her nipples rubbed the thick hair on his chest. Bay stretched out over her body and covered the backs of her hands, linking his fingers with Jake's.

Connected now, with Shannon sandwiched between them, their bodies linked but their thoughts still private, Bay slowly began moving his hips. He was the one who directed them, sliding deep inside Shannon, his erection slipping past Jake's, separated by nothing more than the thin membrane dividing her passages.

She imagined their cocks: smooth skin over muscle, swollen with blood and hard as baseball bats, slowly penetrating and retreating, one past the other deep inside her body. She tried to imagine the sensation, what her men were feeling with each pull and thrust. It was something she'd shared with both of them before.

Imagination was good, but Shannon wanted reality. She

opened her mind to her lovers, slipping quietly into their thoughts and feelings, grasping at once the deep, lush sensuality of two men, lovers and friends, slowly but surely fucking each other through the woman they loved.

They didn't so much make love to Shannon as they loved each other within her body. Feeling as much like a beloved vessel as a participant, Shannon lost herself to sensation, to the coarse hair on Jake's chest scraping her tender nipples, to the hard muscles of Bay's chest and the softer, silkier hair that spread over his. She loved the way it brushed against her back, loved the small tremors she felt in his body as he fought the rising level of excitement threatening his control.

She slipped into Bay's mind, awash in his love for Jake and for herself, a pure, unquestioned love for both of them, and the hope he had to satisfy their needs and desires. She allowed herself a moment of pure sensation, the tight slide deep inside her rectum and the way her body pulled at Bay's cock, the way her muscles clenched tightly around the base of his penis like a hot, wet fist.

Bay felt it from his spine to his balls, that tight, needy pull against him, but the sensations were secondary to the solid contact between his cock and Jake's. Shannon realized she was clenching her muscles even tighter, responding to Bay's need to be closer to Jake, closer to her.

She slipped her searching thoughts free of Bay then, concentrating instead on Jake. His love was unquestionable, his pride in her almost undoing her. As caught in sensation as Bay, Jake still made love to Shannon first, to Bay second. He held on to control by a thread. Each rhythmic contraction of Shannon's sex brought him closer to the edge, but he fought it with everything he had.

Bay's cock slid past Jake's, and Jake shuddered beneath her. Shannon rubbed her taut nipples across Jake's chest and felt his pectoral muscles jerk in response. She tightened her sex, clenching both men in her velvet clasp.

Short gasps escaped them as the breath hitched in their throats. At the same time, she sensed a silent communication pass between her lovers; she felt their muscles tense and their huge cocks, if possible, grow larger.

Jake let go of Shannon's hands, tilted his hips, and drew his knees up on either side of her, lifting her higher, dragging the full length of his cock over her clit on both retreat and entry. Bay shifted just a bit, driving deeper inside with every well-aimed thrust. Shannon felt the solid pressure against her perineum and knew their sacs pressed tightly together with each stroke, knew their trembling bodies fought the need to come.

Shannon fought it as well, even as the intensity of their loving grew, as her body shivered and her legs trembled with pleasure. Sensory overload flooded her mind. The combination of both Jake and Bay, of their arousal, of their overwhelming desire, of their love in all its myriad forms filled her thoughts, became Shannon's thoughts and she cried out with the unbelievable surge of sensations.

Her scream was the trigger, the key that sent both men into climax. Jake's thrust lifted her into Bay. Bay's cock drove deep, but he didn't hold at the point of orgasm.

Instead he thrust harder, sliding deep into her with Jake, both of them going in and out in tandem, each one filling her with their seed. Their groans enveloped her senses; their semen, hot and thick, filled her body.

Her eyes refused to focus, and her thoughts scattered. Shannon's entire body clenched in one spasmodic tremor with muscles locked, holding both men inside. Her heart pounded in her chest and sweat covered her body front and back, soaking the bedding. Hers? Bay's? Jake's?

Shannon's legs trembled beneath Bay's; her breasts, swollen and tender, throbbed in time with her racing heart. Her vision refused to clear. Little black spots wavered in front of her eyes.

Lungs heaving, she dragged in deep, ragged breaths of air.

Her breasts pressed against Jake's rising and falling chest; her back felt compressed by Bay's weight. When she finally thought to open her thoughts to her men, there was a sense of surprise in both their minds, that the sex could be this good, this hot, time after time, two men with one woman.

Their woman.

Hadn't they always fantasized two women, one man?

Shannon would have smiled if she'd had the energy. Enervated, she lay there, compressed between Bay and Jake, welcoming Bay's weight, Jake's strength.

Her vision cleared slowly, the spots fading as her heart settled once again into its normal rhythm. Still she sprawled bonelessly over Jake's body, loving the feeling of both men and the knowledge they loved her, and that, after so many years searching, she'd finally found love.

Jake swept her tangled hair back from her forehead. "Anyway," he said, as if he'd not once again rocked her world, "I really think it would be an adventure to take the bike out to California. What do you say?"

Bay tilted his hips, pressing against her buttocks. His cock was no longer hard as a post, but she still felt him deep inside her. "Say yes, Shannon. Please?"

"Oh Lord, that feels good. You're cheating."

Laughing, Bay slipped free of Shannon's body and rolled to one side. He groaned. "Okay, no more undue influence." Bay swatted her on the butt, then crawled off the bed and headed for the bathroom.

Shannon sighed and tightened her vaginal muscles around Jake's cock. He'd softened a bit as well but still managed to fill her with sensation. "How will I carry enough clothes? We're supposed to have a bachelorette party for Tia, and I'll need something for the wedding and . . ."

"The bike's got big panniers, but we're going to San Francisco.

They have stores. You can buy all new clothes when we get there and mail them home when it's time to leave. In fact, you can even fly home if you like and Bay and I will ride back on our own. Please, sweetie? It'll be such a cool adventure."

Laughing, Shannon lowered her head to Jake's chest. "You're willing to bribe me with a shopping trip in San Francisco? Your credit card?" He nodded. "That's cheating. I may be a wolf at heart, but it doesn't affect my shopping gene." She rubbed her nose against his chest, licked the nipple over his heart, then grumbled, "As if I have any say in the matter? Yes, we'll take the bikes to San Francisco. But I'll be damned if I sleep in a tent. Nice motels all the way, good restaurants, and stops whenever my butt gets tired or I have to pee. And backrubs. I insist on backrubs."

"Damn, woman. You drive a hard bargain." Jake lifted her chin with his hands and kissed her soundly. Shannon kissed him back and wondered what kind of fool she was.

Jake ended the kiss with a shout. "Hey! Baylor . . . we won! She said yes!"

Over three thousand miles on a motorcycle? Shannon dropped her forehead against Jake's chest. She must be nuts.

Anton Cheval checked the calendar one more time, then gazed steadily at his very pregnant mate. She stood in the doorway to his office with all the grace of an African queen: elegant, self-confident, and sexy as hell, despite the fact she was into her eighth month of pregnancy. "We're pushing it, love, flying to San Francisco for your cousin's wedding. What if you deliver early?"

Keisha laughed and Anton knew he was going to cave. So many were in awe of him, but never this lovely woman. No respect from her at all. He had to bite back a smile.

"Then you, my love, will deliver our daughter." She stepped

into the room, covered his hand with hers, and placed her other palm over his heart.

He felt the damned thing skip a beat. She had no idea how much power she held over him, how much he needed her. Anton covered her hand and pressed it against his chest. "It's not something to joke about. I'm terrified of anything happening to . . ."

"Nothing will happen. Besides, we'll have Stefan and Xandi along, and Oliver, too. I imagine he knows how to deliver babies, right?"

"Oliver is good at many things, but I'm not sure the practice of obstetrics is in his repertoire. We have two weeks. If you're still feeling this good, then we can . . ."

Keisha shook her head. "No, we don't have two weeks. We need to be there in less than a week. I am not going to miss Tia's bachelorette party, even if I can't drink those fuzzy little concoctions she loves."

Stefan and Xandi wandered into the room. Anton looked up and shrugged his shoulders. Stefan was the brother he'd never had, the son he loved, and the lover who kept him sane at times like these. "How do you feel about this trip, Stefan? I'm concerned about the girls traveling so far this late in their pregnancies. I could fly down on my own, perform the ceremony as I promised Tia and . . ."

"Not in this life you won't!" Keisha stood and glared at Anton. She reached for Xandi and the two women clasped hands.

He knew then the battle was a foregone conclusion. Stefan caught his eye, shrugged his shoulders once again, and then burst into laughter. "It is a matriarchal society, you know." He leaned over and kissed his mate. "When you mate with a Chanku bitch, she gets the balls."

Anton raised his eyes to the heavens . . . actually, to the large chandelier over the dining room table. "There are days, Stefan, when I wish I'd never divulged that bit of information."

Keisha stood up. Her body was heavy with her pregnancy, but he'd never seen her more beautiful. Nor, Anton thought, had she ever been more powerful, more sure of herself. "Your divulging information makes no difference. We are what we are. We need to leave by Thursday. Can you make arrangements so the plane is ready to go by then?"

Anton nodded, but the sense of misgiving wouldn't leave him. Xandi's pregnancy wasn't quite as far along as Keisha's, but both women were well beyond the time when doctors would normally allow them to travel. However, their doctor, one of the few familiar with the Chanku species, had found no reason to inhibit travel, at least for another few weeks.

Damned charlatan. Unfortunately, the man was brilliant and someone Anton had learned to respect.

"The plane will be ready. As will I. We leave on Thursday." He glanced over Keisha's head and caught Stefan's eyes. The bastard had a grin on his face a mile wide, but then he loved it when Anton lost a battle. Damn, if he didn't love the man, he'd kill him where he stood.

Tala held the tiny baby in her arms for one last look. The infant stared up at her, fearless, filled with trust. Her innocence made Tala think of how much she'd had to learn to trust over the past few months. How much farther she still had to go. Blinking back tears, she handed the child over to the paramedic and signaled to the two large wolves sitting patiently beside her. It was time to go home.

The Alabama police chief who'd called in the team from Pack Dynamics caught Tala before she could gather her crew and leave. "We found the kidnapper back in the swamp. Was it necessary to rip out his throat?" He glanced nervously at the wolves sitting calmly beside Tala. "I had no idea they were killers."

"So was the man who died." Tala nodded toward the helicopter lifting off with the child safely inside. Dust and leaves swirled in the golden rays of the late afternoon sun as the chopper whirled away toward Mobile. The baby would be returned to her mother: safe, unharmed, and hopefully young enough that this terrible incident would be forgotten. "The kidnapper didn't hesitate to kill the nanny. The child would have died the moment the ransom was paid. You knew it. We knew it. The bastard's killed before. This time he made a mistake when he went after my wolves with a gun. They had no choice."

The police chief shook his head. "Amazing animals. They look so calm sitting there, so intelligent. You'd never guess they killed a man not an hour ago. As tiny as you are, don't you ever worry about them? I was surprised to see they hadn't been castrated, that you worked with intact males. They can be so aggressive."

Tala immediately threw up her mental blocks. No way could she carry on an intelligent conversation with the reaction she was certain the guys had to the chief's innocent comment. Biting back laughter, she shook her head. If only the man knew . . . "No. We don't believe in neutering. We need their aggressive tendencies. They're very well trained." She patted both animals on their heads. The larger one growled. The police chief took a step back.

"I sure hope so." He held out his hand. Tala took his in a firm grasp, and they shook hands. Another crisis averted.

"We'll be going now. I have a long drive back to the airport, and my boys need some rest before the flight. You have Ulrich Mason's number if you need to reach us, and of course we'll be available should there be any hearings. I'm glad we were able to help." Tala turned and walked away with the two huge wolves following close behind. She felt the chief's gaze on her back all the way to her SUV. She'd left the rental vehicle with its darkly tinted windows parked at the side of the road.

"Okay guys. Get in." She opened the door and both animals jumped into the back seat. Tala climbed in, fastened her seat belt, and pulled out onto the pavement, heading off into the setting sun. It felt good, knowing their intervention had saved that little girl's life.

Tala glanced into the rearview mirror at the two unbelievably beautiful naked men slipping into jeans and shirts. Mik Fuentes looked up and caught her eye. The smile that spread slowly across his face made her heart beat a little faster and the muscles in her pussy clench in anticipation. He shoved his long, black hair out of his eyes and winked.

"Neutered, eh? Not this puppy."

AJ Temple pulled his knit shirt over his head and nudged Mik. "Maybe that's your problem. No balls." He winked. Tala returned his grin in the reflection in the rearview mirror. With his curling dark hair and thick black lashes around those amber eyes, he was absolutely gorgeous . . . and full of the devil.

Mik leaned back in the seat and folded his muscular arms behind his head. "You were sucking on something of mine last night, and it wasn't my cock. That piece of meat was resting comfortably deep inside our lady's lovely little pussy."

AJ laughed, but he squirmed in his seat. Tala wished she was tall enough to see more of him in the mirror because she was absolutely positive he'd gotten hard just thinking about sucking Mik's balls. Her pussy clenched in sympathy. There was something so hot about sex in a motel room with two absolutely gorgeous men.

Her men. Her bonded mates. Damn, how had she ever gotten so lucky? Tala turned her attention toward the road west. Musing aloud, she asked, "What do you guys think of driving instead of flying home? There's a lot of country I haven't seen between here and California." *And a lot of motel rooms . . .* For a retired prostitute who'd really loved her work, roadside motels were pretty special places.

"Sounds good." Mik fastened his seatbelt and nudged AJ. "You know how it is with Tala and those seedy little motels . . ."

2

Shannon fastened her helmet, settled her butt against the smooth leather seat, and wondered once again how the hell she'd let herself get talked into traveling three thousand miles on a motorcycle. She glanced over her shoulder just as Bay threw his leg over the saddle of his bike, one identical to Jake's.

Dressed similarly to Jake in full black leathers with a full-face black helmet, Bay looked just as tall, lean, and dangerous as her bonded mate . . . Both of them were sexy as hell. Jake started his bike just as Bay turned the key in his. The low rumble sent a shiver of arousal through Shannon's pussy and she wrapped her arms around Jake's waist.

He gave Bay a thumbs up and pulled slowly out of their driveway. The early morning air was crisp and cool, the sky already fading from pink to blue, and the road beckoned. Shannon shifted on the seat of the big bike and held on tight as they picked up speed and headed out.

Eight hours and almost four hundred miles later, Shannon was more than ready to call it a day. They pulled into a nice motel in a forested region, but for the life of her she couldn't even say what state they were in. All that mattered was a hot shower and a bed with clean sheets. She wasn't even sure she'd be able to eat.

Her pussy no longer felt the vibrations. The poor thing was numb. Bay took care of getting them a room with two king-sized beds. Shannon claimed one for herself. "I am sleeping alone. Tonight, and quite possibly every night hereafter. I can't believe you two talked me into this." She flopped backward on the mattress and covered her eyes with the back of her hand.

Chuckling quietly, Jake and Bay went in search of dinner. Shannon waited until they left and then headed for the shower. It even hurt to walk.

An hour later, she pushed herself away from the table littered with Chinese take-out cartons. "I'm exhausted. Bedtime for me. My butt will never be the same and my crotch has been vibrated beyond repair."

"Would a massage help?" Bay sat back in his chair with his feet on the edge of the bed and stretched. He wore nothing but jeans, the zipper only partially raised, the taut muscles of his belly glistening in the low light. "I'm sore, but I imagine your muscles are really tight." He locked his fingers behind his head and stretched again.

"Good idea," Jake said, before she'd even had a chance to reply. Somehow, within seconds, Shannon was naked and spread out on her tummy on the bed she'd claimed with a man kneeling on either side of her.

Jake squirted lotion into his hand and passed the bottle to Bay. She heard squishy sounds as the men warmed it between their hands and then groaned aloud as two sets of fingers spread out across her back and buttocks.

There were no words. None. Shannon couldn't have described the unbelievable bliss of strong hands working her stiff and oh-so-sore muscles if she'd tried.

She closed her eyes and moaned occasionally, just so they'd

know she was awake. It seemed to work. Jake hummed as he rubbed; his big hands, so familiar with her body, finding every tight muscle, every aching bone. Baylor concentrated more on her buttocks, massaging and kneading each cheek and bringing life back to the muscles along the backs of her upper thighs.

It was purely accidental, wasn't it, when his fingers slipped between her pussy lips, when his thumb found her clit?

The guys talked softly about the day's journey. It was obvious they'd loved every minute. Meaningless words and phrases passed above her head, and she could tell by the strength of their massage that both men got off on the power of their bikes, the big engines, and the pure joy of the ride.

She got off on their joy, but the massage wasn't bad either. At some point, the men both lost their clothes. She wasn't sure when it happened but noticed the occasional thump of a hard erection against her thigh, the damp slide of a smooth crown, slick with moisture, along her back.

The massage grew more languorous, the touch more erotic. Her breasts received their fair share of attention, as did the cleft of her butt and the soft lips between her thighs. She wasn't sure if the slippery cream Bay used to rub her tired muscles came from a tube of lotion or the slick fluids between her legs. Maybe he swept it from the end of his cock . . . it didn't matter, so long as his hands worked their magic.

They took her together, finally. Jake lay on his back and pulled Shannon over on top of him. Her skin tingled with arousal, but her muscles were so relaxed she merely lay there, draped across his hard body while he used his fingers to open her slit. He stroked her for less than a minute, sliding easily in her slick juices before slipping his big cock into her greedy sex. Thrusting hard and deep, he found just the right sweet spot to bring her off before he fully entered her.

She sighed through the sweet vibrations of her climax, barely aware of Bay kneeling behind her. His fingers stroked the taut little pucker of her ass, pressing and rubbing until he could press his cock against her and slip through her tight sphincter without effort. He kept on pushing and slid smoothly along her channel.

When his soft tangle of pubic hair brushed her cheeks, she came again, another small ripple of pleasure. Shannon sighed as Bay slowly withdrew, then just as slowly filled her. Jake held perfectly still, his cock clenched deep inside her sheath. Shannon knew he felt Bay's cock each time their packmate thrust, felt the thick intrusion of the other man's erection sliding past his own.

She was stuffed full with Bay's erection gliding in and out of her backside and Jake's sizeable cock filling her pussy. She loved this sensation, her body sandwiched between two lovers, men who loved one another almost as deeply as they loved her. Her entire body was so relaxed she felt like overheated Jello, a mere blob of sensation for two men to fuck.

But they did more than that. So much more. Shannon nuzzled the thick hair on Jake's chest and figured it was worth sitting on a motorcycle for all those long hours if this was the way they planned to treat her at the end of the day.

Bay quickened his pace just as Jake arched his hips and drove deep inside her sex. His big hands grasped both her breasts, kneading and rubbing while flicking at her nipples with his thumbs. Jake's touch sent a zing of current from her breasts to her clit. Bay's short, sharp breaths against her spine told her how close he was to coming; the tight grasp of his fingers around her hips dragged her back against him with each deep thrust.

Sensation built upon sensation; arousal stole the breath from her lungs and any coherent thoughts from her mind. Shannon opened to Bay and Jake and found a level of arousal even higher than her own, a dark swirl of carnal desire filled with flickering pinpoints of light.

Light and love. Desire and need, a sense of unity not to be denied. Bay let out a strangled cry. His groin pressed against her ass as he filled her. Jake groaned, lifted his hips, and his cock met Bay's deep inside Shannon. She tumbled with them, free-falling through waves of sensation. Her inner muscles rippled the length of two erections, hot jets of ejaculate from both men tipping her into even another climax. Crying out, Shannon arched her body in what could only be described as a river of current: live, electric current tying them into a single pulsing, gasping, shuddering organism.

They lay there for long moments. The three of them were locked together, Bay's arms holding them all close, their hearts pounding, lungs heaving. Finally, after a long recovery, Bay slipped free of Shannon's body first and went for a quick shower. She drifted, still sprawled across Jake's chest with his fingers tracing lazy trails along her spine, and Shannon thought she could stay this way forever.

When Jake finally slipped his penis free of her sex and dragged her into the shower for a quick rinse, Shannon practically fell asleep in his arms. He dried her like a child, toweled as much water out of her hair as he could, and then carried Shannon to the bed. Her last conscious thought for the night was how wonderful it was to press her nose into Bay's smooth back while Jake snuggled close against hers. She didn't even mind the fact both men shared her chosen bed.

Anton Cheval set the phone back in its cradle and stretched his long fingers together to form a steeple. He rested his chin on his forefingers and stared out the window, though it was obvious he knew Keisha had entered the room. "I've sent Oliver on ahead," he said. "He'll arrange our rooms—I've got the California Suite at the Mark Hopkins for the four of us for the next two weeks, so we should at least be comfortable during our visit."

Keisha laughed out loud at what had to be a classic Anton understatement. "*You'll* be quite comfortable. You and Stefan.

I'm almost nine months pregnant and Xandi's not far behind. *Comfortable* is no longer part of our vocabulary." She wrapped her arms around his shoulders and kissed the top of his head. "Thank you, my love. What's that cost? It's got to be around thirty thousand a week."

Anton chuckled as she rubbed her belly against his back. "Yep. And worth every penny. I hope you realize our daughter just kicked me in the back."

"You deserve it, for being such a poop about taking me on this trip." She slipped around to his side, slid her once slim fig-ure down onto Anton's lap, and draped her arms over his shoulders. "Stop obsessing, okay? I will be fine. Xandi will be fine, and the babies will come on time. Relax. We'll have fun. There is no way I'm going to miss Luc and Tia's wedding."

Anton wrapped his fingers around the back of her head, tan-gled them in the thick, wavy mass of her hair, and pulled her face toward his. He kissed her, slow and deep, his tongue brushing the full curve of her lower lip, raking over her teeth, and then tangling with her tongue.

He fucked her mouth slowly, sucking at her lips, his tongue taking her on a smooth, sensual journey that had Keisha mewl-ing deep in her throat, squirming against his growing erection, and kissing him back until both of them strained against the clothing keeping them apart.

"Are you sure?" Anton's palm smoothed over her gauzy maternity top, following the curve of her belly. "I'm so big," he said, and she knew it wasn't bragging or male ego talking but merely a description of the body she loved. "I'm afraid I'll hurt you or the baby."

Keisha pulled back far enough to see all of his face, his beloved features creased with worry, the telltale flush to his high cheekbones that told her exactly how aroused he was. How much he wanted her. "So long as we're careful, big guy . . ."

His expression never changed, but he lifted Keisha and carried her across the room to their bed where he stretched her out on the ivory coverlet. She felt like a beached whale. Her belly had grown so big her own body felt alien. Her breasts were ponderous, barely supported in the serviceable bra she'd had to start wearing. How Anton could find this body sexy, Keisha would never understand.

He undressed her slowly, kissing each bit of skin as he bared it. When he slipped her panties down her legs—thank goodness *they* at least still looked trim—he trailed his fingers lightly along her thigh to her ankle. Then he dragged his fingertips the length of her leg, leaving shivers in his path. He caressed the curve of her belly where she'd once had a tiny waist, tracing the dark line that ran from her navel to her mound. His feather-light touch left her entire body tingling.

The last thing he removed was her plain white cotton bra. Her breasts spilled out like huge, brown melons, the areolas wide and flat, her nipples stretched taut. Keisha wanted to cover them, but Anton leaned close and suckled the nipple of first her right breast, then her left. When he pulled away, his lips were shining; her nipples were hard and wet and her sex clenched in needy longing.

Feeling unaccountably shy, Keisha looked up at his face. The love in Anton's eyes was almost her undoing. No matter how she felt about herself, she knew Anton looked at her with eyes of love. Worshipped her body now, even in this gravid state.

He rubbed his thumb over her nipple and the shock went straight to her clit. "No, sweetheart," he said. "Even more, if that's possible."

"That's not fair." She reached up and touched his chest, feeling his heart thundering beneath the crisp white shirt he wore. "You're snooping in my head."

"Of course I am. I love you. Don't ever think I would find you unattractive. Far from it . . . you're lovelier now than ever." Anton brushed her hair away from her eyes, then stood back and stared at her for so long Keisha almost used her hands to cover herself. Almost.

Then he removed his clothing, item by item, folding each piece neatly and placing it on the dresser. When he turned back to her he was fully aroused, his cock flushed a dark red, rising up out of its nest of black hair in a long, powerful, gravity-defying arc to his belly. He stood there and stared at her as if memorizing her, and his eyes glittered with emotion. *There are no words . . .*

His thoughts, obviously not meant to be shared, slipped un-expectedly into her mind. Such a slip was unusual for a man of Anton's power. With his words flowed the feelings he'd been trying to control—his need, his fear for her, his unquenchable love. Keisha held up a hand in invitation. Anton sighed, wrapped her fingers in his, and lay carefully on the bed beside her. He spread his other hand over her belly, his long fingers looking al-most ghostly against her dark skin.

She tried to imagine this child of theirs, born of two races, and wondered if she would be dark like her mother, fair like her father, or a beautiful blend of the them both, like Tia.

"She'll be perfect."

Keisha almost laughed. There were no secrets with this man. Anton leaned close and kissed her stomach, just below her pro-truding belly button. She moaned, surprised by the intensity of sensation from a simple kiss. The sound slipped effortlessly from her throat. He traced the curve from hip to groin, his touch gentle yet unaccountably arousing. When he finally dipped his fingers between the swollen folds of her pussy, Keisha cried out and arched into his touch. *Damn!* She was so sensitive there, all wet and swollen with a combination of pregnancy and desire.

It felt so good when Anton trailed his long fingers across all her sensitive folds and furrows. When he circled her clit with the tip of one finger, Keisha suddenly climaxed in a warm gush of fluids and a low groan. Gasping for air, she wrapped her fingers around his wrist. "Enough," she said, laughing. "I'm so sensitive right now."

Anton lifted his fingers to his mouth and sucked them clean of her juices. His cock bobbed against her hip but he made no move to enter her. She knew he wouldn't, especially after she'd grabbed his fingers away from her clit.

Direct touching was a bit much, but there was no way she was going to stop now, not with her body vibrating with ripples of pleasure. Moving awkwardly, Keisha managed to push Anton to his back. "This way I control how deep and what angle, so quit worrying, okay?"

"If you say so." He didn't sound at all certain, but he wrapped his hands around her hips and helped Keisha find a comfortable position.

She straddled him, rising up on her knees and guiding his erection carefully toward her center. They'd not made love like this for ages, not since she'd gotten so big. As much as she liked oral sex, they'd had to be extra careful even with that . . . and besides, Keisha needed the feeling of him deep inside, the sense of connection that came only when they made love the old-fashioned way.

She'd not shifted for what felt like forever, either. Even though her doctor thought it would be okay, none of them knew for sure if there might be any danger to her growing baby. She wasn't about to risk her baby's health. Instinctively, all the female Chanku knew, in theory, how to keep the fetus safe when they shifted. Still, after about her sixth month, when she began feeling as awkward on four legs as two, it hadn't seemed worth the risk.

As Keisha tilted her hips to the slick length of Anton's cock slipping over the mouth of her womb, she realized just how very much she'd missed this connection. Even more, how much she missed the powerful sexual union they shared as wolves.

Her nether lips kissed the thick mat of hair at the root of his penis and she sighed, settling her hips on his upper thighs, tightening her inner muscles around his length and breadth.

Anton sighed as well. She heard him swallow, and she opened her eyes and saw tears at the corners of his. Keisha reached down and swept the moisture away with her thumbs. "No fear, okay? Make love to me. I'll tell you if it's too much. Right now I need you. I need to feel you rocking my world. You make me feel like a woman instead of Moby Keisha."

"Moby Keisha? Is that how you see yourself?" He finally smiled, clasped her hips even tighter in his long fingers, and helped her as she lifted herself slowly off his cock then just as carefully slid back down his hard length. He groaned, but there was laughter in his voice when he whispered, "You're the prettiest whale I ever made love to."

"Gee, thanks." She flicked her nails over his nipples and dragged a choppy "Ah" from his lips. Then she curled her fingers in the dark hair covering his chest and continued her slow rise and fall along his silky cock.

She wondered what she felt like to him, how it was to have his cock squeezed into a space made much tighter by their growing child. As she let herself wonder, suddenly she knew. Anton opened his thoughts, brought her into his with a facility that never ceased to amaze her. Brilliant, mentally more powerful than any other Chanku, Anton shared the sensations as he experienced them in a link of scintillating clarity.

Not only was she hotter, tighter, and wetter than usual, her inner muscles seemed to ripple with a new purpose. She clasped him in slick, wet silk, binding him inside her, holding him so that he struggled not to tip over the edge.

She wanted to tip. Hell, she wanted to fly, wanted that lightness of being only Anton could give her. Faster, deeper, Keisha rode him almost to orgasm, sliding up and down his smooth shaft as sensation built upon sensation, as even Anton's eyes took on that glazed, pre-orgasmic glow.

He turned loose of her hips, slipped a thumb beneath her swollen belly and found her clit. The bud was slippery with her juices, more receptive now to his touch. He stroked her, matching the sweep of his thumb to her quickening pace, but it was the flat of his hand, his palm pressed against her belly while he stroked her, that brought a strangled cry to Keisha's lips, a surge of electricity from deep inside her body, and the sweet, all-consuming rush of orgasm.

Anton came with her, though she sensed his struggle for control all the way through to the last spasm of his cock. There was no lunging thrust at the end, no endless penetration.

Instead, he wrapped his arms around her and pulled her close against his chest. Kissed her sweat-tangled hair and nuzzled the soft swell of her ponderous breasts. Moments later, once their breathing slowed, he nuzzled her ear. "I hate to change the subject, my love, but the plane leaves at ten in the morning." He leaned over and licked the sharp point of her nipple. "I hope you and Xandi know what you're doing."

Keisha kissed him long and hard. When she came up for air, Anton looked a bit shell-shocked. Good. It was nice to know she hadn't lost her touch. "If you can make me come like that without setting off any contractions, a little flight to San Francisco will be a snap."

"If you say so," he answered, but there was no smile behind his words.

Tala rested, stretched out half-asleep in the back seat of the rented SUV. She always felt so keyed up during a job, but now she knew she could finally relax. All was as it should be—they'd rescued the child and both her men were safe. AJ was at his usual place behind the wheel with Mik riding shotgun.

It was still hard, sometimes, to realize how her life had changed since she'd first stowed away in the back of their car so many months ago, since she'd first learned of her Chanku heritage and the amazing abilities her genetics made possible. From streetwalker to private detective was one hell of a leap.

Tala still wasn't sure exactly who Pack Dynamics answered to, whether they were a government agency or merely took jobs no one else could handle. She only knew to follow orders, get her assignment done safely, and high-tail it back to San Francisco for another job.

She absolutely loved every minute.

Of course, she hadn't minded her life as a whore all that much, though her pimp had been a jerk. At least she'd had steady work doing what she loved. Thank goodness Mik and AJ understood her over-the-top libido.

They had the same problem . . . if you could call it a problem. Tala hoped they'd find a place soon to stop for the night. Damn, but she was so horny after a job, and there was something special about sex in a motel room with these two.

It always reminded her of their very first time.

Watching AJ and Mik make love to each other, joining them for the most amazing sexual experience of her life, linking with two men in a mental communion unlike anything she'd ever imagined . . . damn. Tala's pussy clenched and suddenly creamed with the memory. Mik turned and glanced over the seat in her direction. She watched him surreptitiously through the thick fall of hair covering her eyes. His nostrils flared. He raised an eyebrow, grinned broadly, then nudged AJ. "Time to find a motel for the night. I think someone's getting impatient."

"Works for me. Let's look for something rural, though. I need to stretch my legs." AJ nodded in Tala's direction. "Then I think we both need to stretch something else."

She pretended to sleep. Obviously the guys knew she was awake. And aroused. They scented her arousal the moment her juices quickened. *Damned wolves . . . damned, wonderful creatures.* Tala's fingers stole beneath the elastic band on her shorts and slipped between her legs. No reason to suffer while AJ hunted for a room. At least this would help the time pass more quickly.

Within an hour they'd found a motel deep in the woods, unloaded the car, and slipped out into the darkness, headed for a deep stretch of forest bordering the small motel. "It's like walking into another world, isn't it?" Tala felt a need to whisper as she followed Mik's silent footsteps deeper into the woods. Trees towered overhead and night sounds created their own song.

It is another world. It's our world. AJ slipped out of his clothing and stuffed everything into a small sack he'd carried with him. He pushed it under a thick tangle of brambles and waited: a naked, dark-haired god of the night.

Tala's heart pounded as she did the same. Would she ever get used to this, to the mystery of turning herself from woman to wolf, from small-town girl to the alpha bitch for two incredibly sexy males?

Mik touched her shoulder. She craned her neck to look up at him, and caught her breath against the swell of desire coursing from his body to hers. Broad shouldered and bronze skinned, with black hair falling straight and thick to his waist, Mik carried himself like a chieftain of some ancient civilization, as powerful, as mesmerizing, as either human or wolf.

Ready?

There was no need to answer his silent query. Tala merely shifted, making the change from woman to wolf in less than a heartbeat. She hit the ground running with the other two right behind her.

It was after two before they dragged back to the motel room, showered, and crawled into bed. Tala wrapped a towel around her long hair and quietly shut off the light in the bathroom so she wouldn't wake the guys. Her silence wasn't at all necessary.

She paused in the doorway and watched her two men on the big bed, memories of her first night with Mik and AJ flooding her mind. They'd rescued her without realizing it when she'd hidden in their car to escape her angry pimp. Badly beaten and traumatized from a gang rape, she'd wanted nothing more than a hiding place, a dark cave to hide in.

She'd found herself with AJ and Mik. Once they'd realized her predicament, they'd done everything possible to protect her, even before they'd known she was Chanku. But that very first night, waking up in her lonely bed next to Mik and AJ, she'd watched the two of them making love. It had been a revelation for her. Two men fucking each other right before her eyes wasn't unusual, considering her occupation, but this had been so much more than that. They'd made love to one another, and their tenderness had dragged her in, had caught her in their silken net.

Just as it now caught her once again. AJ lay on his back, his ankles looped over Mik's broad shoulders. Mik knelt between his thighs, pumping his big cock slowly in and out of AJ's ass. Mik's head was thrown back and his black hair swayed like a slow-motion metronome across his butt with each deep thrust. His eyes were closed, his mouth set in a tight grimace that only hinted at the level of his arousal.

AJ's fingers had fisted in the blankets on either side of his hips. His cock curved up and over so that the tip rested against his belly. His balls cushioned the top of Mik's sizeable erection on each penetrating thrust.

It was the lonely look of AJ's cock, the plum-sized head weeping a single white tear at the end, that drew Tala into the room. She stood beside the bed, licked her lips as she imagined the familiar taste of him, and reached out one finger. With the tip, she caught the drop of fluid and brought it to her lips.

Suddenly, AJ's hand tightened around her wrist. "Suck it. Please, Tala. I need your mouth on me." His voice had roughened with passion. His quiet plea made her sex tighten and her nipples ache.

"This way." He tugged her close and pulled her over him so that her sex rode astride his face, her hungry cunt just above his mouth, his cock within reach of her tongue.

She licked him, swirling her tongue around the tiny eye, and felt his groan against her labia. His fingers wrapped around the backs of her thighs as she lowered her mouth over his erection. Her tongue swept the sensitive ridge beneath the broad crown, her teeth scraped the smooth, satiny top. Once again he groaned, and the low rumble vibrated her folds and valleys.

Mik continued his same steady rhythm, driving all the way inside his lover, retreating, then pushing back, deep and slow. He moved like a man in a dream, totally focused on sensation, on his own pleasure, no matter how much he was pleasing AJ. Tala focused on the size and strength of AJ's cock in her mouth, on the slide of satiny skin over smooth muscle. She hummed against her mouthful just as AJ hummed against her pussy, sharing their vibrations while Mik continued his slow and silent thrusts.

Caught in their passion, trapped by the lush beauty of their combined sensations, Tala opened to her men, guarding herself from the full thrust of their arousal, but loving them both, loving the way they focused on their own pleasure as much as each other's. This single-minded drive for their ultimate sensation, the mind-shattering desire that coursed through each of them, doubled back upon itself when shared through their mutual link.

This was the drug that ruled her life, this loving, fucking, heart-pounding sweep of desire, shared among three, experienced as one.

Only seconds into the link, Tala pulled away and softened

the blow of AJ's arousal. Too much at once, it threatened to tip her over the edge. Instead, she slipped into Mik's mind and almost screamed with the slow, dark agony he endured, the pleasure and pain of holding his lust in check. He wanted to come, wanted to bury himself hard and fast in his lover, but the sharp edge of stimulation he skated over was more powerful than the finish.

How long, how long, how long can I hold on? Hold on. Oh, shit. Hold on.

Mik's fervent prayer made Tala smile around AJ's cock, but the tongue that speared deep inside her sex, the need she felt in Mik—neither had the power of AJ's growing excitement.

Slowly, as if peeling back a blanket to peer beneath the covers, she opened herself to AJ, slipped in beside him, in essence *became* him. Her own flavors struck her first, the tangy taste of woman on his tongue, the softness of her plump lips, the brush of pubic hair grown softer with each shift.

She let herself think of the changes for just a moment, the physical manifestations of her growth from human to Chanku. With each shift her hair grew softer. Even the coarse pubic thatch between her legs had softened and lost its wiry feel. Little things, like the way she perceived light and color, her now acute hearing and sharper eyesight. So much easier to accept than the easy shift from human to wolf.

Steeling herself to maintain control, Tala focused on AJ. She studied the way her lips felt on his cock; the smooth glide over the engorged length, the way her teeth scraped the ridge around the crown, and how the big vein along the underside felt against her tongue. She sensed how much he loved it when she dipped her tongue into the tiny slit at the end, so she did exactly that. She held the crown in her teeth, licking the pre-cum from the end as if she savored a fiery popsicle, licking and sucking, twirling her tongue around him. When she sucked the tiny eye and teased him with her mouth, she felt every lick and nip as if it were her own cock, her own pending orgasm.

But Mik . . . ah, what Mik could do to him . . . for him. AJ's oldest love, his first love, Mik thrust his huge cock deep inside, filling AJ, bringing both pleasure and pain in equal measure. Tala felt Mik's struggle to make it last, this lush and carnal act he craved as strongly as AJ. She felt the rush of sensation as both men balanced precariously on a dangerous cliff of their own creation.

Suddenly, her thoughts were swept up, connecting even more deeply, connecting on a visceral, cellular level. Body trembling, Tala glanced up, her lips still surrounding the tip of AJ's erection. She caught Mik staring at her, a look of intense concentration masking his sharply defined features. Then he cocked one dark-winged brow, arched his hips and drove even deeper into his partner.

Tala felt it all the way to her heart. She cried out, swept up in the intensity of sensation, the overwhelming emotions as Mik raced AJ toward the precipice.

AJ stabbed her pussy with his tongue, and Tala almost laughed with the joy of it all, the inclusion within their bond, a solemn covenant that linked the three of them as tightly as one. Racing with them both, giving over to the combined power of three bodies reaching climax as one, she flung herself over the edge and tumbled, free-falling into the whirling maelstrom of pure sensation.

Her vaginal muscles pulsed with her climax, and she sucked down on AJ's cock, as if anchoring herself with his body. The salty, almost bitter taste of his ejaculate filled her mouth and she struggled to swallow it all while her body writhed in the solid grip of his strong hands.

Mik's thrusts sped up and he arched his back and cried out, a long, low howl of release before slumping weakly against the backs of AJ's raised thighs. All of them pulsed with the rhythm of orgasm, lungs gasping, bodies trembling.

Tala slipped out of the link as both Mik and AJ stroked her shivering body with their large hands. She imagined the picture they must make as they lay there, two large men and one small woman tangled hopelessly together. Their bodies were still connected and all three were still sweaty and panting as if they'd just raced a mile. Mik stroked lazy circles over her breast; AJ patted her buttocks.

Their minds were gloriously blank, their thoughts at rest, content. She laughed with the pure joy of the moment, overwhelmed by a most amazing love shared, times three.

3

Anton checked Keisha's seatbelt as the pilot went through his pre-flight list. He was new, though he'd come highly recommended by their copilot, a quiet man who'd flown for Anton a few times in the past. The copilot checked to make sure all their bags were properly stowed for the flight to San Francisco, passed out bottled water to each of them, then took his seat in the cockpit beside the pilot. He reached back and closed the door between the cockpit and the cabin, giving the passengers privacy.

Listening with only part of his mind to the sound of the engines warming up and the women's voices, Anton sat across the aisle from his mate and fastened his own belt. He hadn't slept well the night before. His dreams had been uncomfortable yet meaningless vignettes that woke him over and over in a cold sweat. He couldn't shake the feeling something wasn't right, that they should not be making this trip, but Keisha was so excited to be going Anton couldn't have said no for anything.

He'd never been one for premonitions. His dreams were

merely manifestations of his own concerns. Keisha was right. He really did worry too much.

She and Xandi chattered like a couple of schoolgirls. Anton sipped his water and bit back a tired grin as he listened to their stream of laughing conversation. It never ceased to amaze him how two women who shared the same house, and quite often the same bed, could still find so much to talk about.

Sitting directly behind Anton, Stefan reached over the seat and touched his shoulder. "Relax, bro. The girls will be fine."

Anton covered Stefan's hand with his. "I know, but one of us needs to worry."

Stefan laughed. He sat back in his seat and tightened his belt. "Well, knowing you're on the job will give me a chance to relax. Wake me when we get to San Francisco."

"I'll do that," Anton said. Then he settled back in his seat for the flight to California. He actually felt himself begin to relax as the powerful Hawker 1000 blasted into the air. The corporate-sized jet he'd purchased a few years earlier was one of the best and safest on the market, and Keisha's doctor had assured him she would be fine traveling in such comfort. His mate was right. If he couldn't find something to worry about, he'd make something up. With that thought in mind, Anton finally closed his eyes and drifted into sleep.

Keisha's voice in his mind was the first solid inclination of things gone terribly wrong. *Anton? Are you awake? Something's wrong. I just woke up, but we appear to be flying east, not south-west.*

Startled awake, Anton shook his head. He felt as if he'd been drugged when he glanced out the window. The sun should be to the left of the jet. Instead, it shone brightly through the starboard window, practically blinding him. *Stefan! Wake up. We have a problem.*

What's up? Stefan's mental voice sounded groggy.

Did you drink any of the bottled water?

Yeah. Finished mine. Why?

It appears we're heading the wrong direction. We've all been asleep. I believe the water was drugged. Do you think there's a chance we've been skyjacked?

Shit. No wonder I've got a headache. Can you read the pilot? I don't recognize him, but the copilot's flown with us before.

Anton held up his hand for silence and closed his eyes in concentration. Then he turned around and stared at Stefan, experiencing, for the first time in his life, a sense of pure terror. He narrowed his mindtalking to Stefan alone. *It appears Secretary Bosworth's plan for a Chanku breeding farm did not die with him.* There'd been fear, even after Bosworth's death, that more of his group might still exist. Still, Jacob Trent and Baylor Quinn had been unable to find tangible evidence.

Now, unfortunately, Anton feared the group might have all the evidence it needed . . . and then some. What better target than two pregnant female Chanku?

He and Stefan, of course, were expendable.

Keisha's angry mental voice slammed into Anton's head. He spun around to catch her looking daggers in his direction. *What the hell's going on? Why are you talking over our heads? Xandi and I are not children.*

Anton sighed. *I know, my love. Old habits. Plus, I didn't want to alarm you until I knew for certain. I think the water we had was drugged. All of us have been asleep, something which rarely happens when we fly. I believe we're being kidnapped. I want you and Xandi in the back of the plane. Grab all the blankets and pillows you can, just in case we have a problem. I want you to try and contact someone at Pack Dynamics. They may be using something that will jam your cell phones, but possibly your combined mental voice will reach another of our kind. Let them know what's happening. Stefan and I need to have a talk with our pilot.*

Xandi grabbed Stefan's arm as Keisha did the same to

Anton. *Be careful,* Keisha said. Her amber eyes glittered with tears, but she had a look of such resolute power, Anton took strength from her touch.

Keisha glanced toward Stefan. *Both of you. More than our lives depend on your success.* Anton noticed both woman cradled their bellies protectively, most likely without even realizing what they did. Keisha kissed him hard and fast before she turned his arm free.

Anton helped Keisha out of her seat and nodded to Stefan as the women moved silently to the back of the plane. Stefan quickly slipped out of his clothing and shifted. *By the way, Anton. You do know how to fly a jet, don't you?*

But of course. Moving quietly, he gestured to Stefan to stay out of sight. There was no doubt, from the conversation he'd managed to glean from the pilot's thoughts, that the men were heavily armed with both live ammunition and tranquilizer darts.

Taking their captors alive was not an option. Nor was discovery. Anton glanced back at Keisha and Xandi, who were carefully strapping themselves into the rear seats. God how he loved her. His heart stuttered with fear, not for himself, but for his mate and their unborn daughter. He would die before he would allow anyone to take a single member of his pack, but if anyone touched his mate, harmed his child . . . Anton's nostrils flared and his chest swelled as he gave the anger free rein. He took strength from it, felt it literally burning in his veins.

With a single harsh breath, Anton turned and stepped to the doorway. He tried the handle. Locked. He should have guessed. The jet was modified for security with a locking door into the cockpit . . . one that locked independently from either side. He rapped sharply on the door, but, as he expected, got no answer. Flying at elevation, there was no reason for a pilot to worry about his passengers escaping.

Anton stepped back from the door, touched one hand to Stefan's furred shoulder for more power, touched the door with the other, and concentrated on the lock.

Electricity snapped. Sparks flew. The acrid smell of burning wires filled the cabin. Anton's hair stood on end, and he felt the current flowing through his body, flowing from the wolf who was his lover, his friend, his packmate. It flowed from Stefan, filling Anton and growing exponentially as it passed through his mind to the circuitry within the locks on the door.

Suddenly the door burst open. The copilot rushed through, his pistol aimed straight at Anton. Before he could fire, the wolf charged, grabbed the man by the throat, and threw him to the deck. There was a sickening crunching noise as the vertebrae in his neck shattered. To be on the safe side, Stefan bit down, clamping his powerful jaws around his target's windpipe without drawing blood.

Paralyzed, with a broken neck, the copilot could only stare in horror at the wolf who killed him. Anton grabbed the gun and rushed through the door the minute Stefan nailed the copilot. As the pilot turned at the sounds of the attack, Anton shot him just above the heart.

The hollow-point round tore a hole the size of a dinner plate out of the man's back. He was dead when he hit the deck.

Unfortunately, so were most of the controls on the jet.

Anton shoved the pilot's body out of his way and slipped into his seat, but he realized his error the minute he glanced at the myriad dials and graphs, all of them blank. His burst of mental power had fried the circuitry in the cockpit as well as the lock.

He checked the radio. Dead.

They were losing altitude quickly, though the plane dropped in a downward glide rather than an out-of-control spin. Whether the controls had locked in position or the auto-pilot might still be functioning, if only marginally, was anyone's guess. Anton had no idea where they were. Clouds blocked the view to the ground. Stefan ran into the cockpit, tugging on his jeans as he entered. "What's happening?"

"Radio's out, we're losing altitude. Still have some engine power. I need to find a place to set down. Get the girls cushioned with anything soft you can find. Pile it around them. I want you back there with them in case I really fuck this one up worse than I already have."

"Anton, you did not fuck up anything. Those bastards are responsible. But I'll give you this—get us on the ground in one piece and I'll never bitch about being the bottom again."

Anton swung his head around to look at Stefan. The fool was grinning ear to ear. He leaned down and kissed Anton on the mouth, hard. "I'll take care of the girls," he said. "You land this sonofabitch."

"Tell Keisha I love her."

"Don't worry. She knows. But I'll remind her." Stefan turned around and headed back to the women, still talking. "We'll try and get word to the Pack. If stress helps power a message, we should be able to reach them with no trouble at all."

"That's sex," Anton said, gritting his teeth. "Not stress." He grabbed the stick and watched as a cottony wall of clouds engulfed the jet.

Ulrich Mason stared at the computer screen, but his mind was on his daughter's wedding, less than two weeks away. He hoped he didn't break down and cry walking Tia down the aisle. Though it wasn't really an aisle, he thought. Not if the wedding was held on the beach.

Damn, he wished Camille could be here to share this day. At least her baby girl was going to get married, just as his late wife had wished.

He shook his head, grinning. Camille usually got her way. Even now, over twenty years after her death, she still called the shots.

A frantic pounding on the front door brought Ulrich out of his daydreams and leaping to his feet. He raced down the hallway and threw open the front door.

Anton Cheval's personal assistant stood on the porch. The little man's uniform was rumpled, his dark face stricken. He appeared to tremble uncontrollably.

"Oliver? My God! What's the matter, man? Come inside."

Oliver grabbed Ulrich by the forearms. "Mr. Cheval. All of them. His lady Keisha, Stefan, Alexandria. They are missing. Their plane was late." He stopped to catch his breath. "I checked with the airport. They filed a flight plan and should have arrived hours ago. There's no sign of them anywhere. You must help me find them! Please!"

Shannon wasn't sure what state they were in. With plenty of time left to make it to the wedding, they'd meandered a bit, checking out the back roads and small towns, following a path of no actual plan beyond their ultimate destination. San Francisco was *that* way, and they'd get there eventually, with plenty of time to spare for the bachelorette party and the wedding.

The weather'd been unseasonably warm, so they'd stayed to the northern routes, circling the southern shores of the Great Lakes, enjoying the ride. They'd found this tiny motel in the depths of the forest somewhere in Minnesota—at least Shannon thought it was Minnesota—and while it was early yet, they'd started out before dawn and the dark woods looked so inviting they'd decided to call it a day.

Shannon giggled as she tugged off her helmet and shook out her sweaty hair. She wasn't about to admit to the guys just how much fun she'd been having, hanging on to Jake all morning on the back of his big BMW GS, her clit vibrating with the power-ful engine, her breasts pressed against Jake's leather-clad back.

She could get used to this, really fast.

The best part had been the last couple of nights, with both Jake and Bay rubbing her feet, her hands, her butt. She sighed as she followed Jake inside the motel office. The forest loomed all around them and the day was clear and cool.

Already her pussy clenched in anticipation.

Jake signed the receipt for their room, handed the slip back to the clerk, and held out his hand for the room key. Shannon couldn't help but notice the dreamy-eyed gaze from the young woman behind the counter and the way she sighed when Jake smiled in thanks.

If he weren't already hers, she'd be drooling over him too. Jacob Trent was gorgeous no matter what he wore, with his sun-streaked brown hair curling around his collar and the cocky sparkle in his amber eyes. In black leather motorcycle gear, he was sexy enough to make any warm-blooded woman drool. Right now, Shannon's blood practically boiled.

He tossed the key in the air, snatched it in his fist and grabbed Shannon's elbow. "How about a run? Do you think Bay'd be up for it?"

The door closed behind the office and the starstruck motel clerk as Shannon and Jake walked out into the brilliant sun-light. She laughed. "When is Bay ever *not* up?"

Dressed in jogging gear, the three of them headed out from their motel room, following a well-traveled path into the forest. Once beyond sight of the motel, they dipped into the thick brush and cut cross-country until they found a small meadow where they could safely undress and shift. They tucked their clothing beneath a shrub, disguising everything with the branches, shifted to wolven form and took off at a full run. The woods here were thick and cool, the air was damp and filled with scents, and the game appeared to be plentiful. Racing beside and just behind Shannon, his wolven paws tearing clumps from the thick humus coating the forest floor, Jake kept his nose to the ground and his senses alert.

They ran for miles at a fast, easy pace that covered the ground without effort. Still, it was much too easy for Jake to get sidetracked by the gorgeous she-wolf he followed. His alpha bitch. Would he ever get used to the fact she'd chosen him above all others? Not that he'd given her all that much chance, but Bay had been there before they mated, and he certainly wasn't hard on the eyes.

Jake glanced in Bay's direction, then concentrated once again on Shannon. Jake knew his packmate wanted her, knew Bay'd give anything to mate with Jake's woman, to bond, but she was Jake's. Only Jake's. Bay respected that and honored their bond.

Otherwise, lover or not, he'd be dead by now.

Shannon spotted the buck first, an older animal standing near a small pond. It paused as if listening for a threat, but they'd caught it unawares and she leaped without breaking stride. Locking her powerful jaws around the animal's throat, Shannon broke its neck with the weight of her body as she threw the animal to the ground. Bay and Jake moved in for the kill. The deer went still, dying without a struggle.

Shannon stood over the warm body, growling low in her throat, teeth bared and eyes narrowed. Jake and Bay backed off, caught up in her bloodlust, their tails low and ears laid back.

Watching her feed while his own belly rumbled, Jake felt nothing but pride. Damn, but she was perfect. His woman. Beautiful, wild. His. He glanced toward Baylor, saw the gleam in the other wolf's eyes, and growled. Bay glanced his way, then tucked low to the ground.

A guy can dream, can't he? Bay licked his lips but, like Jake, waited patiently for their alpha bitch to feed.

Any other time, after running and feeding they would have gone back to the motel to fuck and sleep and fuck some more, but the day was too beautiful for that, and the sky was such a perfect cerulean blue. Their blood was running hot from the kill. Shannon nipped at Jake's shoulder, dipped head to paws in play, then whirled about and waved her bushy tail under his nose.

Okay, so he didn't usually mate with her when Bay was nearby, purely out of masculine courtesy, but she was so damned hot and he needed her. Badly. He'd felt her leather-clad pussy against his butt all morning long and had fantasized about making love to her on the motorcycle, in the tall grass beside the road, in just about every motel they'd passed.

Hell, he wanted her all the time, wherever she would let him love her. Was there ever a time when he didn't want to be inside her, buried in her wet heat? Wolf or woman, so long as it was Shannon.

Jake nipped her flank, pawed her shoulder, and received a teasing growl in response. Bay waited off to one side, head cocked, eyes shining almost green in the sunlight.

Deeply aware of his packmate nearby, Jake mounted Shannon before she could twist out of his way, thrusting fast and hard and finally plundering her hot center. His paws raking her shoulders with each deep penetration, he panted with a combination of bestial lust and pure physical effort. She planted her legs and he filled her, his wolven cock plunging deep, the huge knot sliding past her tight vaginal opening, locking them, tying them together.

He'd not linked, not yet. There'd been no need, so caught up had he been in the sensation of fucking as wolves, in the lush yet carnal act of animals mating in the forest. With his blood running hot from the kill, from the pure joy of racing through an ancient forest, he'd stayed totally within his own thoughts. Now, locked to his mate, Jake opened his mind.

Shannon was there: glorious, passionate, her body ripe and ready for his.

And Bay? Snarling, Jake whipped his head to one side and saw Bay behind him, his black coat glistening in the sunlight. Bay's ears lay flat against his skull, his teeth were bared, and his paw was raised to rake Jake's shoulder, to mount him as Jake mounted Shannon.

Jake should have growled, should have warned his packmate off. Should have, but didn't. Couldn't. Not loving Bay as he did. Wanting him so much. Jake planted his feet, clasped his front legs tightly around Shannon, seated his swollen cock hard and fast inside her, and snarled at Bay. He opened his thoughts to Shannon, then opened to his packmate, welcoming him.

And bracing himself for something totally new.

The sharp jab of Bay's cock took Jake's breath. He clasped Shannon tighter and felt her legs steadying them both. Once again, slower this time, Bay's sharp thrust of his wolven penis took him deep inside Jake's body.

The sensation was new, totally unlike a human penetration. Harsh and unforgiving, Bay's erection slipped inside Jake, past nerves every bit as sensitive as their human counterparts. Bay's thrusting body sandwiched Jake forcefully against Shannon, shoved his cock even deeper inside her heat. Still pulsing from his climax with Shannon, Jake felt the thick swell of Bay's knot and knew his own cock was growing long and firm once again. His level of arousal spiked once more and his mind filled with the combination of Shannon's lust, his own . . . and Baylor's.

Their lust grew higher, spiraling with the intense sensations of the wild, building in their minds, one sensation upon the other. The link invaded Jake's mind: the deeper Chanku mating bond that signaled a connection much more powerful than that of mere packmates. This was something higher, something beyond anything he'd ever experienced except his bond with Shannon.

His body trembled with the combined sensations—his wolven cock locked tightly within Shannon's pulsing folds, Bay's sharp claws digging into his shoulders, Bay's penis jerking hard and fast within his ass. And more.

Something unexpected: There, on the very edge of climax, he caught another voice. Before he could single it out, orgasm took him, a powerful spike of energy that whipped through Jake, Shannon, and Bay. It lifted them, a dynamic pulse of energy combining hearts and minds, a synergetic cataclysm of power.

At the very peak, amplified by their release, was the sound of two unknown voices crying out in pain and fear. The unknown yet somehow familiar voices exploded into Jake's mind, into Shannon and Bay, shaking all three with an intensity more profound even than their mating.

He knew. Though he'd never met them before, Jake knew who called out, who cried for help. Keisha and Xandi! *Trouble!* Somewhere over the skies, somewhere east of their Montana home. *Find us!* The cries echoed within their three-way link. *Find us! Our plane is going down . . .*

Scrambling to their feet, the three of them separated and shifted as one. Jake grabbed Shannon's arm as she stumbled, holding out a hand to Bay. "Okay," he said, fully aware his voice shook. Was it in reaction to the voices they'd heard or the most amazing sexual experience the three of them had shared in wolven form? He'd need time, later, to think about what they'd done.

"We all heard that," Jake said. "We need to get back to the motel, call Luc, and see what the hell is going on."

Bay stopped him. "He might not even know there's a problem yet. Let's see if we can reach them again."

"Good idea." Jake took a deep breath, then grabbed his packmates' hands. After a few futile moments, he shook his head and laughed ruefully. "I guess it takes a three-way fuck to get any distance. Lord only knows how far away they are." He paused, then glanced off into the distance, replaying what he'd heard. "Shouldn't they be on their way to San Francisco for the wedding? Luc told me the Montana pack was planning on coming a couple weeks early. Why would their plane be going down east of Montana, not southwest?" He shook his head. "Makes no sense. C'mon. Let's head back. I won't relax until I talk to Luc."

They shifted back to their wolven forms, melting seamlessly from human to lupine in a heartbeat. They'd run long and far and it took awhile to make it back to the clearing, change clothes, and return to the motel. There was no signal for any of their cell phones and the phone in their room was dead. Luc slammed the headset for the ancient rotary phone down in the cradle. "I'll go try the office."

Two minutes later, he was back. "Sign on the door says they'll be back at five. We can't wait that long."

"I've got our stuff packed." Shannon was already pulling on her black boots.

Baylor stepped out of the bathroom with their overnight kits. "Let's go. Any idea which direction their voices came from?"

Jake nodded. "Due west of us, I think, but I can't be sure. We'll head that way, at least until we either find a phone or a signal for the cells. Damn, I keep telling myself I need satellite access." He shook his head, staring at the useless bit of technology in his hand. "Once we get back on a main road we need to find out what the fuck is going on."

After making a last minute sweep of the room to check for belongings, Jake followed Shannon and Bay out the door. He realized he hadn't stopped shaking since Keisha and Xandi's terrified voices had filled his mind. With a last glance at the funky little motel where they'd not even taken time to shower, Jake started his bike and followed Bay down the road.

* * *

Luc rolled his chair away from the computer, yawned, and rubbed his eyes. "There was a visual sighting, but it doesn't make sense. A Hawker 1000 was spotted at about eleven this morning, Central time, near Bismarck, North Dakota, heading east. The pilot noticed the plane because he's interested in buying one like it. He got the number off the tail. It was Anton's."

"East?" Tia grabbed a map off the desk. "Where would that put him? How fast do they go?"

"Over five hundred miles per hour, with a range of thirty-four hundred miles. They could be anywhere." Luc Stone, Tia's mate, stood and leaned over her shoulder to study the map. "Oliver said they were scheduled to leave Anton's private air strip at ten this morning. Shit. You're right. They could be anywhere, but unless they refueled, they're on the ground somewhere by now."

"Oh, God." Tia shoved her fist in her mouth. "What if they've crashed?"

Tinker McClintock looked up from his set of maps. His usual smile was gone, replaced by a look of grim determination. "This is Anton Cheval we're talking about. He's okay."

Luc focused on Ulrich. "You're sure Bosworth is dead?"

Ulrich nodded. "The secretary is definitely dead. However, his program may live on." He turned toward Tinker. "Contact Jake and Bay. See what you can find out about their hunt for any of Bosworth's cronies. Lisa, you see if you can get hold of AJ, Mik, and Tala. We need to pull everyone in on this. If Bosworth's program is still functioning, the Montana pack could be in much more danger than we suspect."

Lisa glanced up, frowning. She felt like a fifth wheel here among all the established agents of Pack Dynamics. As the newest member, she was still learning the names of the players. "Who's Bosworth?"

Tia got up from her desk and came over to sit by Lisa. "He was part of the President's cabinet, the head of Homeland Security, but in many ways he was a rogue." She glanced toward Ulrich Mason, and Lisa sensed both fear and pain in Tia's thoughts. "He kidnapped Dad a few months ago. Anton and his packmates helped us rescue him, but even though he was a member of the President's cabinet, the man was horrible. He wanted to create a breeding farm for Chanku. We're not really sure exactly why . . . maybe merely to prove our existence . . . but there is some concern he wanted to breed shapeshifters to work undercover for some secret branch of the government."

"Isn't that what Pack Dynamics is doing now? Working undercover?" Lisa glanced at Tinker, her mate, but he was buried in computer printouts. No help there.

Tia nodded. "Yep. But we do it of our own free will. Not because we've been bred and trained for some specific purpose." She flipped through a Rolodex on the desk. "Here. This is Mik's cell phone and here's AJ's. Looks like we don't have Tala's in the file yet. You should be able to get hold of one of the guys. Let Luc or Dad know if you reach them."

Tia went back to her computer. Lisa held the two small white cards in her hand. AJ and Mik were her sister's mates. The sister she hadn't seen in over ten years. She blinked back tears. It was one thing to know she would meet her brother and sister for the first time in all these years at Tia's wedding, but this wasn't how she pictured her first contact with her sister. Lisa wiped her hand across her streaming eyes and picked up the phone. *It's not about you, Lisa. Get over it.*

She tried AJ's number first. There was no answer, but she left a message for him to call headquarters. Taking a deep breath, she punched in Mik's number.

* * *

Tala swam slowly to the surface of consciousness, aware of a heavy weight across her thighs and a moving pillow beneath her head. As she blinked her way into awareness, she realized she'd fallen asleep still sucking languidly on AJ's lovely cock, with her head pillowed on Mik's fabulous butt. AJ sprawled across her legs, pinning her to the bed.

His flaccid penis lay beside her cheek. She leaned over and licked him, a long, slow stroke over the soft crown. She suckled the smooth skin between her lips and ended with a swirl of her tongue at the tip. AJ slept on, but his cock slowly elongated, pressing against her mouth.

It was a marvelous way to awaken; if only she didn't have to pee. The room was still dark and she had no idea what time it was. Easing herself out from under AJ's body was tricky, but Tala managed to roll him aside without waking him. Mik merely grunted when she carefully clambered over his body and slipped off the side of the bed.

As far as motels went, she'd give this one a ten.

The sex tonight had been magnificent.

The clock in the bathroom blinked midnight. She used the toilet and washed her hands, staring blankly at her tousled image in the mirror. Her long hair hung in thick, dark tangles to her waist and her lips were swollen from kisses. There were pale bruises on her breasts, and her nipples glistened deep red from all the sucking, licking, and pinching. She rubbed her palm over one and the tingle went straight to her core. There was no doubt at all; she looked like a woman well and truly loved, and her body ached in the most wonderful places.

Still smiling at herself, she'd turned away and started back to bed when Mik's phone rang. He'd left it in his overnight bag in the bathroom. Not wanting to awaken the guys, Tala answered it.

"Hello?"

She waited through a long silence. Then a voice she'd not thought she'd hear again until she'd got to San Francisco said, "Mary Ellen? Is that you?"

"Lisa?" Clasping the phone to her ear, Tala slid down the wall to the floor. "What are you . . . ?"

"My God. Mary Ellen . . . Tala. They said you're Tala now. Look, sweetie, I want to talk to you so badly, but there's been a horrible emergency. Are Mik and AJ there?"

Tala nodded, realized Lisa couldn't hear her, and choked out a strangled "Yes. I'll get them. What's wrong?"

"I'll fill you in later. Right now I'm giving the phone to Lucien Stone."

Luc? Shit. If Luc was in on this it must be an emergency. Scrambling to her feet, Tala ran back into the bedroom. "Guys, wake up. Something's happened!"

Mik was on his feet reaching for his phone before she'd gotten the words out of her mouth. AJ rolled over and off the bed, alert, as if he'd been waiting for Lisa's call. Both Tala and AJ immediately keyed into Mik's thoughts.

Anton Cheval and his mate, Stefan Aragat, and Xandi . . . all of them were missing: their plane either hijacked or downed. Tala realized she'd clasped AJ's hand in hers. They drew close and his arm came around her shoulders. He squeezed her in a comforting hug.

Lord help her, all she could think of was Lisa's voice. Damn, she'd missed her sister so much. Ten long years. She didn't even know the members of the Wyoming pack but she'd loved Lisa with all her heart. After their father's trial for murdering their mother, after all the tension and stress within an already totally dysfunctional family . . . they'd shattered. Each had gone their own way, had been lost in their own hell.

She knew Lisa had taken her shot at happiness with her mate in San Francisco, and knew also that Bay was part of a successful ménage in Maine with Jacob Trent and Shannon Murphy, but they'd not all been together since discovering their Chanku roots. Not for over ten years.

Tala shivered, listening to Mik's terse replies while he talked to Lucien Stone, remembering Lisa, wondering about all the years they'd lost. Wondering as well, and worrying, about those who were missing: the Montana Chanku, the four everyone spoke of with voices laden with awe. She slipped her arm around AJ's waist and held tight to one who loved her.

"I've left messages on all three of their phones, but they must be in an area that's out of service. I've been trying to get them all afternoon." *Damn Jake and his harebrained idea to come west on the bikes.* Tinker rubbed his fist over his eyes. It all felt like a nightmare. Nothing could happen to Anton Cheval. Not to him or his beautiful lady or their packmates. Anton was the key to all their mysteries, the one who always had the answers.

Where the hell was he now?

Lisa appeared and grabbed Tinker gently by the arm. "Mik, Tala, and AJ know, and we'll hear from the others soon enough. Sweetheart, you need to sleep. Worrying won't help. Even Oliver finally went to bed. Come with me."

Tinker looked around Ulrich's messy office and realized he'd been talking to an empty room. He leaned over and kissed Lisa's forehead and then wrapped his arms around her slim waist. "Anton won't let anything happen to Keisha. Not if he's still alive. I think that's what scares me so much. The man is so powerful, so brilliant. We need him. All of us do, and I'm scared to death something terrible has happened."

Lisa reached up and cupped Tinker's cheek in her palm. Her voice was husky, filled with emotion and love. "Have I told you lately how very much I love you? Now come to bed so I can show you."

Tinker gave in. He was exhausted, sick with worry, and terrified all his fears might be true. Lisa offered peace. She was his refuge of calm within chaos, the pacemaker that steadied his racing heart. He followed her down the hall to the guestroom they'd share tonight with Luc and Tia, thankful once again for the lovely lady who owned his life.

4

A sharp stab of pain in his shoulder brought Stefan awake and his first thought was *good:* he hurt; he must be alive. His second thought was for Xandi.

It was dark. So dark he needed to shift to see clearly, but he couldn't risk a shift, not until he knew where they'd come down and how secure their position was. "Xandi? Keisha? Can you hear me?" His voice sounded small, unsure. He needed to get hold of himself. Figure out where and what and how . . . shit. Everything seemed out of sync; his thoughts were scrambled. He searched for the women with his mind even as he called for them, but the silence was deafening.

He listened for Anton's mental voice. Nothing. Damn, it was so dark. Even with his excellent human night vision, he couldn't see a thing. There were emergency flashlights attached to the bulkhead near the door to the cabin, but Stefan's seat had torn loose and was lying on its side. He wasn't sure if he was inside the plane or out, and the smell of jet fuel was strong.

He recognized the scent of fuel and rotting vegetation, as if there were a swamp nearby. Stefan's left arm was useless and the pain almost blinding. He must have broken his shoulder in the crash, but he managed to unhook his seatbelt with his right hand and ease out of the shredded seat. Clouds parted at just that moment and a shaft of pale moonlight aided his night vision. The plane had broken in two. The nose tilted down into muck; the tail section he was in lay off to one side.

He stumbled, shuffling awkwardly toward the back of the plane. Both Keisha and Xandi were still in their seats, almost buried in the blankets and pillows he'd piled around them. Stefan checked Xandi first. He placed his trembling fingers against the big artery in her throat and felt the slow, steady beat of her pulse.

His legs gave out then. Relief? Fear? He collapsed at her feet. "Xandi? Can you hear me?"

There was no movement, but she lived. He refused to think of anything but that she still breathed. He touched her belly. A small foot kicked against his palm and Stefan almost wept with relief. Alexandria Olanet was his life. She had saved his sorry soul on more than one occasion, had brought him out of a living hell into what could only be termed paradise in her arms. He couldn't survive without her.

She lived. So did their child.

Moving carefully, Stefan drew closer to Keisha. A soft moan drifted out of the darkness. "Keisha? Are you okay?"

He heard her rapid breathing. Another groan. Then her voice, hoarse with pain. "Shit, Stefan. Anton's going to love this. I'm in labor. I will never hear the end of it." She reached out and grabbed his forearm. "Is he okay? I can't reach him. I've been trying."

There was only the slightest tremor in her voice. She must be sick with worry, with pain, but Keisha held it all under control . . . the perfect mate for Anton. The true alpha bitch in their pack. Stefan covered her hand with his and squeezed her fingers. "I just came to. Hang in there, sweetie. I'll go check."

"How's Xandi? Is she okay?"

Stefan tried to answer, but his voice cracked. He couldn't think about Xandi, not now. Not until he knew if Anton was alive. "She's unconscious but alive. Don't move. The plane seems stable, but I haven't found a flashlight to check it out yet." He loosened Keisha's seatbelt, patted her hand, and moved toward the nose of the plane. He couldn't remember the crash. Nothing beyond the first solid impact when they hit the ground: Keisha's scream, Xandi's curse.

It had been daylight then. As dark as it was now, they'd been here for hours. Thank goodness the plane hadn't burned. The smell of fuel was almost overwhelming. He needed to get the girls away, get them to fresh air as soon as possible.

He found a couple of flashlights still strapped to the wall. He turned one on and took the other back to Keisha. She looked ghastly in the harsh beam of light, her face drawn with pain and tracks of tears on her dark cheeks, yet she thanked him as if he'd handed her a precious gift and calmly waved him off to find Anton.

Stefan walked back down the length of the fuselage and aimed the powerful beam out of the ripped wall of the cabin. Light sliced across an open marsh, highlighting the body of the copilot lying partially submerged in dark water next to the wreckage. Stefan ignored the corpse and checked out the rest of the plane. The tail section where the girls were lay at a ninety degree angle to the nose of the plane and the cockpit. Moving carefully, Stefan climbed down through the gutted aircraft and sunk to his knees in mud and reeds.

He waded the short distance to the cockpit, but he soon saw it was going to be difficult to get inside. The nose had plowed into the soft ground and stood at a sharp angle. Somehow, he had to climb up the jagged edge in order to reach Anton. Stefan set the flashlight on a tangle of shredded metal, pulled his belt out of his pants, and, using his teeth, managed to wrap it around his torso, trapping his left arm against his side.

He pulled the belt tight and fastened it. The pain was excruciating, but immobilizing his arm and shoulder should help. He tucked the flashlight into his rear pocket and used a jagged strip of metal as a ladder, pulling himself slowly and painfully up a snarl of shredded cables with his right hand until he could throw a leg over the broken edge of the cockpit.

The smell of fuel left him lightheaded. The smell of death terrified him. When he finally got inside, Stefan propped himself against the bulkhead, panting with the effort. He tugged the flashlight out of his pocket and swept it around the relatively intact cockpit. The pilot's body lay shoved up under the control panel. There was a dark, bloody hole in his back. All he could see of Anton was his right arm, hanging limply to one side behind the seat.

Blood stained the white sleeve of his shirt and dripped from the ends of Anton's motionless fingers into a spreading crimson pool.

Stefan sent out a mental call as tears choked his throat and almost stopped his breath. Nothing. His heart ached. They'd come down hard and fast. No one in the cockpit could have survived. Not even Anton Cheval.

Mesmerized by the slow drip of blood, Stefan took a deep breath and used the back of the copilot's seat to pull himself upright. Sliding against the sharp angle, he worked his way closer to Anton.

Dead men don't bleed. Stephan saw a long slash across Anton's right temple and a steady stream of blood still dripping from the wound. Other than that, he appeared uninjured.

Stefan propped himself against the control panel and touched Anton's neck. A pulse beat there, weak but steady. Stefan gasped for air, felt the tears running down his face.

He'd never felt so helpless. There were two pregnant women,

one in labor. His leader, his lover, was possibly badly injured. His own shoulder was most likely broken and he had no idea where the hell they'd gone down. Breathing quickly, heart pounding, Stefan carefully unhooked Anton's seatbelt and lowered the padded arm of the chair.

He needed to get Anton out of there, get him down close to the women. He needed to get all of them away from the plane in case something set off the highly flammable fuel, or the soft, wet earth swallowed them all. Heart pounding, aware his imagination was working far too well, Stefan eased Anton out of the seat and managed to drag him up the small incline to the torn edge of the plane.

It was actually easier getting Anton down than it had been climbing in by himself. Using a broad strip of aluminum as a slide, he eased Anton partway down the incline and then draped him over his good shoulder in a fireman's carry. Anton didn't have an ounce of fat on his long, lean frame, but he still weighed a ton. Slowly, carefully, Stefan walked through the sucking mud toward the fuselage, carrying Anton.

"Stefan! Is he okay? How is Anton?"

Her voice came from somewhere off to his right. "Keisha? I've got him. He's alive. Where the hell are you?"

"Over here. Xandi too. I cut her seatbelt and helped her out and we found dry ground. She's shaky but awake and okay."

Thank the goddess. He wanted to laugh but could only manage a grunt. "I thought you were in labor."

"It seems to have stopped. I didn't like sitting in the middle of all that leaking fuel."

"Smart girl."

He stuck the flashlight in his left armpit and carried Anton through the muck and weeds with his right arm slung over Anton's hips. The women waited on a small rise not twenty yards from the plane. Still, they should be far enough away to be safe should there be a fire.

They had the blankets and both first aid kits that had been in the plane, as well as the emergency rations of water. "How'd you move all this stuff?"

"You've been gone almost an hour, Stefan." Xandi's hand covered his forearm as he eased Anton to the ground with Keisha's help. "I love you. I was so scared. I was conscious right after the crash. I called and used mindtalking, and no one answered. I could see your chair ripped away from the plane, but I couldn't see you and I couldn't get my seatbelt undone." She ran trembling hands over his chest. "I can't believe you're okay."

"Battered but okay." He caught Xandi's hand in his, kissed her fingers, and held her palm against his heart. "How's Anton?"

Keisha was carefully washing and bandaging the gash on his head. "He needs stitches. It's going to leave a scar without them, and I don't know how much blood he's lost. This is pretty deep, and head wounds always bleed so much. I wish he'd regain consciousness. It's scaring me, that he's staying out so long."

"We can try and bring him out of it." Stefan slipped his hands between deep tears in the once-pristine white shirt and placed his palm on Anton's chest. He felt the shallow rise and fall of his pack leader's lungs, felt the warmth of living flesh. Keisha pressed her palm close to Stefan's. Xandi moved close and touched Anton's forehead.

Stefan felt the power of their link, the boundless love each of them held for Anton. There was no fear, no sense of danger, merely deep, endless love and an overwhelming desire that he come back. Calling on the power of Chanku, Stefan willed his beloved packmate to awaken.

Shannon stared at the two motorcycles parked side by side along the lonely stretch of road and wanted to scream. There were flat tires on both of them, with no cell service this far out in the boonies, and the Montana pack was possibly in terrible danger.

And what did she and Jake do but sit here and stare at the bikes. *Damn.* She checked her watch. Bay had hitched a ride into the nearest town with a wheel under each arm almost two hours ago. She couldn't believe they'd both picked up nails along the same stretch of forsaken highway, but it appeared someone had dropped an entire box of them just up the road.

She'd killed some time picking up as many as she could find in order to protect other drivers, but now she waited and watched while the sun disappeared over the nearby hills. Headlights glimmered in the distance. Shannon glanced at Jake. He sat on a large boulder, staring at the lights. Finally he jumped down and strode quickly across the hard ground to where Shannon stood on the side of the road. He gestured toward the oncoming lights. "It's Bay. He talked to Lucien. Anton Cheval's plane went down somewhere today, probably at the exact time we heard the cry for help. Our timing may help them pinpoint the location. Mik, AJ, and Tala are headed this way and shouldn't be far behind us. We're to get the bikes going, head into North Dakota, and keep listening for any contact from the Montana group. If they're alive, they should be able to project quite a distance."

"Do you know any of them?" Shannon had only heard of the four from Montana.

Jake shook his head. "No, but with any luck, we'll meet them soon. Here's Bay."

The state trooper who delivered Baylor and the patched tires helped them get the wheels back on the bikes before he left. They rode in silence, taking a direct route this time, aiming for the heart of North Dakota. Shannon hung on to Jake and kept her thoughts wide open.

Exhaustion finally forced them to stop in a tiny town east of

Bismarck. They ate at a small diner, then went directly to their shared room. Running tonight was not an option, not with lives at stake.

Jake's cell phone rang just as they stepped through the door. Shannon carried their bags in while Jake talked quietly. His voice sounded harsh, rough with exhaustion. After a moment's conversation, Shannon heard him say, "We're about half an hour east of Bismarck, on Interstate ninety-four."

She'd stripped out of her leathers and stopped on her way into the shower to listen. Jake gave the name of their motel, then cut the connection. "That was AJ," he said. "Bay, call the desk, okay? See if you can get the connecting room to ours for Mik, AJ, and Tala. They should be here before too long."

Bay grabbed the phone between the two king beds. Shannon headed for the shower, warmed the water, and slipped beneath the spray. Jake stepped into the shower before she could pull the curtain. His arms were hard and warm around her waist, his chest a solid wall of muscle at her back.

She sighed and leaned against him. His cock pressed between her cheeks, solid and warm but not fully erect. "Do you think they're okay?"

His erection grew harder, longer. "I hope so. For one reason or another, I've never met any of them, but AJ and Mik have. I'm hoping with our combined energy, and with Mik and AJ's familiarity with the mental signals of the Montana pack, we'll be able to make contact."

Shannon felt his long sigh against the top of her head. He sounded tired and depressed and more hopeless than she'd ever heard him. "I've never been tested like this," he said. "AJ and Mik were involved in Ulrich's rescue. They know how it works. I don't. Damn. I feel so helpless."

Shannon turned in Jake's embrace and found his mouth with hers. The hot water beat a rapid tattoo down her spine and his cock was a firebrand against her belly. She kissed him, shaping her body to his as she whispered against his mouth, "We're all learning, sweetie. None of us really knows that much about who and what we are, or even what we're capable of. Even Anton admits he's still learning. That's what Tia said."

Jake broke the kiss and leaned his forehead against Shannon's. "All the more reason why we need to save him. He's got answers to questions we haven't even thought to ask." His hands swept along her spine, raising shivers wherever they passed.

"Anybody welcome in here, or is this a private party?" Bay slipped into the shower behind Shannon and grabbed a washcloth off the metal rack on the wall above the showerhead. He leaned over and kissed Shannon's neck. "I got the room and called Mik to let them know. The key will be waiting for them at the desk."

Shannon turned to look Bay in the eye. Damn, he got prettier every day. She thought of how he'd looked when they first met: the upright, uptight Secret Service agent with the close-cropped hair and button-down collar. Now his hair curled around his nape and, under the needles of water, hung in his eyes. His face was leaner, his muscles more pronounced.

There was still a twinkle in his amber eyes, though it was dimmed now from exhaustion and worry. He stood almost as tall as Jake, his shoulders as broad, his cock as big. Very big, in fact, Shannon noticed as he washed himself under the spray, taking most of the water that had been spilling over Jake and Shannon.

"He's hogging the shower again, Ma." Jake nuzzled kisses along Shannon's jaw.

Bay laughed, but he moved aside and put Shannon in his place. "Ma?" He reached overhead and adjusted the shower nozzle so the spray covered the three of them. "She doesn't look like any mother I remember."

Shannon finished washing herself, then scrubbed both men's backs and then their fronts. By the time she'd finished, their cocks curved out and up and their balls looked as if they were trying to crawl back inside their bodies.

She left them like that and got out of the shower. Her skin tingled under the rough cotton towel. Her sex throbbed, hot and swollen, and her nipples ached with arousal, with a need that went beyond pure sex. She glanced back at the two men finishing up their shower and willed them to hurry.

Shannon was hanging the damp towel when the phone in their room rang. Mik told her a message for the guys. An important one. Laughing, wondering how she'd deliver the message, Shannon quickly dressed in her flannel pajama bottoms and a black tank top.

Jake came out of the bathroom first. He spotted Shannon lying on the bed, fully dressed, and stopped in his tracks. Bay walked right into him. "You're dressed," Jake said. He looked over his shoulder at Bay. "She's dressed." He looked back at Shannon. "I thought . . ." He stroked his cock, running his big fist down its full length, stretching the foreskin over the tip, then sliding it back behind the crown.

Shannon patted the side of the bed. "No sex. Mik called. Sexual frustration strengthens our mental signal. They'll be over here in a couple minutes and we'll try and link with the Montana pack."

"No sex?" Bay stood beside Jake. "Well, crap." He took a deep breath and let it out with a loud *whoosh*. "Okay. I can do this."

There was a light tap on the connecting door. Jake reached for it while Bay slipped on a pair of running shorts. He shrugged while Shannon watched him dress. "Hell. Tala's my sister. I'm not running around naked in front of my kid sister."

"It doesn't seem to bother Jake any." Shannon watched Jake

swing the door wide and welcome AJ and Mik with open arms. Tala got a hug too, though she was such a tiny little thing Jake's cock practically reached her breasts.

Tala eyed Jake's sizeable erection up close. "Looks like you got Mik's message. Hope that thing doesn't hurt too much." She ran a finger along his length and Jake groaned.

"That is so not fair."

"All for the good of the cause," Tala said. "Hi Shannon. Hey! Baylor . . ." Tala slipped past Jake and hugged her brother. "I talked to Lisa. She's with Tinker in San Francisco. Can you believe it?"

Jake grabbed a pair of jeans as Mik and AJ entered the room. Shannon scooted over on the bed to make room for Tala. Mik sat next to Bay on the extra bed, while AJ and Jake grabbed the two chairs from a small table near the window.

Mik spoke first. "I know you guys are probably exhausted, but we need to try connecting with the Montana pack. As tired as we are, they could be badly hurt, lost, and scared to death."

"If they're even alive," AJ added.

Mik held up a hand. "I don't believe they're dead. I think we'd have felt something if any of them had died."

"We heard a cry for help," Bay said. "We were . . ." He glanced toward Shannon and she caught a telltale darkening across the sharp slash of his cheekbones. Bay? Blushing?

Remembering exactly what they'd been doing when they heard Keisha and Xandi brought a flush to her face as well. Not from embarrassment. No, it was arousal, pure and simple.

She wanted to do it again.

"Probably at the height of orgasm, right?" Mik's bald statement was not at all flippant. Shannon realized he was dead serious. "It heightens senses, but you were also a couple hundred miles farther away from here. I think we're closer to where the plane went down, within a few hundred miles according to Luc's estimates, so we shouldn't have to actually be fucking to reach them."

"So you're thinking sexual frustration should be enough?"

"Jake, if that's the case, I'm ready." Bay's dry comment brought laughter and agreement from the rest. "Mik, you and AJ were part of Ulrich's rescue when he was kidnapped, right?"

AJ nodded. "Yeah, but we arrived after they did the mind link. That was just Tia, Luc, and Tinker. Luc explained how it's done, though. They reached Ulrich all the way in Virginia from Montana. In fact, they even sent Anton's spirit. He was able to enter the body of a crow and get the layout around the place where they held Ulrich. Absolutely mind-blowing stuff. We only need to cast our thoughts out a couple hundred miles at most. Both Mik and I have met the Montana pack and know their mental signatures. Let's give it a try. If it doesn't work, we'll get some sleep and try again in the morning.".

AJ turned down the lights. Mik arranged them in a circle. Jake held Tala's hand, sitting beside her on one bed. Across from them, Shannon held Mik's on the other. Bay took a chair between Jake and Mik while AJ sat in a chair between Tala and Shannon. They linked hands. Mik took the lead. His naturally deep voice seemed to drop an octave.

Shannon realized she was trembling.

"You'll like the first part," Mik said. "Anton is a wizard with abilities far beyond ours, but he says we're all capable of magic, that it's not a thing we pull out of some crystal ball or get when we wave a magic wand. It's what's inside us. Sex is the most powerful magic of all. We'll use that to drive our search. Anton formed a circle just like this one when they contacted Ulrich. He had everyone in the circle imagine making wild monkey sex to the person on their right."

Shannon glanced up into Mik's shining eyes. "So, you'll be thinking of me . . . ?"

"Exactly. And you'll imagine fucking AJ. Get creative. He likes that. AJ will be thinking of Tala, which he does way too much of the time anyway, and she'll be concentrating on Jake, who will, for what it's worth, imagine screwing Bay."

"I'm good at that." Jake laughed. "You're the bottom, Bay."

"Gee, thanks." Bay glanced at Mik and grinned. "Just like I know where I'm putting Mik."

Shannon noticed the growing tent in Mik's jogging shorts at the same time Bay did. "I don't think Mik minds," she said.

Bay laughed.

"Okay. That's enough. Down, boy," Mik said, glancing at his shorts. His cock obviously chose not to pay attention. "We're just going to take a few minutes. Long enough to get our systems revved up. Then we'll try and reach them."

Mik bowed his head and closed his eyes. The others followed suit and Shannon had to bite back the giggles. They looked like a group at prayer.

In a way, they were, praying for the strength to send their thoughts winging out across a desolate state in search of their missing friends. Sighing, Shannon focused her attention on AJ and turned her most carnal, libidinous and kinky desires loose.

He was more than pleasing to the eye. He made her think of cowboys and late nights under the stars, with his tall, whipcord lean body and thick, dark brown hair curling over his forehead and around behind his ears. His chest was almost smooth, his muscles well defined. She'd had sex with him on more than one occasion, though not since he'd bonded with Mik, and now Tala. She knew AJ was a sensual and considerate lover. Still, he was a man who loved more than anything to have a woman suck his cock—suck him deep and swallow every drop of his cum.

But what could he do for Shannon? What fantasy would leave her squirming in her chair, unable to free herself from his touch? In her mind's eye, Shannon saw herself tied firmly, her arms bound behind her back on an old-fashioned chair, the kind found in funky diners. It had an aluminum frame and padded seat and back. She felt the cold vinyl beneath her naked butt, and her thighs ached from the way her captor had her legs spread uncomfortably wide and her ankles tied to the back legs of the chair.

She couldn't have been more exposed. Her pussy throbbed in the cold air; a trickle of moisture ran from her slit to her ass. Her nipples puckered and she realized there was a breeze, but it was from air conditioning. She was inside an auditorium of some kind; her chair sat dead-center on a huge stage. An audience of thousands watched, waiting, wondering what would happen to her next.

AJ walked out onto the stage. He wore a leather harness, the kind fetishists choose, with huge buckles and straps crossing his broad chest, arrowing down over his flat belly and crossing between his legs. The strips of thick leather were fastened to a cock strap, also of leather, but with metal rings that held his erect cock straight up. His balls were separated and stretched wide with more straps, fully visible beneath his erection.

She couldn't see his back, but imagined the strip of leather riding up his ass. She wondered if he wore a butt plug and decided he definitely had a big one inserted.

One that vibrated.

This was, after all, her fantasy.

He moved close enough to stand between her thighs. The chair was just the right height, and the tip of his cock rubbed between her sensitive lips. She got a better look at the metal rings running the length of his cock. They'd obviously been put on before he got an erection. Now the dark red skin bulged out between the rings, which had knobs all around each one.

While she stared at his cock, a small bubble of white appeared at the tip. So intent was she on watching the big vein pulsing between the metal rings on the underside and the precum at the tip, she didn't realize he was attaching clips to both her nipples. When he snapped them on her breasts, she cried out.

The sharp pain subsided to a dull ache. Her nipples pulsed now, in time with her sex. She felt the power of her growing arousal and knew her climax was close. Teetering on the edge, she panted as AJ pressed the broad crown of his penis against her slit then slowly drove its ringed length inside, inch by maddening inch. Her juices eased the way, but she felt every ring as each one bumped its way along her sheath.

Tala felt overwhelmed by the people in this room: all of them, at one time or another, lovers. She'd met Jake and Shannon, had reconnected with Bay on a visit to Maine, but they were all so self-assured, so certain of their place within the pack.

She had to concentrate on Jake, on finding some sort of fantasy to turn her on. The man was definitely sexy and, in his own way, every bit as beautiful as AJ. It was hard, though, to think of other men when she really only wanted AJ and Mik.

She had to do it, though. She'd never met the Montana Chanku, but Keisha's story had become part of her own: the fact Keisha had been brutally attacked, had turned into a wolf without realizing she had that power, and then had killed her attackers in a most satisfying manner.

Tala'd done the same thing, though she'd been so traumatized it had left her with amnesia for three whole years. Only the final act of bonding with AJ and Mik when the three of them mated had set her free; it had returned her identity, her memories, her soul.

Time was passing, and she still couldn't work up any feelings for Jake. He was nice enough, but he was Shannon's mate, not hers. Tala glanced at Mik. His head was down, his eyes were closed, and he was obviously having his merry way with Shannon.

He'd never know, would he, if Tala fantasized about the two of them? Now that was something she could get into. Shannon was wonderful. Ballsy and tough, yet still feminine and beautiful, and so tall, at least from Tala's point of view. Tala pictured Shannon on her knees in the middle of that big, soft rug in Jake's cabin, her butt raised while Mik fucked her hard and fast in the ass.

Tala'd stand there in front of her, her short legs spread wide, her fingers holding her pussy lips open so Shannon could suck and lick her. She'd want it right on her clit, the smooth sweep of Shannon's tongue swirling around her button, her lips sucking on that little nub like it was a nipple, sucking gently while she used a big vibrating dildo and rammed it in and out of Tala's pussy.

She'd grab hold of Shannon's shoulders to steady herself, and her fingers would tangle in all that long red hair. Mik would be smiling, his eyes glazed with lust, but he'd be grinning like the cat that got the canary because he'd be fucking one woman while she was sucking off another.

Tala realized she'd clamped her legs together, so real had her imaginary scene grown in her thoughts. It all felt so good, but she wanted Mik to feel more too, so she put Jake behind him, with that big cock of his. He'd lube up Mik's butt and use his fingers first. Then he'd work his way slowly inside while Mik did Shannon.

And Shannon did Tala.

Squirming in her seat, Tala decided she needed to fantasize more often because this was a hell of a lot more fun than she'd ever realized. She was so damned horny she'd probably leave a wet spot on the bed. Wasn't that what Mik wanted, though? She hoped she didn't have to last much longer, especially since she couldn't even use her fingers to bring herself off. In the meantime, she went back to imagining Shannon's lips on her clit and the look on Mik's face as Jake slowly pumped in and out of his ass.

"Okay." Mik's face was flushed as he cast an odd look in Tala's direction. She did her best to look innocent, but she had the horrible feeling Mik might have checked out her fantasies. He was a lot better at getting into her thoughts than she was at getting into his.

"No matter where you are in your fantasy, I want you to end it, and give me your attention before we end up with a group orgasm and waste all that wonderful energy." He waited while everyone laughed, but his eyes were still on Tala. "Okay," he said, turning his attention back to the group. "Hold hands and concentrate. AJ and I know Anton and Stefan's mental signatures the best, but I've usually got more range, so I want you to concentrate on me. Help me push my thoughts out there. Picture a long cable made up of many threads . . . our phone line, so to speak. That's what we'll use to reach the guys."

He looked around the circle and made eye contact with each of them. "Once we reach them, concentrate on the mental signature, on the route we took to find them. That way, if the link is broken, each of us should have the ability to stay in contact with our targets."

Tala'd never seen Mik like this: so in control, taking charge of the rescue this way. So often he deferred to AJ, or even to her. Now, though, he had so much purpose, an innate power she'd never realized.

A very sexy innate power.

Damn, she was wet and horny and frustrated as hell. The minute after they made contact, once they knew everyone was okay, then *Mik, look out.*

Jake squeezed her hand. So did AJ. Tala concentrated on the subject at hand.

Mik wasn't used to being the center of attention, but he put his nervousness aside. Only their mission mattered, not how uncomfortable he was in the leader's role.

He'd always been a better follower, but right now he was the most qualified and he'd damned well better get it right. He sort of wished he hadn't checked out Tala's fantasy. Damn, it made it hard to hold Jake's hand and keep things focused. He'd been looking for sexual frustration, though, and by golly he'd gotten it.

Mik emptied his mind of all thoughts, then drew on the joined minds, on their power and focus. He built up a fresh image, a long cable unraveling out into the ether, drifting through a midnight-blue void, searching for Anton and Stefan. He felt the other strands joining his and was surprised to see that each person there had chosen a different color. The strands wove together, building a multi-hued bridge, a road leading out into the night.

The power grew, and Mik struggled to control it, to direct it. He kept the focus on Stefan and Anton, felt the others focusing on him. The night was dark and the distance great, but the line snaked onward, out into the darkness. The colorful strands continued to weave about its length and lend it strength. He was only vaguely aware of the others in the room, sensing them as generators, as tools to help him on his quest.

Suddenly, he sensed a flash of consciousness, a familiar mental touch. *Stefan? Anton?* Mik called out to them both. He tightened his grip on Jake's and Shannon's hands and opened his mind to the signature of the Montana Chanku.

Mik? Is that you? Where are you?

Stefan! We're near Bismarck, North Dakota. We're trying to find you. Where are you?

I don't know. We were headed east out of Montana when the

plane went down. We're in a swamp or shallow water some-where. It was dark when we regained consciousness. The girls are okay. Anton is unconscious. We're trying to bring him around. Help us. When you contacted me, he groaned.

Mik didn't answer. Instead, he pressed their joint focus toward Anton Cheval. Called out to him, begging him to awaken. There was a sense of surprise, of anger, almost, at having been disturbed. Then Anton's voice, weak yet familiar, filled Mik's mind.

I'm here. I'm alive. How is Keisha? Is everyone okay?

Mik almost collapsed with relief. "He's alive," he said. "They all are. Now we just have to find out where in the hell they went down."

Mik? You need to find us fast. There was an edge of panic to Stefan's voice. *I think Keisha's water just broke.*

5

Is there a transponder on the plane? Mik asked

Probably fried. Anton didn't waste energy explaining how. *Now that we've established a mental link, you can use that to find us. Can you sense the direction to search?*

Anton waited for what seemed like an interminable amount of time.

Northwest from our location, I think. Let me check.

Mik's voice disappeared again. Anton wondered whom he conferred with. There were other minds in the link, but he could identify only Mik's partner, AJ.

Keisha needed him, but Stefan was with her. Right now Anton knew that, even with his head injury, his range was the greatest. Where the hell were Mik and AJ?

As if on cue, Mik's voice popped into his thoughts. *Jacob Trent, Baylor Quinn, and Shannon Murphy are heading out now. They've got your mental signature locked in and are on big all-terrain bikes that will take them just about anywhere. AJ, Tala, and I are going to follow in our SUV. We've got four-wheel drive, but the bikes are better for off-road. Jake was a paramedic. Shannon has some medical training as well. They've got some medical supplies and blankets. Don't worry. We'll find you. Just keep on broadcasting.*

"There it is!" Jake turned the bike off the dirt road he'd been following through the early morning shadows and headed cross country. He'd assured Shannon that Anton's voice grew stronger in his mind with each passing mile, but she hadn't been able to lock on to the wizard as well as Jake. She hung on for dear life, and suddenly she saw the rising sun glinting off the upended, twisted nose section of what could only be Anton Cheval's jet.

They skidded through mud and weeds, with Bay following close behind. The bikes were big and heavy enough to break through overgrowth, but mud flew in all directions. The four members of the Montana pack waited on a small knoll near a swampy area blanketed in a tangle of willows and tules.

A steamy mist rose off the shallow water, and the smell of jet fuel was overpowering.

Jake parked the bike on a dry spot and grabbed the first-aid kit. "Cheval? Aragat? I'm Jacob Trent."

"Thank goodness." The tall man who stood looked exactly as Shannon had pictured him. Slim and elegant, even in a blood-stained white shirt and torn dark slacks, he might have been a musician or a poet with his flowing black hair and aristocratic demeanor. The bloodied gash across his temple and his ashen complexion did little to detract from his sophisticated look and beautiful features. He held out his hand, his fingers every bit as graceful as the rest of him.

Jake grasped it. There would be no posturing today. No alpha wolves sizing one another up, no need to establish who was on top. Shannon marveled at the way their pack dynamics changed when another Chanku needed help.

"I'm Anton Cheval. My mate, Keisha, appears to be in labor.

She's a few weeks early. Xandi's fine but I think Stefan has a broken shoulder. He's immobilized it as well as he could."

Shannon nodded at Cheval and went directly to his mate's side. Keisha lay on a dry blanket, propped up against part of one of the airplane's seats that someone must have hauled from the wreckage. Her hair hung in silky black tangles past her shoulders. Xandi sat next to her, equally disheveled, holding Keisha's hand.

Both of them were heavily pregnant, with their faces and bodies streaked with mud from the swamp, but they still had the kind of looks that caught a person's attention. Shannon had seen photographs, but Xandi and Keisha in person took her breath. These were women like her. Chanku, but so drop-dead gorgeous . . .

"I'm Shannon," she said, touching Keisha lightly on the shoulder and sensing the woman's pain. "I've been wanting so much to meet you, but I never imagined it would be like this. Are you doing okay?"

Keisha laughed. "Much better, now the troops have arrived. It was feeling pretty lonely out here."

"I bet. The reserves will be here soon." Shannon chuckled and sat next to the women. Stefan Aragat had joined the men.

Jake had obviously taken charge and was looking at Stefan's injured shoulder, but he turned to introduce Bay. "This is Baylor Quinn, our packmate. Bay, see if you've got a signal on the cell, call Luc, and give them coordinates for the chopper. They were southwest of Rapid City last time I talked to him." He gestured toward Shannon. "Cheval, that's my mate, Shannon Murphy. Hon, see if you can contact Mik and AJ. They should be close enough for mindtalking. Let them know exactly where we are, and that, other than Keisha in labor and Stefan with a broken shoulder, everyone appears to be okay."

He flashed her a cheeky grin when he said it, and Shannon

felt herself relax. She sat back and concentrated, reaching out for their brethren.

Half an hour later, Baylor finished up his third conversation with Lucien Stone and stuck the cell phone back in his pocket. "The chopper should be here before long. They had to refuel. How's Keisha?"

"Her contractions are coming every four minutes," Shannon said. She knelt on one side of Keisha; Xandi and Tala were on the other. Tala, Mik, and AJ had arrived a few minutes earlier, and Tala had taken up her position with the laboring woman almost immediately.

Anton sat behind his mate and held both her hands. Shannon placed her palm over Keisha's belly. Keisha arched and groaned, obviously having a hard contraction. Shannon checked her watch, then glanced up at Bay. "It's going to be a race between the chopper and the baby."

Bay nodded at Shannon, then turned away. He felt a need to give Keisha privacy, so he joined Mik and AJ sitting on the ground with Stefan and Jake. Stefan stood up, as if to join the women, but Bay stopped him with a glance. "I know you want to be with your packmates, but we're going to need a story for the authorities. I imagine we've got at least a couple of bodies to explain away. What happened?"

Stefan nodded in agreement. "It was a hijacking, pure and simple. Looks like both the pilot and copilot were in on it." He rubbed his left arm and shifted his position, as if trying to get comfortable. His eyes appeared both pain-glazed and troubled. "I can't believe we didn't pick up something from these guys, some sense of danger. The only thing we can figure is that they drugged our water. We all had bottled water during takeoff, and we were all asleep within minutes of one another. Once we were out, they must have changed course and headed due east. Luckily Keisha had taken only a few swallows and wasn't as deeply under. She's the one who noticed we were headed in the wrong direction and woke the rest of us up."

"Okay. What kind of injuries do we need to explain? How'd you overpower them? Any particularly unusual damage to the plane?" Bay rubbed his temples. They'd been awake now for over twenty-four hours and he was fading fast. He hoped he wasn't missing something important here.

"Broken neck on the copilot, probably a crushed windpipe, but I managed not to rip his throat. Anton shot the pilot, point blank, just above the heart. We crashed because Anton fried the controls when he used his mind to burn out the locking system on the door to the cockpit. I imagine that could be explained as an electrical malfunction, though I hate to say that. The Hawker's a great airplane."

Bay thought a moment, imagining the terror Anton and Stefan must have felt—their women on board, the pilot and copilot taking them to some unknown destination. "How about the copilot shot the pilot and tried to take over the plane. You and Anton took out the copilot but the plane was damaged in the struggle. You're both very wealthy men. Kidnapping for profit would make a plausible story."

Stefan nodded. "Works for me and seems to cover everything. Run it by Anton. See if he agrees."

Bay glanced at the group gathered around Keisha, then back at Stefan. "Looks to me as if Anton's otherwise occupied. Jake, aren't you supposed to be catching the baby?"

"Shit." Jake grabbed the first-aid kit and raced to help.

Anton supported Keisha as she cried out and raised her head. Tala, Shannon, and Xandi had grown quiet. Each of them touched Keisha: her arm, her shoulder, her leg. Bay wondered if they used the power of their Chanku link to help ease Keisha's pain.

All of a sudden, things happened very fast. Keisha grabbed

her ankles and drew her heels back tight against her thighs. Anton rose up on his knees to better support her back. She cried out once more, Jake scrambled to find a position between her legs, and Anton hung on to Keisha's hands as she strained to push her baby into the world.

The sight and sound of Keisha's dark-haired daughter slipping out of her mother's wet birth canal was something Bay would never forget. He stood, transfixed, as her dark scalp appeared, still covered in membrane, then as the perfect little body slipped into Jake's big hands.

"Got her." He held her upside down long enough to clear her air passages, and she opened her mouth in a strong, wailing cry. The women applauded, and Keisha lay back against Anton, obviously exhausted, but smiling ear to ear. Jake took the soft towel Bay handed to him and wrapped the tiny baby before tying off her umbilical cord. Stefan used his one good hand to clamp and cut the cord with the sterile scissors Jake had given him from the first-aid kit. Jake handed the baby girl to Anton, then pressed his hand on Keisha's midsection to help her expel the afterbirth.

Anton's calm exterior crumbled. Tears coursed down his cheeks as he gazed into his daughter's eyes for the first time. His voice cracked and he took a second to gather himself, and then his words were for Keisha. "She looks just like you," he whispered. "Exactly like you." He leaned over and kissed his mate, kissing away her tears as he cried his own.

Bay felt his own eyes tearing up. He glanced at Jake and saw that his cheeks were streaked as well. He'd removed his rubber gloves and now his fingers were firmly entangled with Shannon's. Stefan wept openly, but he gazed upon his pregnant mate, not the child Anton held.

AJ and Mik stood silently to one side, their arms wrapped around Tala, and it was obvious they were as emotionally touched as everyone else. Bay glanced up and caught Shannon watching him. Was it so obvious, he wondered? Was his pain, the fact there was no mate to bear his child, written in bold letters on his face?

He'd never felt outside the circle before. Never once questioned the loving relationship he had with Jake and Shannon.

Shannon was Jake's mate. Someday she would make babies with Jake and Jake alone. She smiled at Bay, but her thoughts were blocked when she turned her attention back to Keisha and the beautiful baby in her arms.

Sighing, Bay welcomed the distant *thump, thump, thump* of the approaching helicopter. He rose to his feet and held out his hand to Anton in congratulations. Then he gave him the story they would need to agree on for the report the authorities were sure to demand.

The helicopter lifted into the air with Stefan, Xandi, Anton, Keisha, and her daughter tucked safely aboard. Luc stayed behind because of weight limits on the chopper, but he'd gone out to the plane and grabbed what personal items he could recover for the Montana pack.

A crash investigation team was on the way in. Luc had listened to Bay's scenario and agreed it made the most sense, but they weren't waiting around. Mik and AJ loaded the bags into their SUV and Shannon hugged Tala. Luc was riding with them on to Billings.

"Shannon?" Jake brushed Shannon's hair back out of her eyes and gave her a tired smile. "You're sure you don't want to go with Tala and the guys? They've got a flight from Billings into San Francisco that'll get them there by tonight. Warm, clean beds, hot showers, maybe a nice restaurant for dinner?"

She wrapped her fingers around his wrist, turned his hand, and kissed the palm. "You sound like you're trying to get rid of me. You don't think I'd leave now and miss the excitement of a cross country motorcycle trip, do you? I don't think so!" On a more serious note she added, "Besides, Tala's so excited about seeing her sister. I don't want to interrupt their reunion. We'll be in San Francisco in a few days."

His smile lit up his entire face and made Shannon so glad she'd answered as she had. *Damn.* She did love the man something fierce.

"No reason to wait around, then," Jake said. "Bay? You ready?"

"Ready as I'll ever be." Bay fastened his helmet and threw his leg over the big bike. He gave Jake a thumbs up.

Shannon settled in behind Jake and wrapped her arms around his waist. She still felt shaken after watching Keisha give birth and still hurt from the labor pains she'd somehow, instinctively known how to take on herself. All the women had helped to ease Keisha's pain, something none of them had realized was possible. Her Chanku instincts brought one surprise after another.

She'd definitely want these women with her when her time came. Would she ever have Jake's baby? They'd never really talked about it, not that much, and for so many years she'd thought herself incapable of having children. Now, though . . . Shannon thought of the tiny infant she'd held for just moments while Keisha was strapped into her stretcher for the helicopter ride. Remembered the warm little body, the bright eyes looking directly into hers. What a life that little girl was going to have! With Anton and Keisha for parents and Xandi and Stefan as godparents . . . talk about your perfect family.

Jake shifted into gear. Shannon tightened her grip on his trim waist and they headed out. Bay followed. She put all her worries aside, concentrating on the wind in her face and the beautiful day still ahead. Grinning like a fool, Shannon cut loose with a long, loud howl. Damn, she'd never imagined how much fun this could be.

* * *

They found a beautiful little hotel in an old town close to the Colorado border, one with a restaurant on the first floor and all the amenities a guest could want in a private suite on the third. Shannon giggled when Jake whipped out the Pack Dynamics credit card to pay the exorbitant charges for the room, but when she saw the massive bed in the middle of it and the hot tub on its private deck, she decided she agreed with Jake. They had earned this one.

Bay ordered in room service and was still on the phone when Shannon stripped out of her leathers. Totally exhausted, she grabbed the shower first. No way was she crawling into a bubbling hot tub with leg stubble. When she finally, reluctantly, dragged herself out, Shannon found dinner warming under covered lids and champagne chilling in a bucket of ice. She ignored dinner and headed for the hot tub, where she slipped into the steamy, bubbling water with a full crystal flute and smooth legs.

Jake and Bay showered and joined her in the tub. They'd not really talked since the morning's rescue. Now they merely wanted to enjoy the peace that came with a job well done.

Sipping champagne with two gorgeous hunks: It just didn't get any better than this.

Then Bay proved Shannon wrong. It really could get better. He set his champagne aside and knelt between Shannon's legs. The water bubbled and churned around her and steam rose into the night sky. The deck was totally private, screened on all sides but open to the stars.

Jake scooted over. He lifted Shannon and settled her on his lap. His cock rode the crease between her thighs until Bay wrapped his hands around her waist and lifted her. She felt Jake's cock slip between her cheeks and press against her ass. Bay's tongue found her clit. Sighing with the doubled sensation of two men pleasuring her tired body, Shannon drifted in a world of fantasy and sensual contact.

Jake used his fingers to relax her sphincter and slipped his cock past the tight ring with very little pressure. Bay rose over her body and penetrated vaginally, driving deep inside as he kissed and suckled her sensitive breasts. The water was almost too hot, but not nearly as hot as the men who loved her. Their bodies pressed hers on either side, their hard muscles rippling and bunching with each thrust and withdrawal.

Shannon moaned, caught up in pure sensation, in the mental connection with men she loved. There was desperation, though. She felt it in Bay. A sense that all was not well. He thrust into her hard and fast, his cock driving deep, pounding against her womb. Jake's thrusts were slow and careful, her comfort his every concern, but Bay took her hard, his face a mask of need and anger.

Why, Bay? What's wrong?

He stopped, blinked as if coming back to the present, and slumped in her arms. Slowly, he withdrew, leaving Shannon feeling bereft, empty. "I'm sorry. So very sorry. I didn't mean . . ."

Jake reached for his packmate, but his words were for Shannon. "Are you okay?"

She nodded, covered Jake's hand where it clasped Bay's forearm. "Are you?"

"I don't know. Today was . . ."

Shannon smiled. "Intense. Very intense. We saved lives, delivered a baby, lied to the government inspectors. All the makings for a great book."

"Yeah, but I guess I want that happy ending." Bay bowed his head.

"You want a mate. A woman for your own. One to make babies with." Shannon reached up and cupped his cheek. "It'll happen, Bay. There's someone out there for you. Until then, you know you've got us."

He sighed. Nodded. "I know. Today, it just hit home. Hard."

Shannon leaned forward and kissed him. "Make love to us,

Bay. Love me. We'll sleep, we'll go forward. You'll find someone. I feel it in my heart."

He kissed her on the nose. Then he thrust his hips forward and filled her once again. He brought all of them to climax until they were shuddering in each other's arms, floating in the lazy bubbles of the hot tub.

But Shannon sensed Bay's anxiety, his need for something else, something more, and while she loved him with all her heart, she knew it wasn't enough to keep him.

Tala crawled into the big bed and managed to snuggle herself in between AJ and Mik. There was a definite plus to being small. They moved apart and made room for her without any complaints.

She didn't want sex. Not now. She wanted to lie in between her men and think about the evening she'd spent with her sister. Lisa was so healthy and happy and alive. Tala didn't realize how much she'd missed her until she stepped out of the cab and saw Lisa standing there, tucked under Tinker McClintock's strong arm, her long hair swinging behind her and a big grin on her face.

They'd spent all evening together catching up, talking about the huge changes in their lives. Both of them Chanku shapeshifters. But the two had agreed that the best part of it all had been finding love.

If only Baylor had someone of his own. Tala lay there between AJ and Mik and wondered who was out there for her brother. There had to be someone: a woman somewhere who would love him for himself, who would be Chanku, just like Bay.

Mik rolled over and nuzzled against Tala's breasts. She felt his tongue come out and wrap around the nipple that suddenly sprang to life. AJ's hand slipped over her hip, snaked around her side, and dove directly between her legs.

Tala sighed. She might not have felt as if she wanted sex when she crawled into bed, but these two could be *so* persuasive. Wriggling her hips, she found the perfect spot against AJ's groin, made room for Mik's broad chest against her breasts, and smiled into the darkness.

The big house where the men from Pack Dynamics lived, where she and the guys would stay through the wedding, might not be a motel, but damn it all, Tala was sure it was going to rate a ten anyway.

Anton sat in the darkness wearing soft cotton knit pants and nothing more, vaguely aware of traffic noises on the street below their luxury suite in the heart of San Francisco, yet almost preternaturally aware of the small life he held against his bare chest. *Lily Milina:* Lily because lilies were Keisha's favorite flower; Milina for Anton's Serbian grandmother, a name meaning pleasure, charm, and grace. He brushed the blanket back from her eyes with a fingertip and stared at her perfect face.

Lily was definitely a pleasure to hold. She was exceedingly charming and, if she proved to be anything like her mother, destined to be filled with grace. No matter, his daughter slept soundly, wrapped in a light blanket and cradled in his arms. He absorbed her sweet new-baby smell, the sounds she made in her sleep, the feeling he might burst for the joy filling his heart and soul.

Joy tempered by lingering fear.

He'd come so close to losing them today. So very close. Luc worked, even now, on finding the bastards behind the attempted kidnapping. Anton's heart raced at the mere thought of how close he'd come to losing everything that mattered in his life. He studied his daughter's perfect features: the tiny nose and pouting lips. Never again would he allow harm to come to her or her mother. *Never.*

Keisha slept, exhausted but content, just a few feet away.

The doctor had pronounced mother and daughter in perfect health and sent them home after a cursory examination. Home, of course, would be this hotel until after the wedding, but it could be anywhere, Anton realized, as long as he had his family and packmates beside him.

Xandi and Stefan slept in the room next door, both of them exhausted. He sensed Stefan's pain, but he'd learned much from the women today when they'd gathered together to take away so many of Keisha's labor pains. It had been purely instinctual, something he'd not realized the Chanku could do. He'd never guessed them capable of such a powerful and selfless act. Of course, he learned daily just how amazing a Chanku bitch could be. Not only his mate, but every one of the females he'd met were amazing. All of them were strong and self-assured. Indomitable, yet possessing a capacity to love that left him shaken with its intensity.

He'd watched and learned, and now he knew how to use his mind to help Stefan deal with the worst of it, by taking part of Stefan's pain into himself. The mild discomfort Anton felt increased his respect for the women even more.

They had the doctor's assurance Stefan's shoulder should knit without any problems. Of course, shifting was out of the question until the sling came off, unless, of course, he wanted to walk on three legs. Anton wondered, though, if shifting might not help Stefan heal faster.

They needed to talk about that. There was so much they still had to learn about themselves. Especially now. How could they teach their children if they didn't know for themselves? He gazed down at his daughter and smiled as she pursed her lips and blew a tiny bubble. Then he sighed as she stole his worries away.

Tia stared at her reflection in the bathroom mirror. Her face looked drawn; her eyes drooped. Face it, she looked like hell. Even her students had asked if she was sick.

No, not sick, merely stressed to the point of flipping out. Why, she wondered, did this wedding have her so on edge? All she was doing was marrying the man she'd already promised her life to, the one man in all the world she could love this deeply. Instead of being happy, or celebrating, she was worrying herself into a nervous breakdown. It made no sense, no sense at all. But the anxiety remained, seething just beneath the surface.

She heard Lisa come into the bedroom and smiled. Lisa and her little sister Tala had spent the evening together; it was the first time they'd seen each other in ten years. Now that must have been a reunion to savor! Tia turned back to the mirror and glared at herself. Lisa walked into the bathroom and caught her.

"Oh. I didn't realize you were in here. I thought you'd already gone to bed." She turned as if to leave.

Tia reached out and caught Lisa's arm. "No. Don't go. How was it? What's your sister like?"

Lisa practically melted against the tile counter, hitched one hip over the edge, and sat. "She's wonderful. So happy and she seems to be totally content for the first time in her life. She's very much in love with both AJ and Mik. They have no intention of adding anyone else to their ménage. They've bonded. Can you believe that? The three of them are, for all intents and purposes, a couple."

Tia sighed. "I wish I could be as sure of my life as all of you are. What's wrong with me?"

Lisa touched her cheek. "I think you're afraid of change, of upsetting the status quo. Afraid that marriage to Luc will somehow alter the dynamics of your life. It won't, you know. You're already married. After Anton says whatever words he plans to say, you'll still have Luc, still have Tinker, and, for better or worse, still have me. It's all good, sweetie. Relax."

Tia raised her eyes and stared at Lisa. Could she be right?

Was it really something that simple? She allowed Lisa to pull her to her feet and followed her newest packmate to the bed. The guys were both sleeping, wound up in each other's arms as if they'd made their own entertainment tonight. Grinning, Tia crawled in on Luc's side while Lisa got in next to Tinker.

Relax, she said. Right. Lying there in the darkness, Tia thought about what Lisa had said, and willed herself to fall asleep.

The bachelorette party was everything she could have wanted, though Keisha's newborn was the center of attention. Lily slept soundly through the off-color jokes, the margaritas, and even the naked guy delivering flowers. Tia still wasn't sure who'd set that one up. Still, she found herself wondering how many babies might arrive before another year passed. All of them were of the right age; all were bonded to men they loved. Her sisters of the heart, each of them, celebrated her marriage to Luc. Tia sipped her drink and wondered if her hands would ever stop trembling. How could she be nervous here, in this private room in a very exclusive restaurant where the waiters outdid themselves with drinks and fine foods?

The guys celebrated in their own way, running as wolves under the moon on Mt. Tam. Thank goodness Stefan had been able to shift. He was sore and not very fast, but they'd discovered that the act of shifting appeared to speed the healing process. Tia grinned, imagining the stories that would be told should anyone see the huge pack of magnificent wolves racing through the forest. Even her father had elected to go . . . eight alpha wolves in their prime. She shivered with incipient arousal, just imagining all that testosterone.

Then she shivered again. The wedding was two days away. Already she felt like running for the hills . . . on two legs or four. It didn't really matter.

* * *

Shannon gave Tia a hug and a kiss, then reached up and kissed Ulrich's cheek. "Break a leg, Dad," she teased. Then she gave Tia one last lingering glance, picked up her bouquet of white roses, and brushed the hem of her blood-red gown. She turned back once and said, "You're a gorgeous bride, honey. Your mom's here in spirit. You know she is." Then she pushed aside the doorway to the tent where'd they'd been waiting. With a last smile for Tia, Shannon walked slowly down the white runner covering the packed sand, keeping in step to the soft rhythm a very talented musician coaxed from his guitar.

Tia watched her go, then turned to her father and sighed. "Dad, why am I so nervous?" Tia smoothed the satin skirt down over her knees for about the hundredth time. She was so aware her mother had worn this dress for her marriage to Ulrich and, in spite of Shannon's well wishes, just as aware her mother wasn't here. Would Camille approve of this match?

Tia frowned. Well, of course Camille would approve. This whole wedding was her idea, wasn't it? Hadn't she been the one to suggest that Tia and Luc marry? So why the nerves?

Lisa had worked wonders, using part of the long train to lengthen the hem so that it hung in shimmering satin ripples almost to Tia's ankles in front and flowed along in the sand behind. Still, Tia's hands trembled and she clasped them in front of herself to still their shaking.

Ulrich covered Tia's hands with his. "You're nervous because you're a bride and it's your wedding day. I think nerves are part of the ceremony. Think about it, sweetheart. You're choosing to make a binding commitment based purely on love. Not on genetics."

Tia swung around to stare at her father. "What do you mean?"

Ulrich smiled. "When you bonded with Luc, you made a choice but it was one limited by the fact you knew he was your mate, as if the bonding had been predestined. Your DNA had pretty well determined your match, the fact you were both Chanku. Face it, I made sure the two of you got together." He laughed, a low chuckle that told Tia exactly how pleased he was at his own part in her life with Luc. "Now, though," he said, straightening one of the red roses tucked in her hair, "those vows you'll take today? You're choosing to make them, choosing to commit publicly and say this is the man you love." Her father paused, then tilted his head and stared at her. "You do love Lucien, don't you?"

"With all my heart." Even as she said the words, Tia realized the truth in them, the power. She did love Luc. Loved him more than life.

"Good. Then you have no need to be nervous. He loves you just as much, if not more."

With that, Ulrich held out his elbow and Tia looped her fingers over the smooth black fabric. She took a deep breath and stepped out into the early morning sunshine.

They were all here, all the ones who cared for her, who loved her. Students from the class she taught and their parents and her principal, and the others who, like Tia, shared the same Chanku genes. She paused a moment, seeing each person smiling back at her. Suddenly her hands stopped trembling, and her heart settled into a natural rhythm.

It hit her, then—such an amazing yet simple revelation. She'd been so afraid of change, yet that's all her life was about. Wasn't change exactly what had made her happiest these past months? She'd left her safe yet dull life with Shannon and found Luc. She'd left her small apartment near the school and discovered life with Tinker and, of course, Luc, and now Lisa.

More change. Wonderful change. She'd watched AJ and Mik expand their same-sex bond and fall deeper and deeper into love with Tala, and she'd rejoiced in Jake's newfound confidence and love for Shannon. As much as Tia missed them both, she knew Jake and Shannon would never leave Maine. Not as long as they had Baylor.

Bay was ready for change, though. She caught his eye and winked. He had the look of a man who wanted a mate of his own.

Tia turned and smiled at her father, so proud, standing beside her. Handsome and still young. They'd put her mother's soul to rest. Someday, Tia hoped her dad would find a new love. Someone to take Ulrich Mason into his retiring years, especially now that Luc was handling more and more of Pack Dynamics. Someone who'd give him the sass he missed from Camille.

Tia took another step forward. Luc waited, standing so proudly between Tinker and Anton Cheval: tall, dark and twice as good looking as either of the other men. On the other hand . . . Tinker was truly a hunk and Anton certainly had his own charm. It was hard to believe the Chanku wizard used to intimidate the hell out of her. He didn't anymore, not since she'd seen him in his new role as daddy. Anton's tenderness toward tiny Lily Milina brought tears to her eyes and a sense of potential and possibility to her heart.

It was all good. All new, and damned if she couldn't wait to see what might come next. Tia raised her eyes and caught Luc smiling only at her. She opened her heart and felt him. Opened her mind and heard him.

I love you. I will always love you. You are every beat of my heart, every breath I take.

Luc's words. They were powerful words that made her want to laugh out loud, words that drew Tia forward with the strength of their truth. *As I love you,* she said. *As I will always love you.*

Walking with her father, so strong and handsome beside her, Tia felt the brush of her mother's love. She glanced to her left and sensed a shimmer at the edge of her vision, scented a hint of rose sachet, felt the warmth of a hug, a soft kiss on her cheek. *Camille.* She was close beside her, sharing her special day.

Smiling broadly through tears of joy, Tia almost flew the last few steps to Luc's side.

Anton stood at the front of the small group gathered on the quiet stretch of private beach and knew that all those who mattered to him, all those he loved, were here, together, in this one place. He glanced to his right and winked at Keisha. She held Lily in her arms, their lovely, perfect little girl. Their future. He glanced up as Tia and Ulrich appeared at the doorway in the small tent where Tia'd gotten ready, and wondered what it would feel like to be in Ulrich's shoes, walking his daughter down the aisle, giving her to another man.

It made his blood run cold. *Damn.* He'd never thought of marriage along those lines. Give her away? Never. Keisha raised an eyebrow in his direction, and Anton reined in his thoughts. Thank goodness he'd not been broadcasting. Only Keisha appeared to hear, but then Keisha always knew what he was thinking.

He glanced at the small group of guests. Most of them were Chanku, but a few of Tia's students in the crowd sat proudly with their parents. She taught special needs kids, and Anton knew her students and their parents loved her deeply.

He turned his attention where it belonged, to the bride drawing close with a glorious smile on her lips and tears flowing down her cheeks, to Luc standing expectantly beside him, smiling every bit as broadly as Tia. Luc's eyes looked suspiciously damp as well. Tinker stood just beyond Luc, obviously taking his best man duties quite seriously.

Shannon Murphy had found her position on Anton's right as the maid of honor. Her eyes weren't on Tia, though. She hadn't stopped sighing over her mate, though Anton had to agree the resident bad boy looked pretty good in a tux. All of them did. Chanku certainly cleaned up well.

Ulrich stopped directly in front of Anton, kissed Tia's cheek, and stepped aside, smoothly handing her off to Lucien. It couldn't have been all that difficult. Ulrich had chosen Luc for her, after all. Anton was grinning at the thought of choosing someone for his precious child when Shannon took the bouquet of red roses from Tia, and then it was just the three of them. Anton looked first into Tia's eyes and then into Luc's. He felt pride and a very deep sense of love, as if he were a parent to these two exceptional people.

With that thought in mind, Anton held up his hands for a very personal blessing, one that would unite Lucien Stone and Tianna Mason even more strongly than their bonding so many months ago. Just as he opened his mouth to speak, he caught a slight sense of movement, a shimmering figure hovering at the edges of his peripheral vision.

Camille? Ah . . . Tia's mother had made it. He should have known a spirit as strong as hers wouldn't stay away. From the spark of light shining in Tia's eyes, it was obvious she knew her mother was close. Only Ulrich seemed oblivious, as he should be. He'd put his late wife's spirit to rest. It was time for him to move on, time for change.

Anton looked at the expectant faces, glanced once more at Luc and Tia, and began. "We are gathered here today . . ."

With a most traditional opening, Anton knew he set the stage for a wonderfully non-traditional marriage.

Epilogue

They met at the Top of the Mark for Sunday brunch: everyone, of course, except for Luc and Tia, who'd gone to the Pack Dynamics cabin in the Sierras for their honeymoon.

Bay sipped his coffee and felt, once more, that sense of being apart from the whole. He had to admit, though, it was nice having a sister on either side, even better knowing how happy they were in their new relationships.

He glanced up and caught Stefan watching him, smiling broadly. "Take a look at this. I may have found you a woman." He handed Bay a newspaper, a cheap tabloid from the looks of it. The headline screamed across the front, "Wolf Girl Terrifies Rural NY Neighborhood!"

Below was a grainy photo, obviously retouched, of a snarling wolf with just enough human features, including long blond hair, to look truly hideous. Anger fired by pain coursed through Bay. Did everyone find it humorous, that he among them was alone and hating it? It took him a minute to find his voice. He tossed the paper back on the table and snarled, "Not funny, Aragat."

Still smiling, Stefan shook his head. "You don't get it, do you? I'm not kidding, and this is not a joke. Xandi, tell Bay how you found me."

Xandi reached across the table and covered Bay's shaking hand with hers. "Stefan looked almost exactly like the woman in that photo. He'd been stuck like that, in mid-shift, for over five years. That picture's probably not real, but there's often a kernel of truth to tabloid stories. We found Keisha through an article in that same publication. It was just as lurid, but there was enough truth to send us searching for her."

Bay looked carefully at Stefan and tried to imagine the horror of being caught between shifts. "What happened?"

Stefan shook his head. "It's a long story and too intense for a 'breakfast after the wedding' conversation, but the point is, it can happen. There just might be a young woman in upstate New York living the same horror I lived. And you, my friend, might be able to find her and save her."

Bay looked at the article once more with a new sense of purpose. It named a small town in the Adirondack Mountains. He read the entire thing and then glanced at Jake and Shannon. Jake gave him a thumbs up.

Bay stood up, chugged the last of his tepid coffee, and grabbed his helmet and gloves. Already his mind spun with plans and possibilities. "It's been wonderful to see all of you, to meet you," he said, nodding to the Montana pack. "It's been especially wonderful to see you two rats." He leaned down and gave both Lisa and Tala a kiss on the cheek. "But it looks like I'm going to take a little trip east."

Xandi felt a catch in her breath, remembering Stefan, remembering the night she'd found and learned to love the man beneath the body of the wolf. She watched as Bay tucked Stefan's tabloid under his arm, saluted all of them at the table, and strolled out of the restaurant.

Stefan leaned back in his chair, slipping an arm around

Keisha on one side and Xandi on the other. "My work here is done," he said, grinning broadly.

"No." Xandi rubbed her palm along the side of her taut belly where another contraction was already taking her breath away again. "I think it's just beginning."

Kiss of the Dragon

Lacy Danes

To Eric,
You light up my soul, fill my heart, and make me do *very* naughty things.
I adore you.
yours.

While I wrote this story, someone very special's mother passed away quite suddenly.
Barbara S. Weinraub
She loved to read . . . She loved erotic things . . .
This story is for you, Barbara.

Thank you, Eden Bradley, Eva Gale, Crystal Jordan, Emma Petersen, Linda LaRoque, and Shelli Stevens. My fabulous crit group! Without you guys, I wouldn't have made it!

Hugs and kisses,
Lacy

1

Chester Shields stumbled into the bar and headed straight for the loo. Durn said he would meet him here, yet Chet didn't detect his energy in this hell of a place.

The music, some industrial funk, shook the living breath from him as he pushed through the packed crowd. God, he hated night clubs and hated this class of crowd worse. Everyone was dressed in black, with dyed black hair and the pale skin of the dead. Chills chased down his spine. Didn't the men know it was far from hip for them to wear thick black eyeliner and black lipstick? He rolled his eyes and cringed. The powdered wigs of the 17th century made him shudder, but this trend . . . truly repulsive. He would never succumb.

Winding his way to the side of the building, he spied a door with the symbol of a man standing with feet wide, hands on hips and whip in hand. The loo? He shook his head. What did the women's door look like?

Striding towards the male sign, he pushed open the door and stepped onto the gray tiled floor. He lifted his foot and the sucking sound shook up his spine as his shoe pulled from the sticky surface. Bugger. He would have to wash and sanitize his favorite shoes once he left there.

The door swooshed closed behind him, and he absorbed the emptiness of the room's energy. His shoulders relaxed. No one was here. Spying the stall doors, he closed his eyes and scanned for the Royals' presence. Heat prickled his spine as he imagined each stall in his mind. The warmth intensified as he locked his concentration onto the third from the left. He opened his eyes, glanced at the grime on the floor between him and the third door, and cringed. Damn it.

He lurched forward, slamming open the door to the stall. Closing the door, he reached out and stuck his hand down deep into the container with paper seat protectors that hung behind the commode. Ugh. The stall was worse then the main bathroom. The toilet stood half covered with wet toilet paper; the floor was saturated in urine. A shudder wracked him.

Don't think about it, Chet, you will be out of here in two puffs of smoke.

He shifted his hand through the crinkly covers. *Where the bloody hell are you?* Sliding his fingers a bit farther to the right, he hit on a hard, thick paper envelope. He extracted the object of his mission and spun around as he tore open the blue wax seal impressed with the Royals' insignia: a dragonhead with nostrils flared and smoke billowing from the sides of its mouth.

He closed his eyes. Would this assignment be easy or hard? It didn't matter. The Royals chose him because he proved he was the best of the Dragna who vied to accomplish this task.

He sighed, pulled a folded paper out of the torn envelope, and unfolded the parchment with sweaty hands.

Scrolled in heavy dried blood across the ancient paper was *UNCIDON.* Below this in Dragoun were his instructions:

Chet,
The Ralston Company is in the process of developing a

detector of paranormal energies that includes Dragon. As well as others. All research shows this is legitimate. You must obtain this detector and all the research involved. This detector cannot be recreated. Your cloaking skills and flight are the reason we have selected you for this mission. Do not fail us. The security of our race depends on us remaining unknown to humankind.

May Desna follow you.

Rankor

Spying . . . and theft. He sighed. No problem.

Didn't they remember his follies as a kid? He'd always fucked up this type of mission. Besides, stealing went against all he believed. However, the mission was important to the Royals, to the existence of them all, including him. He ran his free hand through his hair.

The door to the men's room swung open and the loud music slammed into the small space, jarring his concentration. Two men laughed as they walked to the urinals. Chet stood still and closed his eyes.

"Did you see the tits on that blonde?" a young male voice slurred.

"Not only did I see her tits, I also got a nice whiff of her wet pussy."

My Desna. Chester cringed and rolled his eyes behind his lids. After three hundred years, the human male's wasted time in talk about possible conquests still appalled him.

The other man laughed, and the door opened then swung shut to muted silence once more.

He glanced down at the letter in his hand and held it above the toilet. His chest warmed and he exhaled a steady stream of fire, catching the parchment aflame. The paper disappeared bit by bit in a shower of red and orange embers. The heat caressed his fingers and he let the last scrap of burning evidence fall into the toilet. Then, with the heel of his favorite shoes, he flushed.

God, it was late. Why Nora was the only one who put any time into getting things done around here, she didn't know.

The detector had fallen behind schedule while Nora was in Hawaii, and now she'd had to spend this—her first day back—working until the wee hours. She sighed. If only she could nail this stupid formula to pick up Shawn's werewolf energies.

The calculations should work . . . In the past, she'd picked up ghost vibrations with no problem. She'd tweaked the crystals many times to pick up different paranormal energies. But now . . . She shook out her hands above the keyboard. She couldn't arrive at the right formula. The detector wouldn't identify Shawn even when Nora could see Shawn's werewolf energy with her own powers. What the hell was she doing wrong? Her eyelids slowly lowered. Man, she needed a cup of Joe.

Nora pushed away from her computer and headed from the lab into the darkened office building toward the kitchen. Ralston had hired three new people while she'd vacationed, and the two she'd met so far didn't have smarts enough to tie their shoes, let alone possess any powers to help solve her problem. The third . . . was apparently her new boss, though she had yet to see him.

She reached for the pot of coffee, poured the dark sludge into her Pluto the Dog cup, and wrinkled her nose. A yawn stretched her cheeks, and she twisted her neck from side to side, trying to ward off the exhaustion creeping into her bones.

Sighing, Nora closed her eyes as another yawn pushed from her lungs. Damn. She would finish this one calculation, then head home. She needed to wake up, though, or the letters and numbers on the computer screen would end up blurred together as she tried to read the formulas again and again. God, she hated that.

Arching her back, she left the kitchen and decided to take the extended way back to the lab by heading down the long corridor. She turned the corner and icy air swirled down the hall as if a window stood open. Shivering in the coolness, her senses awakened and she sighed. Yeah . . . She needed a breath of fresh, crisp fall air.

She headed in the direction of the breeze. The iciness led her to St. John's office. Peeking in the door, she saw that the window stood open. Strange . . . the room was empty. She shrugged her shoulders—*Oh well*—and headed straight to the window, inhaling the sting of the night air.

The moon shone full on this fall night and she wanted nothing more than to stroll down a leaf-covered lane, letting the freshly fallen leaves crunch beneath her feet. The moon's amazing energy would refresh her.

Her vacation . . . what a disappointment. She'd holidayed with the direct intention of having a fling on the sandy beaches of Hawaii, only to discover none of the men there held her interest. They'd either had grey hairs sticking out of their ears or they said *dude* a lot and their pants hung down to their butt cheeks. She couldn't do either type. The Daddy thing or the Ashton and Demi route didn't ring her bell.

John . . . The thought of the soothing heat of him pressed up against her back as she hung suspended from her wrists after play and him whispering to her about her powers slid through her being, leaving a warm, hazy glow of contentedness. She shook herself. *Stop it. He's long gone from your life and happily remarried with the kids he so desperately wanted. That you desperately wanted.*

A frown curved her lips as pain whipped the happy glow from her aura and tears welled in her eyes. Shit. Jet lag messed with her equilibrium. Jalapeño cheese puffs and a Dr. Pepper would cure her when she got home. For some strange reason they always put her to rights. Her stomach grumbled, reminding her that she'd forgotten to eat dinner.

She slid the window shut with a click and headed back out into the hall. Turning into the lab, she jolted to a standstill as her breath locked in her lungs. A tall man hunched in front of the computer on the far wall. She paused in the doorway and tried to get her lungs to expand. His copper hair curled against the collar of his tailored black leather biker jacket, catching the dim glow of the monitor.

His snug, fitted attire showed off his body to perfection. Her eyes widened as she probed past his façade and her body tingled as she saw his entire form glowing with a bluish gold energy. The intensity of the aura pulled at her. She had never experienced anything like his vibrance before. Who was she trying to fool? His energy? Right . . . My gosh, what an awesome ass.

She ran her tongue along her lips, then snagged her lower one between her teeth; the flesh between her thighs tingled. Gosh, she was horny. She'd searched for a dish as yummy as this guy throughout her entire trip in Hawaii.

Must be the new guy, and he no doubt possesses a sixth power. That would be one explanation for the glow.

St. John said he was a wiz and that the project would get past the detector's hurdle because of him. Nora bet a breakthrough hit him in his sleep and, to get the ingenious discovery off his mind, he came in to work. She smiled. Just her luck . . . no one around but her and an incredibly sexy man.

She cleared her throat amidst the computer's hum in the room, and the man turned in slow motion. Her heart seized in her chest and her throat closed, constricting her breath.

Blue eyes, intense, deep, and clear, met hers and wetness slid from her pussy and pooled in her panties. *Oh.* She wanted to shift her stance at the sudden dampness but didn't dare.

His eyes held hers, a smile of pure sex on his face. He was beautiful. His skin, pale and clear, had a sprinkle of small freckles across his nose. Somewhere within her a familiarity tickled, and this moment played in her mind like dejá vu. The corner of his mouth quirked, and his gaze dropped ever so slowly to her lips.

Her mouth parted, and she felt the drag of his lips and his tongue across hers as if she'd kissed him for years. The memory was imprinted deep in her soul. Her limbs trembled, and she shivered, gooseflesh priming her skin.

A man had never aroused her lust so intensely before. Her skin tingled just standing there admiring him. *Oh.* She needed to kiss him, to feel what her subconscious remembered. Desire, a memory, and belonging pulled at not only her sensual self but also at her power.

She couldn't resist.

This was destiny. Not that she was perceptive to what destiny was. Her life played out any way but how she wished. God, just look at how her dad treated her, when he actually took the time to acknowledge her existence. She shuddered, remembering the sting of his words, *'You're crazy'*, as his hard hand had slapped her face and she'd cried. She bit her lip and devoured the blue-eyed man with her stare. It was time to do something she lusted for. She stepped forward, and the man leaned his hip on the counter's edge and watched her with a gaze that said he owned her.

Don't make a fool of yourself. She clutched her Pluto mug and set down the cup by her computer, then continued past the neverending counter to him. God, he wouldn't stop staring at her.

She halted three feet from him and raised her eyebrows.

"Who are you?" The words were so soft they lacked all forti-
tude and held a sense of awe. Could she be any more desperate
to touch him?

"Chester, Chester Shields." He held out his hand in an invitation for her to shake it.

Her eyes widened. Could she touch him? What an odd contradiction. Not one second before, she'd pined for that in every
way. But now . . . She thought it would be better not to be there
at work. One touch from him and without a doubt she wouldn't
be able to stop. She would end up straddling his leg and hump-
ing him like a dog. My God. A lump formed in her throat. She
wanted that. Her gaze took in the lab. No one was here. So
would it matter?

"Nice to meet you, Chet."

His smile broadened and he slowly lowered his hand, placed
his fingers on his thigh, and squeezed his . . . Oh my! Was that
what she thought it was? A hard cock lay against his thigh
under his hand; he squeezed its roundness.

"No, not Chet. Chester," he said, his voice low and husky.
Then he laughed at her.

Her gaze snapped to his face.

His eyes flamed with blue smoke. "Only those bound to me
call me Chet." He winked.

What? What was he talking about?

"Oh." Did he say *bound?* Her brows drew together, and her
nipples pebbled hard. She wouldn't mind being tied up by him
as he did wicked things to her, if that was what he meant. She
wanted to relive the memories in her soul. To relive his kiss.

He shifted and crossed his legs at his ankles, as if waiting for
her to say more. She stared at his black Cole Haans, then let her
gaze wander higher, up his long, lean legs, until it reached the
zipper to his pants. His hand still covered the ridge on his thigh
and his thumb traced the tip of his erection.

The image of his long, naked legs tangled with hers flashed

before her and she gasped. She saw his hips rubbing her bottom, felt the hot skin of his cock pressing into the pucker of her ass. A wave of heat and cold washed through her body and she grew fevered and clammy all at once. She struggled to breathe and squeezed her butt cheeks together. Yum. Anal sex was one of her favorites. She shivered. What an image.

Warmth infused her cheeks, and she slowly raised her eyes to meet his again. One of his brows inched up in question and his smile grew bigger, mocking her. His lips twitched and his chest vibrated as if holding in a chuckle. Were her thoughts that obvious?

"Yes, dear. They are." He reached out and wrapped his searing fingers around her wrist, then pulled her hand to his cock.

Her eyes widened, and her fingers closed around the projection. His flesh twitched beneath her caress. Her tongue slid out and she licked her lips, wanting the taste of his salty skin to flood her mouth. His hand, the one that caressed his cock, raised and traced the line of her jaw, then grasped her chin tight and tilted her head so her eyes met his.

His eyes flickered gold then back to blue. No one possessed eyes like that. She stiffened and his lips came down to stop mere inches from hers. The warmth of his breath heated the tip of her cool nose. Her heart jumped in her chest. Her tongue slid out and traced the seam of his lips.

"Good, Nora."

The salty, sweet spiciness of his words tingled her tongue. Yum. He tasted like curried papaya.

But wait, how does he know my name?

His lips came down hard on hers, leaving her little time to wonder. His hands clutched her hips, and he spun her around, pinning her with his body against the countertop. Her breath pressed from her lungs as he wedged his thighs between her legs.

Heat warmer than the sun in Hawaii washed her skin in a

glow of gold and blue. Their powers mixed and danced. My gosh, his power was strong. Her mind swam with him as he read her thoughts. Mind reading was personal. John had read her thoughts once during sex and the experience still remained imprinted in her mind.

Chester's tongue pushed into her mouth and she sucked, then wrapped hers about his, remembering the pressure, the tangle he liked. How did she know what he desired, what exactly brought him pleasure? This knowledge of him without ever having met him was insane. He groaned and his fingers inched up the fabric of her skirt.

God, she wanted this. She didn't care if he was a coworker. Her boss. She had never screwed anyone after only receiving his name, and for some reason this . . . this contradiction of knowing but not knowing excited her. Yes, she would do this. With this man she didn't know, but who somehow her body and powers did.

She slid her legs farther apart and rocked her crotch into his stomach. His hands pressed her thighs, pinching and digging into the bare flesh, creating delicious pain. His touch branded her, and her skin ached and dewed at his caress. Her pussy dripped thick cream and her panties clung uncomfortably to the folds.

She needed to get her underwear off! Inwardly, she cringed. Damn it, today she had worn her ugliest striped blue cotton ones. He kissed her harder, biting her lower lip as she clutched at his leather coat, trying to find access to the heat of his skin beneath.

His fingers tapped a trail up her inner thigh and under the elastic edge of her panties. She squirmed as more moisture slipped from her and he groaned as he probed at her slick flesh. Arching her hips, she opened her sex farther for him. She needed his fingers in her, screwing her until she couldn't stand the teasing any longer, until he ripped off her panties and then fucked her with his cock until she came. Oh yes, she needed that. She grinned into their kiss.

The tip of his finger slid into her wet lips and grazed her clit. Prickling heat trailed her sex, and she bucked against him, pushing her hips so his finger slid lower. He traced her lips and the opening of her creamy wet hole but didn't enter her hungry pussy.

She wiggled her hips in frustration, trying to get him to penetrate her, but he refused. Groaning into their kiss, she wrapped her hands around his sides and beneath his jacket to his back. His shirt, a crisp brown cotton button up, slid like chocolate silk under her hands. She wanted to tear off his clothes and feel the heat contained by the cotton on her bare skin. She wanted to suck his bare flesh and leave her marks on his body.

Her fingers slid farther around him and touched a projection that ran down the center of his back. What was that? The ridge, too thick to be his spine, rippled beneath his shirt. Her hands jumped to pull back as his finger slid into her pussy and jerked her entire concentration to her sex.

Her body trembled in waves as he stretched her lips and cunt by scissoring his fingers. *Oh . . . oh! Yeah! That's it.* Heat poured into her cunt as he pushed in, and her back arched, pushing harder against his hand. Her hands dug at his back, grasping on to the ridge that only a moment before she'd hesitated to touch.

Feather-like tingles tickled her fingers and wrapped up her arms, engulfing her body. His muscles hardened and caged her to him. She couldn't move. His lips firmed against hers and with deep, thick strokes of his tongue he drank in her soul. His tongue speared into her with fervor; his stubble rasped against her skin as his lips and tongue moved more harshly along hers.

Her breasts ached, wanting to be squeezed by his powerful grip. The desire to feel every bit of this hard, powerful man naked and entangled with her pushed her on. He rocked his body weight into her and her heart jumped, then pounded with his as one.

He released his hand from her leg and tugged at the button to his jeans.

Oh! He wasn't moving fast enough and she needed this . . . his hard cock filling her, fucking her until she screamed out loud. She unfurled her fingers from the ridge on his back but her arms stayed wrapped tightly to his sides as if clutching him in a soul-deep death grip. The memories of him, of this destiny, flooded her like dreams long forgotten. Their powers wove together and her inner being wanted nothing more than this man to stay with her, to be the man wrapped in her arms for eternity. But her mind . . . cautioned her that no man ever had stayed.

His zipper opened with a loud *ZIP,* and he sighed into her mouth. The hot skin of his cock landed heavy against her thigh. She shook, wanting him inside her. His lips plundered her, nipping and sucking on her flesh. He inhaled the air from her lungs and her head grew light.

The fingers still lodged inside her continued to stroke and possess her attention, lighting her entire body aflame with need.

His fingers slipped out of her. It was coming. He would fuck her. A tremor of ecstasy flooded her veins as the smooth, scorching heat of his cock pressed against the folds of her pussy. She shook uncontrollably as the head pressed into her opening and he penetrated her. Her mind and her entire body focused on the electrifying heat of her sex as she opened, stretching to accommodate him. She squirmed.

He stopped and nibbled her tongue, then, with a deliberate rhythm, thrust into her mouth with his tongue.

In-in-out, in-in-out.

Then he licked her teeth. She couldn't move. Her body was at his command. He slid into her again and her swollen flesh clamped around the hot hardness of him. He withdrew and thrust again, picking up the same dance as his tongue. She swayed, mind, body, and soul, to the composition he created. The air hummed, snapping with the tune—

CRASH!

Bright light flashed behind her lids and her eyes snapped open to find the room flooded with light, and then the light extinguished quickly. "Madre de Dios!" The muttered curse in Spanish came from the doorway.

She cringed, then giggled. The cleaning crew.

Still grinning, her eyes focused again on the man in front of her: His eyes and his skin glowed blue and gold . . . his pupils, the shape of a lizards, held her gaze unwaveringly as if waiting for her next move. His rockhard cock joined them together and twitched inside her. Her fingers fluttered on his back and the ridge beneath them rippled. What . . . What *was* that?

Oh, shit! He wasn't human. She'd screwed a life form with intense power . . . like the beings she searched for in her job . . . a *were*something, a monster of sorts. The hair on her neck stood. Oh God, how did she miss that he wasn't normal?

His eyes narrowed. "I'm no monster. I am a Dragon and you are my mate."

"I-I'm your what?" She needed to think . . . She pulled at her hands, desperate to get away and sort this all out. Her wrists released, an unwrapping sensation sliding down her arms. He had tied her to him with an unknown tether. Slipping his hands from her body, he stepped back and his cock slid from her still-dripping sex. The gaping emptiness of her pussy left her longing to pull him back, but this was too weird. She couldn't. As soon as their contact broke he stopped glowing. Turning away from her, he tucked his cock into his pants.

"Nora . . . you are mine. This is not something to be toyed with. I had no idea you worked here. Bugger." Chester spun around. His eyes narrowed and his mouth pursed in a tight frown.

My Desna. She had the look of an angel. There she sat, her rumpled short brown hair and sexy kiss-swollen lips lit up with the combination of the computer's glow and his marks. Her thoughts screamed *I'm not ready to know more* but her emotions and her soul said she belonged to him.

He inhaled and blew out a shaky breath. This was not going to happen tonight. His umbra flickered, his body demanding he come inside her now. The energy drain felt imminent.

Closing his eyes, he shook his head. The Royals were going to have a fit. He'd fucked this mission tonight . . . literally. He would have to return tomorrow . . . only his powers would be down because of her and he needed his powers to get in there. Until he finished initial binding all his energy focused on her. Damn it. He spun back around. She now stood with her arms crossed tightly across her torso.

Her eyes narrowed and her gaze speared him. "Are . . . Are you clean, Chester?"

My Desna. His eyes widened and he shook his head once again. *This* was ridiculous. In one move he caged her with his arms. "Dragons can not contract human diseases." His jaw clenched in frustration.

She turned her head away from him. He grabbed her chin and held her blue gaze to his.

"Nora, you are a dragon mate. My mate. The mother of my offspring. Deep in your soul you know you're mine . You are just not listening to your soul. I will let this go tonight, but not again." He released her, cloaked himself, and walked out the door.

2

Nora slid off her shoes and dropped her keys into the left one as she always did when arriving home so late.

"You know you are a dragon mate in your soul."

Chills raced across her skin. Dragons in the movies always intrigued her. *Dragon Slayer* was one of those horror films that she couldn't tear her eyes from. Her stomach flipped as she remembered the dragon's death at the end of the movie. The story turned her stomach and drew her in all at once.

She'd truly gone loony if she believed what had happened tonight was real. St. John had said weredragons existed but she'd never believed him. Chester's lizard-like eyes and his fin that had rippled beneath her touch was proof they did, indeed, exist. That is, if tonight was real and not a dream she'd had while drooling on her computer keyboard. The hair on her neck rose and lingering arousal dewed her skin.

Stop it! He and this night couldn't be genuine.

Besides, being *a mate* meant you had offspring and *that* she could never do. Her tongue grew thick and tears fell unrestrained down her cheeks. John had left because of her sterility. There was no way she was supposed to be a mystical creature's mate. She couldn't carry a child, and that would be a twisted fate to befall a mystical race.

She had to have dreamed the entire thing, just like the stress dreams she'd had years ago. Jet lag . . . Yeah, that caused her distress. Bed . . . she yawned once again . . . she needed sleep.

Wandering to her bedroom, she felt the flesh on her thigh tingle. The sensation of his hands squeezing that spot returned. She sighed. Some dream; soreness throbbed in her sex and the delightful pressure of his cock filling her hung fresh in her mind. She groaned and the lips of her pussy dripped as she clenched her inner muscles.

Damn, she needed to come even if this night was only the product of her vivid imagination. She lifted her shirt from her body and slid her skirt from her waist. Stepping into the bathroom, she turned on the lights. She slid her hand into the shower and turned on the water. Glancing back at the clock on the nightstand, she groaned. Three A.M. Gosh. She would get only about four hours of sleep.

She turned to the mirror and froze. Her eyes narrowed. Her reflection shone with a golden and blue shimmer from between her breasts straight to the curls of her pussy. On her thighs golden handprints shown. His handprints.

He was real and he'd left his energy on her. She swallowed hard and skimmed her trembling fingers over the clearly identifiable handprints. Branding heat tingled up her spine and she closed her eyes. Blue flashed behind her lids and her body jerked. The image of Chester Shields sitting at a bar as he talked with two other men assaulted her. The men all possessed the same eyes. Chester groaned and their eyes narrowed at him.

"Fuck, Chet." The one with the dark hair speared Chester with his gaze.

Then the blonde touched the dark-haired one's shoulder. "This is not as bad as it seems, Frey."

The dark-haired man shrugged off the blonde's hand. "The new mother is going to fuck with our existence, and it is not all that bad? Look at him, the energy drain has already started." Frey tilted his head toward Chester. "He will never finish the Royals' task and if he doesn't we are all screwed."

"The bloody hell I won't, Frey. And stop talking about me as if I'm not here."

Chester Shields' despair, determination, and anger pounded through Nora. Her gut twisted. What the hell was happening to her? She was used to seeing paranormal energies, they'd plagued her her entire life, though she'd never channeled. Her head spun and she swayed, grasping onto the cool edge of the tile countertop.

Chester pushed from his chair and closed his eyes. Opening them, he placed his hands on the table and leaned forward. "All will be well, brothers."

He spun around and pushed his way through the crowded bar. "My Desna. The connection has started, Nora. Don't deny me. I need you."

Nora spun around in her bathroom. He could talk to her? She shook her head but the image of him and his emotions would not leave her. How could this be? She stepped forward as Chester pushed open the door to the bar and stepped out into the night.

"I will have you this night, Nora."

Her heart leapt in her chest and her nipples pebbled, as if sensing the intense connection they shared. She stepped forward again; unseeing and piercing pain sliced through her head as she slammed into a solid obstacle. She stumbled backward, her vision cleared, and the corner of the door jam stood before her. Ouch! She touched her head and swayed as she slid down onto the floor and closed her eyes.

* * *

Chester swore again. What the hell had just happened? He'd lost the connection with her. No. She was still there. Just as a faint pulse. His head pounded and a shooting pain pierced the center of his nose. *Ah, Nora, what happened?*

He followed her faint call down Wall Street to Fourth, turned the corner, and stood outside the old Chief Seattle building. He cloaked himself so no one could see him, and waited . . . A couple emerged from the entrance, he caught the door just before the latch locked shut, and then he slipped inside.

The smell of new paint and carpet hung heavy in the air. The building was recently renovated but still held all of that old-school charm. The elevator doors were intricately cut Art Deco brass. The lighting held the same Art Deco influence. He took the stairs up to the sixth floor and headed in the direction of Nora.

Mounting the stairs to her floor, Chet noticed a thick burning tar stench, choking the air. An eerie chill pricked up the fin of his spine. Someone in this building searched for the Dragna.

His body warmed, eyes shifting, every Dragna instinct he possessed focusing on that smell. He wanted to stand still, to dare the enemy out into the open so he knew who he was up against. However, Nora lived in this building and she was his first priority.

Lengthening his stride, he traversed the elegant, red-lit carpeted corridor as his heart and lungs clashed in a rhythm that set his blood rushing to the edge of changing.

He stood in front of her door and inhaled. The acrid stench still lingered. Reaching out, he grasped the filigree-turned handle and twisted the heavy brass. The latch didn't budge. The need to hold Nora in his arms and be sure she remained well shook his limbs.

Glancing both ways, he extended his finger and grew his nail into a long, thin point. Inserting it into the lock, he molded the nail to the shape of the key and with the turn of his wrist the latch clicked. *My Desna!* He blew out his breath and turned the handle.

Pushing open the thick wood door, he saw that her apartment stood quiet. Only a small amount of light came from one doorway to the left of the main hall. He shut the door, listened for the click of the lock, and headed in the direction of the light.

All his senses focused on Nora: the smell of her rose-scented skin, the warmth of her touch, the feel of her body tied to his as they'd mated. His skin tingled with the memory of the maddening desire she'd created in him.

He entered the room. Her bed was bathed in light from the bathroom. Nora sprawled on her bed without a stitch of clothing and an icepack perched on her face. Her chest rose and fell in slumber and, as he gazed at her, her nipples pebbled hard. He sucked in through clenched teeth and his groin grew thick. He grazed his finger up her left arm, marveling at the downiness of the hairs on her skin. His body warmed and his umbra glowed blue. The line he traced on her skin glowed in unison.

His mate.

Two hundred years had passed since his last. He sighed with a sense of completeness, of contentedness. His heart and mind soared. This one he would not squander. He would nurture her and bring her to full Dragna capabilities.

She didn't move. He sat on the edge of the bed and sank into the plush surface. Damn, this was his kind of bed: soft, perfect for sleeping and fucking. One by one he unwound her fingers from the ice pack on her nose and tossed the cold lump to the floor. Her petite, lush curves called to him and he hardened in his jeans. He wanted to take her there in that place, but with that smell in the building doing so would be foolish. He needed to get her home and he needed to do so while she still slumbered. Slowly he tugged the blanket beneath her around her body, covering her nakedness from his too-hungry eyes.

He tucked one arm beneath her neck, the other beneath her knees, and lifted her against him. Cradled in his arms, her breath against his shoulder warmed his core and his groin hardened painfully with lust.

He tilted his head to rest on hers and tears of overwhelming gratitude stung his eyes; he had finally found her. They would not part again. He couldn't allow it.

She sighed against him but didn't stir. He would get her to his home, safe in the Dragna community. Then he would have her.

The strain from not completing the joining sapped his energy. He grew weak. The death clock had clicked on when he smelled her enter the room at Ralston. If they didn't complete the initial bind soon . . . All of his thoughts would fill with her . . . He would stop eating, he would stop sleeping and he could die. The hairs stood on his neck. All would be on the right path soon.

He leaned in and kissed her cheek; the smooth texture beneath his lips washed wave upon wave of erotic energy through his veins. His tongue slid out and tasted the sweet surface. He closed his eyes and licked his lips, savoring every minute taste mingling on her skin: salt, lavender, and earthy oregano. She smelled of flowers and spices, he of fire and sweetness. Opposites that complimented each other.

He turned and headed to the apartment door, holding her a bit too tightly, but he couldn't get close enough to her. Opening the heavy solid wood door, he stepped out into the hallway. As the door clicked shut behind him the smell of burning tar engulfed him. His fin expanded beneath his coat and his chest warmed. Whoever the predator was, he or she had traversed this hall only moments before.

Damn it. Expanding his shoulders, he strode towards the stairs with purposeful strides. He needed to get Nora home safely but he couldn't cloak her. If the person approached him, he would stay calm for Nora.

Turning the corner, he saw a gray and brown tabby cat sitting in the middle of the hall staring at him. Bugger! He stopped in his tracks and cold sweat trickled down his forehead. Now what? He stared at the feline.

The cat raised its paw and rubbed its face.

"Move! Damn you!"

The cat tilted its head to the side but did not budge. Its red tongue slid out and moistened its lips.

Chester shook with an irrational fear. He couldn't pass the damn cat. Couldn't get within two feet of any feline—no Dragna could—and the hallway grew too narrow in his mind for him to pass unaffected. He inhaled a breath and used the warmth to send a steady stream of fire toward the cat.

The cat hissed, turned, and stood looking in the opposite direction; then it padded down the hall.

How had this day turned out so bloodied up? He shook his head as he followed two feet away in the cat's wake.

The smell of burning tar increased as he reached the stairs. He glanced around and shifted Nora in his arms. Whoever the person was who possessed that stench grew near.

He stared down the stairway and felt a blizzard-like breeze blow from behind him.

He turned his head to glance at the cause of the sudden chill and saw the cat pounce sideways at him, back arched, hissing.

Bloody hell! He jumped sideways to get away from the feline and tripped off the top step and into the air. Clutching Nora's body tight to his chest, he felt his instinct to fly burst forth. His wings extended and the sound of tearing cloth made him cringe. Bugger! Another one of his favorite coats ruined. Bloody cat!

One hard stroke of his three-foot wings placed them on the red-carpeted landing without harm. His heart hammering in his throat and every muscle taut, he gained his balance and spun about to see where the cursed feline was.

It stood at the top of the steps, eyes flashing at him.

The tormentor seemed to laugh at him. Chester warmed his chest and blew out a stream of fire in the direction of the cat.

The feline hissed and turned back up the hall.

Chester spun, taking the stairs two at a time. He hoped the cat would disappear. He reached the entry and sniffed the air; the smell of burning tar had decreased and the smell of the lovely Nora soothed him. The cat did not follow. He pushed open the front door and walked through it into the dead of night.

3

Cool air fluttered across Nora's skin and she shivered, turning close, like a cat in front of the fire, to the heat she rested against. Beneath her ear the sound *paw-paw-paw* echoed. She trembled and her heart skipped to match the beat. The smell of sweetness clung and swirled in the air around her.

This was heaven, nirvana. The smells and the soothing heat calmed her soul. She didn't want to awaken from this dream. To go back to reality . . . to her life. No, she would sleep a bit longer . . . until the cold receded, until she remained warm, until the fear of being left alone once again subsided.

Nora awoke to velvet blackness. The heat and sweet smells from her dream still emanated in the air. She closed her eyes and absorbed the safety, the permanency of her dream. Similar dreams had soothed her in the past, but not once had calm come with the paranormal visions and energies.

Reaching out her fingers, she jumped as soft warm skin collided with them. Her head pounded. Was she still asleep?

The heat beneath her fingers sparked erotic energy that radiated up her arms and through her body. An ache bloomed, tickling her deep in her belly, and made her groan. Her nipples stood in hard, painful peaks, and the flesh between her thighs overflowed with her cream, dampening her thighs. She needed release, to find comfort in the heated tranquility of her dream mate's body, to take what he offered and give herself in return.

She firmed her touch and slid her hand across a scalding hot stomach. The muscles rippled in a wave beneath her fingers and she moaned in delight at his reaction. Her hand slid deeper into the heat, her mind spinning as visions of passion and erotic body parts with wings floated through the air. *What the hell was that?* She shook her head at the strange dream elements.

Pushing to sit up, she slid her legs across this heated source of her release and forgot the strange visions. He rolled her over, pinning her to whatever she lay upon.

She wanted to gaze upon her dream lover, to touch his cheek and drink in the color of his hair. She strained, trying to pull her eyelids open. They wouldn't budge. Her lids hung tightly closed. Without a doubt she still slept.

The weight of his body pressed into her softness comforted her. She sighed, arching her body into his, and trembled. It didn't matter if she couldn't see him. This was her dream, and he provided everything her body and mind craved. Connection, love, and permanency pulsed through her.

The emotions aroused her and her legs spread wide . . . opening, wanting the release that she craved. She moaned, trembling as the intense arousal engulfed her mind and body.

Weight settled heavy between her thighs, spreading them wider. Wetness drizzled from her opening and slid down to her anus. She needed this sensation, needed to come and come, to feel that sexual bliss snatched from her in the lab.

Her muscles tightened. *Shit, forget about the lab.* This was nirvana . . . a dream coupling just as surreal as the lab but emotionally safe. No worries about when he would leave and take her heart with him.

Hot breath caressed her neck. A tickling feather wrapped around her wrist and pulled her hands up high above her head, leaving her helpless to his desires. His skin on hers sent wave upon wave of lava-like desire through her veins, arching her to him.

His fingers caressed a line of fire down her inner arm to her nipples. Pulling hard on the tips of her peaks, he pinched, then pulled them away from her body. *Oh!* Prickling pleasure shot down her stomach to her clit and her pussy contracted, seeking fulfillment.

She arched her hips against him, wantonly rubbing the slickness of her weeping flesh against the thick weight of his cock between her legs.

His touch caressed every inch of her, gliding from her breasts down her sides to her hip bones. His fingers skidded across her bottom and lifted her. Heated moisture caressed her ear. "You are mine . . . You know you are in your soul."

That deep, demanding voice . . . sounded familiar.

She wrapped her mind around the words . . . Chester Shields. The feel of his hands on her made the glowing marks on her skin blaze with fire. *Stop! Damn it. Get him out of my dream.* This feeling was what she'd wanted her whole life. She would not deny this pleasure.

The hot tip of his cock swirled around her entrance and then penetrated her pussy. She shook as she stretched, the pressure increasing as his dick slid all the way in. The man atop her groaned, the sound vibrating her flesh, deep to her soul.

"Yes . . ." Warm breath hissed by her ear. "I will claim you now. Fill you with my essence." His body jerked. "My Desna. Nora." He pulled back and slid into her again, holding himself fitted to the opening. Circling his hips, he rubbed his cock against the sensitive tissue of her sex, and filled her, stretching her, opening her more for him.

Her body trembled blissfully in overwhelming pleasure and

she licked and nibbled his neck, tasting the salty-sweet spiciness of his skin. She wrapped her legs around him tightly, wanting release, wanting to feel the hot gush of his seed spurt into her wetness.

She wanted this act more then any other in her life.

Rubbing and grinding her pussy and clit along his thick cock, she felt each stroke hit her g-spot with bone-jarring precision. She shook uncontrollably with each pass of his cock's ridge against the spongy flesh. The want for nothing but release blazed in her veins. The threads of reality unwound and she let go of her mind, and felt . . . his skin, the smell of their sex, the way they connected like no other man had with her before. Her body moved with its own desires. The pleasure increased as she wildly thrashed beneath him, her feet slipping down his legs as she gripped him tighter and tighter.

He pushed his cock against the swollen walls of her sex in three harsh strokes. Pleasure shot through her inner core and she whimpered as her muscles crushed her body to him. Wetness gushed out of her sex and melded where they joined.

"Oh . . . Fuck . . . This is it, Nora. I'm swimming in you."

What? Never in her dreams would the man making her feel this good talk to her that way. In fact there would be no talk at all!

She shook her head and pried her eyes open. Blue-gold glow surrounded her and the man on top of her was . . . none other than Chester Shields.

This was no dream.

It was real!

Oh God . . . Did she want this with him? She rolled her shoulders away from him, pulling on her bound wrists as her mind scrambled to answer that question. The soft restraints bit into her skin as he rocked against her clit with his pubis. Desire sparked and her body arched in waves, rubbing against him, wanting more. Her body needed him, needed this. No, becoming his mate was wrong. He needed a true mate, a woman to provide him with children.

Arousal seeped back into her brain, fogging any rational thought. She only wanted more of him, of this pleasure. The desire to have him come inside her drugged her senses.

He grunted as if an orgasm grew near. Sheer desire to carry his child tore through her gut. Her heart ached and tears welled in her eyes, spilling down her face. She could never provide him with a child. This was wrong. He would be bound to a woman who could not *be* his mate. But, oh! How she wanted this, this connection, this comfort that he gave to her without knowing.

His hands cupped her face and she turned her head, sucking his thumb into her mouth as his stiffness penetrated her greedy wet flesh. "Ah, Nora. It has been too long. I can't hold back for much longer." His hand slid into her hair and pulled, arching her neck as he licked down her jaw to her collarbone.

The tears continued to fall as his passion washed through her. He wanted her and he had no way of knowing she couldn't bear a child. She couldn't allow him to do this. She rolled her hips to the side, trying to dislodge him, and the expression on his face twisted in pain as a low moan vibrated in his chest.

"Chester, please."

He glanced up at her, his lips shiny, wet, and swollen from worshipping her. A smile curved his mouth and a pain of longing pierced her heart.

"I will try to hold out for you, sweet." The line of his jaw tightened and he returned his devoted attention to her body by sucking her earlobe into his mouth. Her body trembled.

He'd misunderstood her plea.

Nuzzling her neck, he licked her from ear to shoulder, and sweet trembles of ecstasy possessed her, shooting straight to her womb. All her muscles liquefied and passion washed over her.

Leaning up, she licked his shoulder in the same fashion that he had hers. She tried to concentrate on letting him go, but the pleasure intensified and she swore they were floating. Wrapping her legs tight around his, she rocked her clit against him, bucking and shaking artlessly.

He stilled and a deep purring moan burst from him. "Yea! Oh, yea!"

His cock hardened within her cunt. The flesh of her sex stretched tight and her hips continued to move, milking him as the stretching continued. He filled her beyond full. She trembled at the intense sensations and then screamed as her muscles clenched and her wetness gushed onto him.

He kissed her, nipping and sucking her tongue into his mouth as she blissfully floated on a cloudy haze. His body shook and a pulse of prickles possessed her womb.

"Uh . . ." He pushed into her slickness and pulled out. "Uh . . ." He fucked her harder. "Ooh!"

His cock pulsed and he held still. With each burst of his cum, warmth flooded her womb. She shook, wanting his child. His cock, thick and hard inside her, locked them together. Her hips continued to rock against him, wanting more of him as he settled his weight on her, pinning her beneath him.

She wanted nothing more than to touch him . . . to run her hands across his sweaty back and hold him to her in a spiderweb like embrace. She couldn't move, with her hands still stretched above her. The pounding in her head slowly returned and she closed her eyes, nuzzled into his hair, and allowed the warmth of his embrace to lull her off to sleep.

4

Nora ran her hand through her bangs and skimmed it across her forehead. Hmmm. There was a small bump, but no ache left. She rolled onto her side, then stared at the sun streaming in through wooden shutters and leaving a striped glow that added sophistication to the room.

The room, which she swore the night before had been a black cave, displayed rich cherrywood window casings and shutters. The walls, too, had dark cherrywood wainscoting. The upper parts of the walls were a deep forest green.

Her gaze darted around the room. The bed was a simple slatted sleigh bed with no footboard. Across from the bed stood an armoire, door open, with Chester Shields' shirts hung in crisp straight white lines within the doors. The shirts hung a perfect two inches apart.

She never would have guessed he was a neat freak when she met him last night in the lab. He'd worn a leather cycle jacket and fitted blue jeans. Who was this man . . . this dragon? Her heart wanted nothing more than to find out, but she would not allow any further explorations. He needed to know she couldn't be his mate, that he would have no children if she stayed. She needed to leave. A pain pricked her heart, the blood closing off her throat as she gulped for breath. No, she couldn't hold on to him. She would go.

She would tell him now and walk away before this connection intensified. Tears welled in her eyes. Stupid . . . What an idiot she was. She swallowed hard. God, she wished she'd told him before . . . before she'd slept with him. Her omission of the truth was only that much harder to confide now. Biting her trembling lip, she scrambled to her feet. She needed to do it now. She spun around, her heart beating so hard it choked her with each thump in her breast. Stopping still, she glanced down at her naked body.

She glowed.

Not that pink flush that graced her body after a great night of sex, but a light blue that shimmered gold as she moved. His glow. The one she'd experienced in the lab.

Amazing.

His energy was everywhere: on the palms of her hands, her stomach, her legs, her breasts. There were smudges on her feet and her inner thighs. The beautiful tinge shone everywhere their bodies had touched. His marks. Her chest tightened and she gasped.

My God. She stared unseeing at the blue sky just beyond the shutters. He was . . . a dragon? Her head spun with the knowledge she'd just slept with a mystical beast, and he lived, from all appearances, just like a normal human, in a house that from the inside was like any other. A bird landed on the steep pitch of the house across the street. She tilted her head to the side as it hopped on the roof. Did his neighbors know an otherworldly creature lived in the house right next door?

She rushed to the window and pushed open the heavy wood shutters, curious to see where he lived. Light came blindingly into the room. She glanced out the window. House after cookie-cutter house stood across the street. Each one was less than five years old, with steep, pitched roofs and the fake craftsman details that people craved these days. That was why she'd moved into an old building. Why pay for an imitation when you can have the real deal?

The symmetry of the community went beyond the houses. Each lawn was immaculately cut with alternating stripes on diagonals. The trees were trimmed into perfect uniform triangles or small topiaries. Everything was perfect, exact, like peas in the same pod.

It was all too homogenous.

She glanced at the man across the street as he washed his blue Eclipse. Did he know a dragon lived thirty feet away? At the next house, painted green instead of blue, an older woman in her mid-sixties sat on the front porch step, drinking coffee and smiling. Nora's mouth watered. Coffee. She needed her morning cup of Joe.

A younger man in his thirties came out of the house, the older woman turned, and her smile broadened into an ear-to-ear grin. He leaned down and tenderly kissed her. Nora's smile broadened too . . . He must be a relative. Then the man's head tilted and his lips harshly possessed the older woman's.

Nora's eyes widened. What the heck? The young man dropped to his knees beside the older woman and they continued to make out. Nora almost cringed. She never would have imagined her mother making out with a man her age! She didn't know if she should cheer for the older woman or be disgusted.

The air crackled about her and little electrical shocks caressed her skin as the heat and solidity of Chester's hands connected with the bare skin at her waist. She jumped and closed her eyes.

"Chet."

"Yes. You are bound to me now, Nora." His hands slid firmly across her stomach and pulled her back against him. The heat and crackling in the air increased and seemed to caress her skin. She groaned, sliding her legs apart.

He leaned his head down and kissed her ear. "I see you are checking out the neighborhood."

His breath sent quivers through her muscles in anticipation of him touching her skin everywhere with his lips. "Yes it . . . it's a bit strange."

"You have no idea how much so. This is not a normal community. It is a Dragna community."

"Pardon?" God, he smelled wonderful, like a smoky sweet campfire after roasting marshmallows.

"Every person you see is Dragna or Dragna mate." He glanced out the window, then with his head indicated the couple she watched. "Gal is out front with Mitchel. *That is how a term mate ends.*"

"A term mate? Pardon?" She watched the couple on their front porch with new interest as Chet's hands rubbed her belly and fingered the curls of her sex.

"Mitchel and Gal met when Gal was your age, Nora. They are mates for life. But we Dragna do not age as humans do. I am three hundred years old, Nora." His finger slid, grazing her mound, and snaked back up to her belly, sending pangs of longing through her womb.

She turned her head and stared him in the eyes. He didn't look a day older than thirty-five. She didn't believe him. "So you have been alive since 1707?"

His eyes sparkled and deep within them she could see his past. "I have. You can ask me anything you wish about my life and I will answer you. No secrets. There is no need."

The image of a woman in a full skirt and a wig in the style of the 1700s stood on the cliffs overlooking a sea as the winds whipped her hair. A man appearing to be Chet rode up to her on horseback and wickedly grinned at her. A stab of jealousy speared through Nora. Who was that woman? And why did Nora care if he gazed at the woman the way he did her?

"So . . . am . . . am I your first?" She turned her head away and stared unseeing out the window again, feigning indifference to the answer he would provide.

"I have had one other mate, Nora, when I was young. Too young to know how to appreciate what a mate has to offer." His grip slid around her abdomen and wrapped her tighter against him. "We Dragna can have sex outside of loving just like humans, and do frequently with multiple partners at once. Only we can't spend our seed that way. When we have sex outside of a lifemate it is, by law, with other Dragna only."

She shook her head. He had sex often with multiple other dragons. A prickle of anger touched her spine as John's words filled her mind. *"I'm sorry it came to this Nora. I—I wanted a child of my own and Abby is pregnant. I am sorry love. I need to be with Abby now."*

Abby . . . John's and her play partner. Her heart sank. She knew it was possible to do multiple play without cheating, but her heart just couldn't see past that hurt at the moment. Chet could end up doing the same to her: leave her when she did not produce for the dragon line. Her stomach bottomed out and she flinched at the unease. The thought of him betraying her like John had hurt just the same, more so even. She needed to go home, but where was she? "So where exactly is this community, Chet?"

"We are in a gated community at the base of Cougar Mountain." His breath heated the skin on her neck and wetness coated the lips of her sex. What a contradiction . . . her body wanted him unwaveringly but her mind . . . knew better.

Hmmm . . . maybe he would drive her back to Ralston so she could work this disappointment off. My gosh, she could just imagine how things would be working for him. She frowned and glanced down at his hands wrapped about her body. She would hear his voice and ... "If you keep touching me the way you do, we will never get anything done at work, Chester."

His muscles tensed along her back. "Chet, Nora. You are *mine*." He leaned in and bit the skin on her neck.

Tendrils of fire slid down her body to the flesh of her pussy; the sensation was so intense her sex gaped, waiting to be filled with him.

"I don't work there, Nora." He continued to lick and suck on her neck, his tongue swirling in circles as he tasted her.

"You must." Her words came out a husky whisper. "I—I mean that's how we met."

Come on get a grip Nora ... you need to leave here, not fall back into bed with him.

Chester didn't like the way this line of questioning was going. He wanted only to toss her back on the bed and fuck her brains out once again. "Yes. I—damn ..." If he told her about the mission she would never get back beneath him this morning. "I was there to get something." He licked from her neck to her ear and sucked her lobe into his mouth. She tasted so bloody good.

"At two in the morning?"

Get your shit together, Chet. The mission needs to be completed. IT IS IMPORTANT! You marked her. Initial binding is done. You can now complete your task and save your ass as well as everyone else's. Then you can fuck her all day and night for the rest of her life.

"Okay." He reluctantly unwound his hands from her waist. "Come sit on the bed and I will tell you." He steered her to the bed, visions of her arching beneath him as he kissed and fucked her the night before tempting his senses. His cock sprang to life, standing straight out from his body.

Concentrate, Chet.

He turned her and she sat down, her gaze going to his penis as she licked her lips. Oh, God, what would her mouth on his cock feel like? *Like my Desna.* He groaned, wanting precisely that: her tongue sliding along his stiffness as she licked and sucked him until he could handle no more . . .

Stop it . . . the mission, Chet . . .

He stared down at her. "I was at Ralston to get information about the paranormal detector you are creating. From everything the Royals have heard, the detector works and the Dragna's whereabouts cannot be exposed."

Her brows drew together and she frowned. "You're serious?"

"Yes." His hands fisted by his sides. Damn, he wanted to hold her, but that would lead to fucking her and he needed to get moving on this detector now.

"The detector doesn't work." She bit her lip. "We have not been able to pick up any paranormal life with it. The energy calculations I inputted should work. They've been tested and have worked before on paranormal life forms. The detector's failure has been my frustration for the past year. Each time I make a tweak, sure the change will make the difference, nothing happens."

"The detector does work, Nora. We wouldn't know about the device if it didn't. Maybe it just doesn't work how you think." He turned and sat beside her, grasping her hand and lacing her fingers with his. He couldn't keep his hands from her. The feel of her energy fluttering under his caress both turned him on and soothed him.

"The information the Royals collected show it is *when* you use the detector that makes the difference."

"I don't think so. Anytime Shawn turns it on, it doesn't pick up a thing."

Her hand trembled in his and her uncertainty about him, about them, shook through him. She would try to leave. Bugger. His desire for her inundated him. He hadn't concentrated on her thoughts this morning. He should have known better. He pushed loose his preoccupation and reached out for her mind.

"I have to admit, though, of all the paranormal life I've seen, I've never witnessed a dragon before you. I doubted your kind existed. Ghosts, yes; werewolves, vampires, sure. I've had numerous experiences with them. That's why Ralston hired me. But dragons?"

Chester cringed as he searched her mind. Why did she feel she should leave? Something had happened to her, but as he raced the pathways of her brain searching for that answer, door after door closed to him. She was blocking whatever her past was. Her mind concentrated now on her work. *Damn it.* "What did you aim the detector at so you knew when the device worked, it worked?"

"Umm, well, at Shawn. She's a werewolf."

Interesting. He smoothed the crease out of the fitted bed sheet beside him. "So you work with a werewolf and you have experiences with ghosts."

"Yes." She glanced at him then at the carpet. "I have a small but accurate reputation as a clairvoyant." She glanced at him again from the corner of her eye. *Will he reject me because of this?*

Ah, her guard had dropped again, and she gauged his reaction to this information. She feared rejection because of her power. Why? He probed further into her mind and images assaulted him of a man who had to be her father, his face beet-red, screaming, "You're crazy! Stop all this talk about visions and light!" as she cowered sobbing on the floor.

Bastard. But her fear of his reaction proved she wanted his approval. Deep down she wanted to stay with him. His heart leapt in his chest. She was his, and wanted him, but feared he would hurt her the way her father had. That fear held her back. He was certain of it. "Tell me more, Nora."

Her gaze locked on their hands where his fingers intertwined with hers. "What I do see is real and exact. Ralston hired me to help them see energy levels. That's what I can see, energies." She shrugged. "But since I've been at Ralston I've not observed one unusual energy. Well..." Her head tilted down and her other hand skimmed the blue handprint on her thigh. "Well, not until you."

"The detector works on Dragna when they are vulnerable, Nora. That was what we were told. In the big world, finding a Dragna with its defenses down doesn't happen often. The only sure time is when Dragna mate. I have no idea about the other paranormals. My job is to destroy everything: the prototypes, all the files, every drop of research, so that our race will remain safe from the ever-condescending society of conservatives that would hunt us down and kill us." Yes, that was what was important... if the detector stayed then he and Nora may never have a chance to be together the way they should. They would constantly be running, and he would not put Nora though that kind of hell as he had with his last mate. His failure. He needed to be with her the right way... to prove to himself he was a good mate and not doomed to relive his past mistakes.

"You're going to destroy the lab?" Her shoulders tensed.

It was her work and he went on and on about needing to destroy it without even considering how she would feel about it.

"Nora, I know that you have worked hard on this project. But can't you see this will change our existence forever? We have always been a private race. This invention would force us out into the open. I know this will change your life and that of your coworkers. I am sorry for that, Nora." He mentally shook himself. *Bloody cod, you should have thought about how it would affect her life before this instant.* He was truly sorry he was aiming to destroy everything she'd worked for up until now, but he had no choice.

Nora nodded and bit her lip. "Thank you." Her tongue slid out and wetted her plump skin. "I do understand your need, Chet." Her brow furrowed. "I would like to help you. How will you get the detector?" Her gaze pierced his.

"I have to go back. I only destroyed the formulas from the backups last night before you entered. No one should notice unless a computer crashes and they need the back up. I need to clear the main systems and then destroy the lab."

Her hand fluttered in his grasp. What she was about to say was not good. "The prototype isn't in the lab, Chet. It's locked up someplace. St. John always brings it to us when we need to test and it takes a couple hours for the detector to arrive."

"Bugger. I need to talk to the Royals about this, Nora. I'm not going to leave you here to your own curiosity, though. Come with me."

Chet released Nora's hand and stood. The sudden loss of his contact when she craved more was too much. He had not cringed when she told him about her power. Maybe he would accept she couldn't bear a child, too. Maybe, just maybe, her heart was right about him and despite what her head told her he was truly her soulmate.

She turned to see him in his full nakedness; the sensual curve of his neck and broad masculine shoulders shimmered blue-gold with barely visible scales. A fin stood down his back. The two-inch piece of flesh and scales bent to the side. About halfway down it a gold bar with a ring pierced his flesh. She had never seen anything like it. Her touch on the flesh the night before had brought about wonderful sensations. As if a feather caressed and tickled her desires. Lust flooded her veins at the memory of him binding her to him and joining with her in the lab. Her hands tingled with the urge to reach out and play with the ring, to feel his energy's impression again. She raised her hand to run her finger around the inside circle of the ring. *Stop it!* She dropped her hand and fisted her fingers at her side. *You have no idea what the piercing is for and if you do leave him, it will end up being one more little detail about this mystical creature you'll go over and over each night.* She bit her lip in an attempt to hold back the words, but they tumbled forth.

"Chet, what is the bar on your back for?" She cringed. Where was her self control?

A deep throaty chuckle burst from him, then he shoved his feet into each of his neatly pressed pant legs. "You will see, lovely. You will see."

He turned and his eyes sparkled with images that flashed before her: her tied to him, her arms about his waist and spun silk about her wrists that slid through the ring in his back. She was immobile. Her heart sped and her pussy lips tingled with moisture as he pointed down; she knelt before him, running her tongue up the length of his cock. A moan burst from her lips and his lips curved up as the dreamlike images faded.

"Liked that did you, lovely? Now go ahead and put my clothes on. We will get your wardrobe later today. I will meet you downstairs when you have dressed." He left the room, and the intense erotic images disappeared with him.

5

Chester sprang down the steps and entered the kitchen.

Nora . . . his mate.

He stared out the window, not seeing his backyard beyond. From what he saw of her past she had not had an easy life. He would make sure her time with him was as exciting and erotic as possible. He would be damned if he took her for granted. Reaching for the coffeepot's handle, his hand grasped and grasped at the air. "What the fuck?" He glanced at his hand by the coffeemaker.

No coffeepot.

"Looking for this, dear brother?"

Chester spun about to see Frey sitting on his counter, feet dangling, cup of coffee in hand. "So, is she yours now?" Frey's mouth curved but his eyes remained hard and full of hurt.

"Yes." He grabbed the coffeepot from Frey's hand and poured a steaming black stream into his cup.

"When are you planning to share her with us?"

Chester placed the pot back on the burner and frowned. He didn't want to share her, not yet . . . He wanted to savor her.

Sharing would have to wait. Besides, he had other things that needed to be dealt with. He turned back to his brother and leaned against the opposite counter. "As soon as I can get this detector shit straightened out."

"Hmm. So you're willing to put off the ritual for all of our lives? How gallant of you. I didn't think you had it in you, Chet." His brother's eyes shown with cool indifference, then flashed once again with pain.

"Bugger off, Frey." Chester raised his coffee cup to his lips, not entirely sure how to handle his brother in this mood of his. His brother radiated anger and anguish and pointed those emotions at everyone. Right now, Chester was the one responsible for his pain because by delaying the ritual he extended Frey's anguish. Sharing Nora with him would have healed his broken heart and allowed him to move on with his life. He frowned again. How the bloody hell was he supposed to deal with this on top of his mission and Nora wanting to leave? "I know you are hurting from your loss—"

"Yes, and ready to move on. I can't do that until the ritual is complete and the healing finishes." His brother stared at him with eyes hardened by grief, longing, and memories of love lost.

He sighed and turned, staring again with unseeing eyes out the window. The ritual needed to happen. There was no getting around sharing Nora with Frey and the others. He would have to get through this. Then he could have her to himself. "You arrange it then, Frey. Get everyone together and arrange the final ceremony." He turned back and smiled at his brother. "I simply don't have time right now."

"Done." Frey jumped off the counter and disappeared into thin air.

Chester blew between his teeth and the air crackled as Nora stepped closer to him. His gaze swept to her and rested on her small, shapely form swimmimg in a white button-up shirt tucked into a pair of his green athletic shorts. He grinned, showing all of his teeth.

Even wearing *that*, she was amazingly beautiful.

The slope of her neck gave way to the round swell of her heavy breasts, but the look on her face was what brought him to his knees.

She wanted him: the smoke in her eyes, the slight seductive smile that curved her lips when her eyes met his, shouted it. Even though her thoughts at times denied the fact, *she was his*, and her facial expressions told the entire story.

"So . . ." She fidgeted with the cuff of one of her sleeves. "Who was that and what is the ritual he mentioned?" Her head tilted slightly to the side as her eyes seemed to lick his body from head to toe. His heart skipped in his chest. Delicious.

"That was my brother Frey and the ritual is one Dragna go through when anyone in our family finds a mate. A welcoming of sorts." He couldn't believe he was the next one in queue to have a mate. Durn was who he assumed was next. Nora's nipples pebbled beneath his stare.

The ritual with Nora would blow his mind. She, without a doubt, was one of the most sensual mates he had seen. Exposing her to the Dragna ways would be a sight and experience any Dragna would want to participate in. He held in a burst of prideful laughter.

She frowned and dropped her gaze to her shirt cuffs. "I—I won't be joining your family, Chet."

Really? The laugh he had been restraining burst from his chest and he grinned as he stepped toward her. "You just keep telling yourself that, Nora. You are mine and your soul knows its keeper. But I'm not going to fight you at the moment. I will tell you more about the ritual after we return from seeing the Royals." *And I expose you to Dragna sensuality.* After that experience she would have no doubt Dragna ran in her blood.

With easy strides, he prowled toward her. "Are you ready to see what we dragons are all about?"

She gazed up from beneath her lashes, and searched his eyes. "I want to see the dragons." Pressing up on her tiptoes, she breathed, "Yes, I'll go with you. But don't think this means I'll be joining your family." Her lips touched his.

His head spun with need for her. He cupped the back of her head, harshly gripping her in place so his tongue could taste her sighs. She swayed sweetly toward him, all womanly soft curves and tempting scents of the sex they'd shared the night before. Her chest, nipples hard, feathered against his torso and he hardened fully. His cock pressed into her plush stomach and rounded mound.

Lovely, lovely, Nora.

He wanted to feel the sleek flesh of her oiled cunt wrapped about his hard prick as he drank in the scent of their love. Now was not the time. The detector . . . then Nora, his mate.

He slowed the movements of his lips against hers and she pulled back, trembling.

"Y—You taste like coffee. Can I have some?" Her pupils grew smaller.

He chuckled. Was that desire for coffee or him in her eyes? *My Desna.* "Yes. You may have whatever you wish, Nora." Turning from her, he grabbed a travel cup from the cupboard, and then poured strong coffee into the mug. "We need to get going, so you will have to drink as we go."

She nodded, her short brown curls bobbing.

"We will walk. The Royals live at the crest of the hill."

They turned in unison toward the door. Her hips swayed seductively in his way-too-big shorts as he followed her. Hmmm, well, if they fell off before they reached the crest . . . His prick twitched. *My Desna.* Now *that* he would have no problem with at all. Not at all. Her smooth, rounded bottom would look glorious in the bright sunlight.

"Are you alright?" Nora turned her head towards him.

"Yes, quite well, my lovely."

Chester deliberately hesitated as he reached past her, caging her between him and the closed door. He leaned in and inhaled the mixture of her spicy scent and shirt starch at the crook of her neck, then nuzzled her ear. "Never going to let you go." His hand turned the knob and he opened the door.

All eyes would be on them as they ventured out. A new life mate was a huge deal in the community. Everyone celebrated the event with an outpouring of sensuality that the couple could get caught up in. They stepped across the threshold, and he closed the door behind him.

Nora couldn't believe the eeriness of the community. Door after door opened as they strolled up the walk. People stepped out to watch them. No one talked, but Chet nodded at each person. Her heart pounded. What did they think of her? Would they approve? She shook herself. It didn't matter. She, in all probability, would not be around past today.

As they reached a small play green Nora stopped still. On the green a young boy stood with his mother and a few other children. The mother rubbed the boy's back. Wings, half the size of the boy, unfolded.

Nora's eyes widened. Did she just see that?

The woman leaned in and the boy nodded, then stepped forward and vigorously flapped his wings. He lifted gradually off the ground.

Nora jumped as Chet's finger pressed to her chin, closing her jaw.

"Yes, it is amazing, is it not? That age is special. When the young start to spread their wings and fly."

Nora turned her head and stared at Chet as he walked on. Longing to experience the motherly pride of seeing her child accomplish life skills tickled deep in her belly. She glanced back at the woman on the green. Her smile covered her face and lit the happy tears in her eyes. Yes, watching your child spread his wings gave an entirely new meaning to leaving the nest. She shook her head.

"Come . . . the Royals expect us."

She nodded and ran to catch up. She would never have what that woman had, a child to nurture and watch grow. They strolled past the green and toward a crest. She inhaled again, trying to let the fresh air and powerful dragon auras infuse her soul. Long ago she had put this dream behind her and learned to live with the fact that she was barren. She could do it again. She could relax and just enjoy this once-in-a-lifetime experience.

As they walked across the street and toward the hill, light flashed and a warm, damp breeze flowed over her, making her hair tickle her face. The intensity of the light blinded her and she closed her eyes, letting the heat of its energy infuse her with its power.

"Open your eyes, lovely."

Her lids fluttered open. She no longer stood on the manicured street, but in a dimly lit hall. The dark stone and earth walls were graced with torches at intervals that faded into the darkness down a long corridor. The glow from the flames cast swaths of light along the cobbled floor. It was like nothing she had ever seen. Like a castle, but not; like a dungeon, but not.

"Come, this way." Chet's hand pressed to the small of her back. The heat of his touch made her insides shake as he guided her in the same direction they'd headed moments before. "Not what you thought when I said we were going to see the Royals. Eh?"

"Well, um, no. I imagined a modern mansion: riches and luxury." She struggled to keep up with Chet's long strides.

He laughed. "Well, they do have that. They choose to live here, in the caves where they have been for thousands of years."

She traversed along the uneven cobbles until a brighter light and the sounds of monklike chanting came from up ahead.

"The Royals?"

Chet nodded. "They are having their morning ritual of sustenance."

Rounding the corner, she sucked in a shocked breath. The room was crowded, filled with a mixture of full-form dragons and dragons in half form like Chet. This room was not like the walkway they'd left. At intervals along the room, pillars of solid white marble towered a hundred feet into the sky. The ceiling itself was painted with elaborate scenes of dragons in different activities: flying, blowing smoke, sleeping, and fighting. A pressure circled her legs as if a cat greeted her. She glanced down. A small red and gold dragon, without feet but with wings, fluttered about her legs. Her eyes widened and she jumped backward, away from the ruby-glowing creature.

"It is okay, Nora." Chet rubbed her bicep. "Ruby . . . introduce yourself before taking liberties with my mate."

The red dragon smiled and a forked tongue slid out, tickling the bare skin of Nora's calf. A massaging sensation skimmed her body and aroused wetness tingled along her skin. Nora flinched in surprise at how pleasurable the flick of the little dragon's tongue was. What would that tongue feel like licking the more sensitive parts of her body?

"She is as sweet as she smells." A woman's sultry voice emerged from Ruby's throat and Nora's legs trembled. "And, oh, how responsive."

Chet laughed, drawing Nora's gaze to him. His eyes shown with pure sexual desire and Nora's throat constricted.

"Yes, she is, isn't she?" Chet wrapped a possessive arm about her shoulders and pulled her tight against him. "Now keep your tongue to yourself until I give you permission."

Nora relaxed back against Chet's warm chest, absorbing his

energy, letting it linger and weave an intricate stitch into the cloth of her soul. His words, *". . . until I give you permission,"* shouted ownership. His hold about her shoulder showed every dragon there that she belonged with him. A tremor of arousal, a longing to be just that—*his*—blew into her and wrapped about her heart.

Nora wanted him, Chester Shields, Chet. She desired him in a way she had never wanted a man. Deep down, primal lust pulled at her gut. She wanted to be all he wished of her, both sexually and as a lifemate, but she couldn't. There was that one thing, the one omitted truth still hanging in her heart that she needed to tell him. Sexually she could be all he wished. And maybe, just maybe, he wouldn't care when she told him she couldn't have children.

A high-pitched moan snapped Nora's gaze to a female half-dragon tied to one of the pillars. The dragon woman's pale, scaly skin shone like snow. Her energy, a pure brilliant white, blinded Nora's senses and the urge to run her hands along the woman's white skin made Nora's hands shake. The woman's eyes sparkled pitch black, a striking contrast to the rest of her pale self, and her light dove-gray hair was cropped short.

Nora's eyes widened and she couldn't turn away. She stood, mesmerized, wrapped in Chet's arms. Chet's hand slid lower and his fingers circled her nipple, pebbling the flesh.

The dragon woman's beauty shocked Nora, yet if she'd worn clothing she could have passed for an effeminate male. The dragon woman moaned in ecstasy as another half-dragon pressed his chest against her breasts and rocked his body into her. Rolling his torso, shoulders to pelvis, he caressed her with his body, eliciting a purr of erotic delight from the female.

He, too, was alabaster with the same stunning pure glow that Nora could not resist. Her powers demanded to know more about these two dragons. Her desire to read and see their energies raged hungrily. Drinking in all her surroundings, she focused on the couple. The need to learn more willed her to meet them, touch them, and bask in their energy glow.

The male lifted his face away from the woman's body.

Nora's eyes widened.

He was the same: His face was identical to the woman's, yet his body was hard. A sculpted chest led to a muscle roll about his hips and a long, stiff cock stood between his thighs.

She needed to get a closer look. Nora stepped in their direction.

Chet stepped with her.

Oh . . . She glanced at his face.

He grinned. "The twins are amazing, are they not?"

Her brows drew together. "They . . . they are related?"

"All dragons are related, Nora. The twins are whole without needing a separate mate. They are one together because our goddess, Desna, split one dragon in two creating them. They both can, and do, change sexes. You see they pleasure each other and complete one another in all ways. Enjoy them, Nora. Enjoy their company, their beauty. Especially, enjoy the pleasure they are sure to give to you."

"They were split while living?" And what did he mean by the pleasure they would give her? Would they allow her to explore their energies?

"Indeed, lovely. They used to be one dragon. A snowy white dragon from the depths of crystalline. This dragon was solitary. He had no contact with another soul, so Desna, feeling his anguish, decided to split him in two. She made each half able to shift to pleasure the other in both the male and female forms."

"Amazing." Now she wanted to meet them even more. Did they think alike? Were they in tune with each other?

"Yes, they are, and you shall do more than meet them, my lovely."

"What do you mean, Chet?" She glanced up at him over her

shoulder. The look of desire and mischief in his eyes warmed her through to her toes.

"You will do as I wish, Nora?" His eyebrows rose.

Of course she would ... just look at him. Even if she'd wanted to deny him, that look broke all her resolve. Deep down she desired to be all he wished. Though, what if he asked her to do an act she detested? She bit her lip. "That depends, Chet." Her hands shook. "I—I wish to please you, but I have no idea what you will ask of me."

His smile broadened. "Oh, you will enjoy my request, believe me."

Strangely, she trusted she would. They reached the pillar where the twins coupled with each other.

The male turned his head in their direction and his gaze slid down Nora's body. Excitement and the thrill of the unknown pulled at Nora. Her power surfaced as the pure white light of their auras washed through her. The male snapped his attention to Chet.

"Chester?" The word hissed in the air between them and wetness curled in Nora's sex, making her anxiously shift her stance.

"Foster," Chester nodded, then flourished his hand toward Nora. "My mate, Nora." Chet placed his other hand on the small of her back and pushed her toward the twins.

Nora's legs trembled, her knees weakening, as Foster stepped away from the female twin, leaving her tied to the pillar, spreadeagled for all to admire.

His hand wrapped about Nora's shoulder and pulled her to him. The solidity of his chest hit hers and she groaned. His pure energy pulled at her, arousing a deep urge to touch and be touched by these creatures.

As he rolled his body down hers, every inch of Foster touched her. His large erection pressed to her stomach and electric currents caressed her pores, making the hairs between her thighs tingle with the charge. She groaned as her flesh dewed with his energy. The relaxing, arousing chemistry soaked her, coating her thighs and her sex with her cream. Chet's shorts clung to her dampness. Chet. She stiffened slightly.

Should she be enjoying this as much as she was? Her eyes slid open; he stood a foot away and his positive energy soothed her slight discomfort. Knowing he watched heightened the amazing sensations coursing through her body. His energy warmed her.

Heat that contrasted the twins' icy energy touched her about her waist. Chet. She felt a tugging sensation as he pulled the shirt from her short's waistband. Her eyes fluttered as the soothing heat of Chet's hand traveling up the row of buttons washed over her. Gently he touched her skin beneath the fabric as he undid each button.

The sensations reassured her and loosened her reserve. His touch skimmed her collarbone and pushed the cotton off her shoulders and down her arms. Twisting the fabric about her hands behind her back, he bound her wrists, then slid his shorts from her body.

She tried to move her arms, but her hands didn't move. Her pulse soared, hammering in her chest. They could do as they pleased. Wetness gushed from her pussy and she licked her lips and gazed at Chet. He stood inches from her. His heat mingled with theirs, reassuring her that this was all right, that her desire to experience this was what he wished and expected of her. Her nipples tingled, aching for Chet's touch, as sensations engulfed her.

The twins' hands delved between her legs from both directions and into the wetness of her folds. She quivered as Foster touched her from both front and back. His humid mouth touched her chest above her breasts and her body arched toward him.

Cool energy caressed her back as Foster pressed her up against the twin behind her, pinning her between them. Hard male muscle caressed her front as soft woman's flesh brushed her back. Nora's eyes widened. They'd immobilized her with their bodies, with their energies. Hands caressed her sides; both of their lips caressed her neck. Their cropped hair tickled her skin as they tasted her . . . and that was what they did . . . they fed on her: on her aura, on her sexuality, on her responses to their every touch.

Chet's warm energy soothed her jitters as he watched her. His hand reached between her and Foster and his blazing touch pinched her nipple. She shook and moaned as her body seemed to ignite between the two of them. This was Chet's request of her. To—to . . . be sexual with the twins as he watched and fondled her. Her gaze met his.

His eyes flamed with heat. "Yes," he mouthed and nodded his head.

She did this for him, for them, for herself. A shiver of ecstasy erupted deep in her belly and whispered ever steadily throughout her limbs.

Sex with more than one person . . . Never in her entire life had she experienced such a taboo. Foster's mouth closed on the tip of her breast, and her eyes squeezed shut as his cool energy pulled and coaxed the blazing fire in her body loose. Her desire burst into a wildfire. The flames of her sexual wantonness amazed her. With every touch from their hands, mouths, and bodies, she succumbed to their will with terrifying speed. To Chet's will. Her desires melded, swirled, and churned into his.

"Yes, Nora. Let your Desna come forth. Enjoy this with them. There is nothing in this realm that can exceed foreplay with Crystallines."

Their pure energy flowed, intersected, and wove through her. She was a bead on the thread of their light, sliding back and forth between sensations.

Foster pressed to her chest again, rubbing his hard pear-shaped cock head against her moist mound. Her legs separated and he pushed hard against her, slamming her shoulders back against his twin. A soft, fuzzy, floating feeling surrounded her. Her mind swam and she gulped for air as the sensations submerged her in ecstasy. Her breathing steadied and she noticed the breasts of the twin behind her were gone, as was Foster's cock that had been pressing at the apex of her thighs.

Behind Nora the twin pressed her hips against Nora's buttocks and the hard head of a penis pressed into the crack of her bottom. She trembled. They had changed. Foster was now female and her breasts pressed against Nora's. Their nipples rubbed and caressed each other's.

The twin behind her pressed his cock into the crack of her ass, tapping forward a small fraction and then inching back, each time going farther and farther between the globes of dewed flesh, aiming for her holes. The thought of him fucking her ass as the twin in front kissed and fondled her breasts and clit made her knees shake.

The cock pressing to her rear reached her asshole and she spread her legs wide. As she pressed back against him, the tip of the pear-shaped head tickled her pucker, then retreated once more.

She groaned. Damn it, but oh, when he returned, that next press forward would penetrate her. Her stomach fluttered and a gush of wetness pricked her womb, running down her leg. Chet's humid breath caressed the skin of her ear.

"I will be back, lovely." His touch blazed on the dewed skin of her shoulder. "When I return I will need you desperately. The twins will keep you aroused and ready for me to take you."

The words skittered through her. The twins would provide the foreplay and he would take her when he returned. She would not disappoint him; she enjoyed the twins and would be more than ready for him when he came for her.

The energy grew icy about her. Chet's warming blue-gold presence was gone. He no longer watched her. Nora glanced, eyes hazy with arousal, at where he stood. Chet's wings extended and he flew up to the ceiling. He was going to see the Royals about the detector.

The twin behind her pressed his cock forward; the tip pressed more firmly against her entrance. She quivered; he would not enter her . . . He prepared her for Chet's return. Foster's mouth drank in the tartness of her pussy lips.

Such exquisite torture!

Her body convulsed, yearning for an orgasm she would be denied until Chet returned.

6

Chester watched as the twins pleasured Nora. Her head leaned back against Crysta, lips parted and quivering with lust. She was amazing and fully occupied at the moment.

Come on, Chet, the mission needs your attention. Damn she aroused him, though.

He focused on the Royals' energies surrounding them and stepped back away from Nora. *Goddess Desna, give me strength to deal with the Royals erotic energy.* He hated meeting with the Royals. Their energy oozed sexual hormones into the air. All who wished their guidance left in a state of frantic sexual desire. He continued to recede from Nora, absorbing her energy as he did: her warmth, her vitality, her kind and true heart. The cold earth touched his back. This time his mate was here to release his primal energy into.

"Your Graces, I need your guidance." Chester tilted his head to the sky.

The ceiling's colors shifted . . . and in a cloud of steam the image of a dragon at rest appeared; it opened its mouth. Chester spread his wings. In two hard strokes he reached the ceiling and flew through the open mouth into the Royals' chambers.

The air hung thick with moisture, Frankincense, and heady arousal. The smell reminded him of the old days, of him growing up, of his family. He sighed. He now would start a family of his own. This time, with Nora, would be different. He couldn't allow her to leave. He would do everything in his power to nurture her and not leave her to discover the carnal desires on her own, as he had Jane.

"Chester Shields, Golden Dragon of Sury, what is it you wish to discuss?" The whispers came from all around and feathered his skin like a lover's playful caress.

Chester straightened his shoulders and walked toward the large painting of a red dragon. The hormones oozing from the Royals and into the air caressed his skin and he hardened fully. An elaborately carved ruby dragonhead sat upon a small table before the canvas. Inside the head lay the remains of the Royals. The one thing that held the Dragna and Full Dragons together was contained in a large ruby carving as well as in their spirit words.

He kneeled before the large table. "I have come to seek your guidance in the matter of the detector, your Graces."

"Proceed." The whispers of Desna swirled in the air around him, running up his spine and around his neck before blowing in his ear. He groaned as the smells and soft whispers kindled his desire, rushing blood to his balls, filling them, and pulling them tight to his body.

The Royals' sexual energy dripped in the air. His heart pounded fiercely, the sensations of spending the night before with Nora flooding him. He gritted his teeth as his cock sent wetness from its tip.

No.

He needed to focus. He did not want to share all of the details of his binding with the Royals. The image of Nora lying naked beneath him, her hips rising to accept his penetration, tightened every muscle in his body.

Bugger. *The detector, Chet. That is why you are here.*

"I have not completed the mission . . ." His shoulders trembled. His vision clouded with intense, primitive Dragna arousal. "I met my mate while at Ralston." *Nora. Yes, Nora.* His chest labored for breath. "I have learned through her that the detector is not kept at the lab."

"Indeed. Did you not think we knew of your mate . . . of her location, Chester?" The whispers assaulted him, circling his stiff cock; his nipples hardened. Bugger, he hated this lack of control over his body. He gritted his teeth and inhaled a tight breath, trying to concentrate on their wisdom.

How could they have known where she was? He stared up at the painting as the ruby carving glowed. The site sent his blood rushing; his skin tingled everywhere. *Bloody hell, you know better than to stare at them, Chet. You will end up fucking anything when you leave here if you are not careful.*

"Indeed, we did. That is why we sent you." Their words, their smell, all called to his basest instincts. His hips rocked, fucking the air.

"I don't understand." Only Desna knew where your mate was. How did the Royals know?

"We were aware of her whereabouts as well as her status as Dragna before we sent you. We also knew that without her help we could not obtain the detector."

Chester's heart beat a steady rhythm; his cock spent drops of fluid onto floor he knelt on. Nora would help him get the detector? He couldn't believe it.

A spot on the floor before him opened, allowing him a view of the room below. Nora stood between Foster and Crysta, her mouth greedily feasting on the skin of Foster's neck as Crysta licked her shoulder. Foster's hands pinched her nipples and she cried out. Pain and panic wrapped around his heart and Chester shot to his feet. He needed her . . . only her.

"Your mate is smart, Chester, and wants nothing more than to help you. But she fears your rejection on the basis of a falsehood she was told."

The words pounded through him, each syllable seeming to stroke his dick. He couldn't stand any more. "What falsehood?" He needed to leave, to join with Nora. Chet stared at the ruby carving, once more laboring for breath.

"That is for you to discover. You are dismissed, Chester Shields, Golden Dragon of Sury."

The floor gave way beneath him and he fell . . .

He allowed the pins and needles sensations to caress him, to roll up his body, as his heart pounded in triple time. He spread his wings and landed back on the marble floor of the great room in the exact spot he'd left. His entire body pulsed with intense arousal.

His eyes focused on the pillar where Nora stood engaged with the twins' frolic. Yes, only Nora would do. No other touch could compare. In two strides he was at the Crystallines' sides.

Foster's head rose and his eyes met Chet's. A knowing smile curved his lips and he glanced down at Chester's engorged cock.

"Need some relief, Chester?"

"Don't fuck with me, Foster. Move aside." He stepped closer to them and the scent of Nora's slick wetness locked his lungs. *My Desna.* He needed her. Needed her with a desperation he could not control.

Foster stepped back. "All yours, Chester."

"Yes, she is."

Chet's energy engulfed Nora as Foster pulled back from her. His hands burned the skin of her waist as he pulled her from the second twin behind her and spun her, crushing her to his body. Her body shook, arousal pumping from every pore. She needed him and he needed her.

Her head swam with his energy, as he rotated her again, pressing her up against the marble pillar right next to the bound twin. The twin's icy energy caressing her side paled in comparison to the heat radiating down her front.

Her eyes fluttered open and she gasped at the look of wild, intense passion in Chester's eyes.

His cock nudged the lips of her weeping flesh and she spread her thighs. With a harsh advance of his hips, he penetrated her hungry cunt. She arched into him.

"I need you, Nora. This will not be soft." Goosebumps rose on her skin and she groaned. She didn't want it to be soft. She wanted this primal, aggressive taking, this taking by her mate.

The thought filled her heart. She wanted him in every way.

His hand fisted in her hair and pulled her head back. Lips fused, thirsting for contact, for touch, for tastes of the other. His mouth dragged down her throat as his cock slammed in and out of her flooded pussy. Her legs moved with each thrust. He groaned, growled, and bit her flesh, his hands everywhere on her body, her hands everywhere on his. They ignited; their passion and need for each other made Nora's mind spin. Every thought spilled from her head and she felt the sensation of Chet's energy, of her energy, winding, twisting and weaving into a pattern that could not be undone. She gave her body, mind, and soul over to him. He greedily claimed her.

The cool marble pillar slid against her back. The sounds of his breath, of the wetness of their joining, of people fucking about her, tingled her skin everywhere. Her eyes slid open; the twins fucked right beside them. Foster greedily sucked his mate's nipples and thrust into her. Her legs spread wide and brushed Nora's knee; the touch, so pure, so different, yet so familiar, broke her. She convulsed as Chet bit down on her shoulder. Wetness trickled down and dripped on the floor as Chester cried out and his seed spilled into her open and wanting cunt. The warmth of his seed flooding her tingled every fiber of her cunt and she shook, then shattered once more.

Nora couldn't move. She was bone tired. She collapsed against Chet, her head on his shoulder, as she struggled to catch her breath.

"Are you well, lovely?"

"Umm . . . Yeah, I—I think so . . . just really tired." She inhaled his scent and let the sweet, smoky smell wrap about her in comfort and safety. But what was safety without truth? She needed to tell him. She couldn't feel this way about him and let this go on with out him knowing everything.

She looked around the room. A mass orgy unfolded around them. Dragons and half-dragons caressed, kissed, and screwed everywhere. It was a beautiful and erotic sight. Her energy reached out and listened to them . . . the energy glowed warm yellow. They were welcoming her. This mass coming together was for her. Her heart warmed. A welcoming. She had never had anyone welcome her quite like this. They celebrated her and Chet with uninhibited sexual abandon.

She couldn't let this dragon race perish and, if Chester and the Royals were concerned about the detector doing that, she could help him. Everything about this mystical race was magical and intense. If they wanted to be secluded, then why should she be a part of those who wanted to flush them out? No, she would help him.

Chester wrapped Nora in his arms and cradled her. Without doubt she would crash hard after this. "Time to get you home, lovely. Put your head down and doze if you like."

Nora's head rested on his shoulder and she nodded. He walked through the crowded room as the day's fucking continued. The room radiated power after his joining with her; the entire clan was caught up in their sensuality. It was truly amazing. They welcomed Nora in a way he had not expected.

The little red dragons flew about, licking and frolicking in the air. As well, every Dragna in the room engaged in some form of foreplay or sex. If he didn't have to worry about the detector and if Nora wasn't plain beat, he would have stayed and enjoyed Nora with the group. Her breathing shifted to one of deep slumber. He kissed her hair and continued on home.

He tucked her into bed. Running a fingertip over the blue-gold glow of the bite on her shoulder, he smiled. His heart and soul filled with joy. Today Nora had proved she was truly a Dragna and truly his.

7

Chester arrived at Frey's house to find a complete mess. He had not visited in the past weeks and now that he saw the chaos in the house he was sorry that he'd come.

"Fuck, Frey, what the bloody hell happened in here?"

Frey lifted his head up above the edge of the couch. His eyes were swollen and red; a glass of scotch perched in his hand. "Why, brother, this is called *grief*." His eyes narrowed and he let his head fall back below the edge of the couch.

"Come on now, Frey. I know you're grieving, but what a mess. My Desna."

"Not all of us live to be tidy, Chet. Some of us have more important things than pressing our shirts to deal with."

Ouch. "Bugger off, Frey." Chet sighed. This was what Ann's loss did to him. Well, that and anger at Chet for finding Nora.

Chet walked around the edge of the couch as Frey tucked a paper into the pocket of his pants. Across the table lay books flipped open to inscriptions scrawled in a woman's writing. Ann's. The book on Frey's lap lay open to a page with a postcard settled in the crease.

Chet sat down next to his brother. "We all miss her, Frey."

His brother's eyes narrowed. "Fuck that! No one misses her." His hand ran down the open page and he slammed the book shut. "I have arranged for the ritual. The switch of the guard will be tonight. The book says that to complete the change, you, me, and her are required. The others can attend, and it is recommended, but to complete the ritual, to complete my healing and welcome Nora into the fold, only the past partner of the family couple and the couple are required."

"Tonight?" With the falsehood the Royals mentioned looming there was no way she would be ready to trust him and Frey on that level. "She won't be ready, Frey."

"She needs to be. I can't go on like this, Chet." His brother's anguished stare washed over him.

Chet ran a hand through his hair. "I have never seen a welcoming that the clan didn't all watch. I'm not sure how the energy will be, Frey." Especially after what they'd done that afternoon. This ritual needed to be bigger.

"Doesn't matter."

Chester sighed. There would be no persuading him on that front. Frey was ready to be done with his pain. Chet couldn't blame him.

Light flashed behind his lids and Chet saw Nora pick up his phone and dial. He held up his hand to keep his brother from disrupting his concentration. What was she doing?

"Shawn, hi. I think I have the calculations all figured out. Can you call St. John and request that the detector be brought to the lab later this afternoon?" She glanced around the room. "Yes I'll meet you for coffee and we can head to the lab from there. See you in twenty minutes." She turned and left the house, getting straight into one of the local Dragna cabs.

Chester's jaw clenched. She was going to get the detector without him. Didn't she realize she might be in danger by trying to take it from the lab? Ralston wanted that detector and he would bet that they had a tracker on the thing. Bugger.

"Frey, I need your help. Nora is headed into what I feel is a dangerous situation. I need to get there before her. Can you help me? Your teleporting skill is the only way I can arrive at Ralston before her."

"Under one condition, brother." Frey's lips turned up. "As soon as you have her again we end this thing and welcome her home."

Chet nodded. "Done."

Nora would have to be ready. He would make sure she was. Her safety and comfort were what mattered. He hoped she was not headed into a situation that put her in jeopardy. But in a moment he would know.

Frey stood up. "Well, brother." He held out his hands. "You ready to go on a wild ride?"

"Quite." Damn right, he was. Nora's safety was what mattered. Screw his teleporting sickness. Chet stepped forward and Frey's large black wings spread out from his body and wrapped about the two of them. Chester inhaled a deep, steadying breath and stared his brother in the eyes. The heat of his brother's body increased and the familiar spinning and rolling waves of energy engulfed them both.

Only a minute, Chet.

Only a minute . . .

He blew out a hard breath and clenched his teeth.

This will only take a moment.

His stomach rolled as the circling increased.

Breathe!

Teleporting is almost done . . .

His stomach flipped and he pressed his tongue to the roof of his mouth.

That's it.

Bile rose in his throat.

Bugger...

He swallowed hard, forcing down the acrid liquid.

He refused to cast up his accounts.

Nora pushed open the door to Malgione, her favorite coffee spot. Shawn sat at a table eating quiche and drinking her typical mocha.

"Sweet cheeks!" Shawn's smile lit her entire face. "I've been waiting for you."

"Have you?" She nodded to Daniel behind the counter for her grande drip and a piece of quiche.

"Yep. So I'm dying to know. How did you figure it out?"

Nora's cheeks grew toasty warm. She hated lying to her friend. In fact, she couldn't.

"Shawn, I have to tell you something. Something that I am telling you in the strictest confidence."

Shawn's eyebrows rose. "You know I would never tell a secret, Nora. It goes against all I am."

"Yes, I—I know. But this means a lot to me. I also could use your thoughts and advice on something."

"Now I'm dying to know ... spill, Nora dear."

Daniel set Nora's drip coffee and her quiche in front of her and they waited for him to remove himself from earshot.

"I met a guy ... a fantastic guy, Shawn. He told me I'm his mate. But how can I be anyone's *mate*, when I can't have kids?"

"Oh sweetie, back up here. I'm missing details." Shawn's latte-colored hand lay across hers and she squeezed.

"I was in the lab late last night and when I came back from getting coffee there was this guy there. You should see him. I know you'll drool. Anyway, we fooled around and the cleaning crew interrupted us. That's when I noticed he wasn't human. He told me he's a dragon ... and that I was his mate."

"Whoa! You got it on with a dragon? That's fantastic . . . do you think he would let us try the detector on him?"

Nora sighed. "You're missing the point, Shawn. How can I be a mystical creature's mate when I can't bear a child?"

"You are stressing way too much about this, Nora. Some of us, even if we are mystical, don't want kids. We're just like humans. Though, procreation is a bit more important, because there are a limited number of us. That's one of the reasons I joined Ralston. You see, finding a mate is hard. If I had a detector, I could find out where others like me live. I could find a mate, a pack of my own."

Nora's eyebrows drew together. "That's true." That was what she'd thought all along: that the detector would help the paranormals, not harm them. Though now that she'd met the dragons, had felt their energy and seen how sensual they were, she understood. People would not understand them. Their culture was so radically sexual they would be called *freaks*. Her father's voice echoed in the depths of her mind. *Freak* was a label she totally understood and would never have wished on anyone. She raised her cup to her lips and swallowed the strong, flavorful liquid.

"Did you say you met him in the lab?" Shawn's brow furrowed in concentration.

"Yes." She picked up her fork and stabbed a piece of quiche.

"What was he doing at Ralston?"

Nora fidgeted with her fork as she withdrew the utensil from her mouth. "Well that's why I asked you to bring the detector in today. You see, the dragons believe the detector will wipe out paranormals. *Not* secure them, as you believe."

"Really? Well, of all the paranormals they are the rarest. I can see their concern with being discovered. But, I can see the good in what we are doing, too." Shawn raised her mocha to her lips and took a long swallow. "Nora, are you trying to take the detector?"

Nora bit her lips and heat blazed on her cheeks. Shawn wasn't going to like this. "Yes, Shawn. I have to help them. If you saw them you'd understand why."

Shawn's lips turned down in a frown. "But the detector is what we have been working so hard for. Are you sure? Because I'm not."

Chet was what was important—him and his race. "Yes, I'm positive."

"I'm not saying I'm in on this one hundred percent, sweet cheeks, but we should get to the lab. St. John should have the detector there by now and you know they don't like that thing to sit out too long."

Nora put the last bite of her quiche into her mouth, chewed, and swallowed. "Yes, let's go." She pushed back her chair at the same time Shawn did and they stood. Nora's short stature towered over Shawn's meager four-foot-ten frame.

Shawn touched her arm. "Nora, if you believe this guy could be good for you, just tell him. Get it out of the way now. I'll bet he has no issue with your infertility. Especially seeing as dragons mate for life, sweetie. If he says you're his, then there's no other one for him."

Nora nodded. She should have told Chet before she'd fled to get the detector. She should have told him when he'd first said she was his mate, but she didn't. Offering him the detector rather than telling him of her sterility was a better plan than just crashing all his dreams.

They walked into the empty Ralston building and turned down the long hall toward the lab. No one should be there on the weekend, but . . . Nora glanced about. What if one of scientists was and could read her agenda?

CRASH!

A flash of blue light filled the hall.

"What the hell?" Shawn's energy went on the defensive.

Nora glanced at Shawn and then took off running for the lab. As she arrived, she saw Chet, hunched forward clutching his thighs, in front of his dark-haired brother, Frey.

Nora rushed in and ran to Chet's side. "What did you do to him?"

Frey stared down at her, shook his head, and rolled his eyes. "Why, nothing, new mother. He always hurls when we teleport."

She ran her hands along Chet's back and grabbed on to the ring in the middle. "Can you stand?"

"Yes." Chet unfolded himself inch by inch, assessing his stomach's unease. "Indeed, I'm well." He stood straight.

"Hmmmm, lots of firsts, dear brother. First gallantry, and now, no tossing your cakes after porting?" Frey spun about, taking in the lab. "Not what I was expecting. So, where is the death of our kind?"

"Where is what?" Shawn leaned against the lab door.

Frey's gaze licked Shawn from toes to head. Yes, licked. That was exactly what it did. Nora's mouth dropped open in shock.

"Who are you?" Frey's brows raised.

"Who are you?" Shawn smiled her *I'm up for anything sexy smile*.

"Okay, guys—" Nora stepped between them and spied the detector safely lying on the lab countertop. Stepping past them, she inserted her key into the two-key lock. "Shawn, do you have your key?"

"Yes, but . . ." She stared at Frey. "So, he's a dragon?"

"Yes I'm Dragna, honey. Who and what are you?"

"Shawn?" Nora repeated.

Shawn glanced back and forth between Frey, Chet, and Nora, her gaze settling on the detector. "He is yummy, Nora, but I still don't know."

Chet stepped forward. "I can open it." His hand extended

and his nail grew into a long, thin probe. Nora's eyes widened and she glanced at Shawn, who stood in the same intrigued state.

His nail inserted into the other side of the lock and he twisted. With a *pop* the latch clicked open.

"Amazing." Shawn stared at the box, then at Chet.

Nora picked up the palm-sized box and popped the device into her pocket. "Shawn, we'll be back in a couple of hours. Enjoy Frey." Nora grinned. Then she grabbed Chet's hand and stepped toward the door.

"Sorry, sweet cheeks. Can't let you take the detector and not take me with you."

Frey and Chet glanced back and forth at the two women.

"All right, then come with us." Nora shrugged. Having Shawn with them didn't matter; she would hand the detector to Chet as soon as she could.

Frey grinned. "Yes, please by all means." His shoulders wiggled back and forth.

Nora walked past them and out the door. Seconds later Chet was on her heels, followed by his brother, then Shawn.

They all piled into the elevator and Chet hit the lobby button. "I have my car here; I left it here last night. I can take Nora with me, but not all of us. It's a two seater."

Shawn glanced at Nora, then at Frey. "I have my bike, if you don't mind hanging on to a woman's waist."

"*Not* a problem." Frey licked his lips. "And brother, you will follow us. We need to complete the welcoming. We will do the ritual away from the others. Somewhere public . . . yet accepting."

Chet nodded at Frey. "I don't care where we go, just so long as Nora is safe."

That morning, as Frey had talked to Chet in the kitchen, he'd looked like he was ready to murder in order to stop his grief. Now he practically panted at Shawn.

Nora got into Chet's car in the parking lot and shut the little blue car's door. "So where are we going, Chet?"

"Not sure. We will follow. Frey is ready for the ceremony. He was ready to join with your friend in the lab. You are ready as well, Nora. I can feel the shift in your energy."

"Right." Nora stared out the window . . . She was ready to tell him the truth. How was it she'd wrapped herself around him so quickly? She was ready to give her work to him and tell him her inner secrets just because he was . . .

Her mate?

Insanity.

She glanced at him, at his blue-gold glow filling the car's interior, and tears drizzled down her cheeks. He was an amazing creature. How was she to believe that she, the girl who her family ignored and men feared, belonged with him?

He observed her from the corner of his eye. He knew her. She knew he could also read her thoughts, and there was a good possibility he already knew her secret.

"Chet, how do you read thoughts?"

He glanced at her, then back at the road.

"Well. I have to concentrate on the person. I don't have to be anywhere near them. Just ponder them and wonder what they are experiencing and *poof*. Their thoughts and emotions flood me."

"So you don't just hear everything from everyone that is near you?"

"No. When I was young I had a harder time with it. I would at times think of a person and I would be beaten with their thoughts. To the point that I sometimes thought they were mine." He reached across the seat and grasped her hand. His energy tickled up her arm and her nipples pebbled beneath her T-shirt.

God, she wanted him. They had chemistry, but the emotions were more than that. She wanted him with her heart and soul.

Her desire for him was irrational. They had met only last night, yet she was prepared to change her entire life for him.

"My mother was a dragon. My father was human. My father never understood the mystical properties of being a dragon mate. He loved my mother. He just turned the other way when she used her powers." He sighed and stopped at the red light.

Nora stared at his profile as he watched the light. He was so handsome. She studied the slope of his nose and his full lips leading to his square, dimpled chin.

The light changed to green and he drove on. "When we were born, he treated us as human. When we showed any sign of being dragons, he would get angry and then take it out on our mother. It got to the point where my mother decided that for our safety, she needed something to change." He turned the corner and into a parking lot that was adjacent to several clubs. "She went to the Royals and asked them for help. She arranged for us to be taken in by the Royals and trained to carry out their missions. I am a runner. I am whatever the Royals request me to be. This time I am a thief. Though not a very good one." His mouth quirked.

"Why didn't your mother leave your father?" That was what her mother had always threatened to do.

He leered at her without watching where he was going in the parking lot.

"Nora, you still don't get it, do you? Dragons mate for life. You can't just leave. If you do before your time together ends, you die."

Nora squinted as her heart pounded in her chest. She was bound to him for life. How she wanted that . . . but that couldn't be true. She couldn't be his mate.

"Listen, Nora. If I were to walk away from you this moment my powers would diminish; all of my thoughts would be consumed with you. I would slowly decay and die."

So if he left her he would die. What if she left him?

"The same. You cannot spare me or yourself from whatever it is you are so sure makes you a bad mate. You have blocked your thoughts on that level, Nora. When I try to see why you think you are not suitable, all I get from you is sadness and loss. Why, Nora? Why do you feel you are not worthy of being my mate?"

Her eyes widened and all she could do was stare at him as he turned his attention back to finding a parking space.

He knew she felt unfit for him. Her heart ached to the point of causing tears. All she wanted was to be worthy of him.

"I will not hurt you, Nora. I plan to take care of you for the rest of your life, making sure you are happy, satisfied, and well taken care of." He pulled into a parking space and put the car in park, then turned toward her and grasped both of her hands in his. His gaze locked on to her. "If I don't know why you feel unfit, how can I accomplish that?" His thumbs ran across the backs of her hands. Heat, passion, comfort, and longing sprang forth from her belly and wrapped her soul in their blanket. The intensity warmed her and frightened her all at once. She needed to tell him.

She turned away; she couldn't bear to look him in the eyes as she told him. She couldn't bear to see his beautiful blue-gold energy change to something different, something ugly, as he realized she could never fulfill his dreams. The thought of being without him ripped through her soul like jagged glass. She would feel like . . . like Frey had acted this morning.

"Why is Frey in so much pain?"

His glare heated the backs of her shoulders. "I will answer that question because it is important. But you will answer me, Nora. I have a right to know what is going on. Frey lost his mate two months past. He is grieving. Anna was his second mate that he lost in childbirth. You see, Nora, in our clan one Dragna has a mate at a time. The others in the family support the mating couple. The ceremony tonight will heal Frey. By joining with you, and marking you, he transitions all of the focus to us."

Nora's eyes squeezed shut. They had been a childless dragon family for years, then, and now they thought she could be their salvation? Chills of horror raced across her skin as she sat in shocked silence at the reality that unfolded before her.

"Nora, what is wrong?" His fingers ran along her chin and he grasped it and turned her face to look him in the eyes.

She swallowed hard and her lower lip quivered. "*We* have to be a mistake, Chet. I can't be your mate," she blurted out.

His eyes didn't waver from hers. "You are my mate, Nora. There is no doubt. The question is, why do you feel you are not worthy of the title?" His thumb traced her lips and heat spread through her body, making her stomach flutter and roll all at once.

"I—I . . ." She could not look at him and tell him. Yanking her head away from him, she scooted as far from him as she could in the confines of the car. She stared hard at the black pavement of the parking lot. A deep smoke-colored tabby cat walked by the edge of the door and stared up at her. Its eyes flashed with the brilliance of the sun. "What a strange cat."

"Pardon?" Chet leaned past her and peered out the window. "Where?"

She glanced both ways at the sun-scorched pavement. "I don't know where it went."

The smell of smoky sweetness lit her senses. Chet. She would know him by his scent forever. Leaning forward, she kissed his ear, lightly tracing her tongue around the rim. And his taste: she would forget it. This was insane; her mind said no, yet her heart, body, and soul wanted him with a desperation she could not deny.

"Nora," he moaned as her tongue slid into the cup of his ear.

Her hands grasped the sides of his torso and all her muscles tightened, wanting him inside her, joining with her as they moaned, touched, tasted, and combined their energies into one. He turned his head toward her. His lizard-like eyes opened and shut as his tongue traced his lips.

"We need to go, my lovely, but before we do. . . ." He ran his fingers into her hair and pulled, tilting her head back. "You will answer me, Nora. I need to know."

Tears welled in her eyes and she pulled her head, trying to look away from him.

"No." He frowned and his other hand traced a zigzag pattern into the flesh of her cheek. "I will not harm you, Nora. Not in any way. Now out with it."

She swallowed hard and closed her eyes. She'd never thought she would have to break the dreams of a man she cared for again, like she had with John or herself.

"Now, Nora. I will not let whatever you have swirling in your brain make monsters that will eat us alive."

A lump formed in her throat and wouldn't budge. She swallowed hard, then coughed. "Chet . . . I—" Her heart tore in two; twisting and fluttering in an abyss of grief and pain.

"Go on." His fingers in her hair loosened and his knuckles massaged her scalp.

She closed her eyes. "I can't have children, Chet." The words came out in a whisper. "I was married once; we tried." Tears streamed down her face. "It was determined I didn't have any healthy eggs. John, my ex-husband, took matters into his own hands and created a child with a play friend of ours, then left me for her."

His fingers never once slowed or stopped caressing her. His breath warmed her face and his lips kissed her wet cheeks.

"You see, Chet, I can't be your mate. I—I can't have children."

Her shoulders shook as the pain of wanting children fled her body and relief at having told him flooded her.

His finger traced her chin. "Open your eyes, Nora."

She shook her head no. She couldn't look at him. Not yet.

"Very well, then listen to me. You are wrong. What happened to you was unfortunate. You have always been destined to be a Dragna mate. You see, Dragna eggs are fertilized only by Dragna seed. There is nothing wrong with you, Nora. You were just with the wrong kind of gentleman. I wouldn't doubt you are already carrying my child."

I can have kids? I am carrying his child? Her eyes popped open, and she stared at his blurry face. Hope sparked in her belly. Was he right? Could she be with child? She couldn't even dare hope that was true. Instinctively her hand spread across her stomach. "What?"

His lips curved up and he wiped away her tears with his fingertips. "Yes, Nora."

How could that be? Her lip trembled as she tried to absorb what he'd just told her. Her entire life she had been destined to have dragon children, and that was why her eggs had looked bad. She wanted to believe that.

"So, I—I can have kids?"

"Yes. Nora, you are mine. This is right and true." He leaned in and kissed her on the lips, his tongue gently tracing the seam, then swirling inside. She moaned as his energy infused her once more. Yes, this was right, fate, her destiny. She'd felt it in the lab that first night. When she'd known what he kissed like before even experiencing it. She knew deep down to her bones she belonged with him and that she trusted him.

"I—I believe you, Chet," she breathed against his lips.

He leaned back and gripped the handle of the car door, pushing it open. She blinked at him, then at the open door.

"Now that we have cleared that up," he smiled and winked at her, "let's go take care of saving the Dragna and relieving Frey from his grief."

* * *

Chester sat back as Nora pushed herself from the car seat and out the door. His stomach twisted. She'd thought she couldn't have children, that she was barren, because a Dragna hadn't found her. God, he wished the pain and self doubt evident in her words had never been. He closed his eyes and shoved open the driver-side door.

Nora's fingers brushed her cheek, wiping the salty remnants of tears from her skin. My Desna, she was lovely, even if she'd loved another man enough to marry him. A claw twisted in his heart. Bugger, she was supposed to be his, not another man's. His brows drew together. How the bloody hell had that happened? He sighed and walked toward her, wanting to hold her, to complete the ceremony so she knew without doubt what being part-Dragna was.

8

Chester stood at the edge of the crowded dance floor. Nora and Shawn were in the restroom. Frey approached from the bar, drinks in hand. "Sorry for such a public scene. But the ritual will be easily performed here."

Chester nodded. "She thought she couldn't have a child."

"Pardon?" Frey visibly tensed.

"Nora. She said she couldn't be my mate because she couldn't have children. She was married to a human once."

Frey's eyes widened. "Wow. Sorry, brother. Though that means she has loved. That is not a bad thing."

"You're right, loving is not bad. I just wish I had found her before she went through that kind of pain and self doubt. Jane, you know."

"Yes. I know, brother. You were young . . . Now you know your mate needs attention. That no one can replace your guidance. Jane tried to replace you, and you were more than willing to let her try."

Chet flinched. "Yes, I'd thought if she had her freedom so

would I. In the end neither of us did. We each longed for each other yet never allowed the other close."

Nora appeared at his side. "I have never been to a club like this before. I didn't know they existed." She glanced at Shawn. "And you're a member? How did I not know that?"

Shawn grinned. "You don't know everything about me, sweet cheeks. Plus, if you haven't noticed, all those here are paranormal."

Nora scanned the room again. The red lights placed every so often in the ceiling cast many shadows for people to hide in, but she spied a werecat as well as some sort of half-zombie-looking man. As her eyes settled on each being she felt their energies—red, blue, yellow, green—and she sucked in her breath as she came to a man who stared at her as if she were a meal. His energy shone pure pitch black. She stepped closer to Chet.

Frey smiled. "Indeed, this is a kinky bar for paranormal rogues."

Nora bit her lip. "So what will we do here, Chet?"

"We will finish the welcoming, binding you to me and freeing Frey from his bind."

"How will that happen, Chet?"

"I will share you, Nora. Trust me." His hand brushed a lock of hair from her face. "I would never do anything to harm you."

She believed he wouldn't hurt her, and she wanted do what he wished, but . . . She glanced around the room and her heart leapt in her chest. If she could do as he wished with the twins, she could do as he wished here with her friend and his brother. She nodded. Yes. She could. She would do it.

"Well let's get started." Chet's hand slid across Nora's back and wrapped around her shoulder. "Take your clothes off, lovely."

Nora pulled her shirt over her head, exposing her nipples, peaked and hard. Chet's gaze dropped to them and he licked his lips. Nora smiled a smile she felt all the way to her toes.

"Very well, brother. This way." Frey tugged Chet's arm and he tore his gaze from Nora, walking with Frey to the side of the room where a bar was suspended from the ceiling. "When you are nude, Nora, come to me."

Nora obeyed and followed behind the two brothers to the bar. Her knees shook and she inhaled a shaky breath.

"It's okay, lovely. Give me your hands." Chet reached for her wrists.

She held her hands out in front of her and he wrapped a soft, fur-lined leather cuff about her wrist, pulling the leather strap tight. He then leaned down and pressed his wet lips to her palm. Heat trickled up her arm. She glanced down and saw his kiss shone blue in her palm, and the trail of heat spreading throughout her body shone gold.

He was magnificent. The way he made her feel was divine. Every cell in her body awakened with just the touch of his lips to her skin. She wanted him, wanted to do as he wished no matter what that was.

He moved on to the other wrist, wrapping the soft leather around it. Frey grasped the first wrist and raised it into the air. With a clip of a clasp, her wrist was securely fashioned above her head. She wiggled her fingers and pulled, testing the strength of the cuffs. Could her hand slip out if she wiggled it? She twisted her wrist as she pulled, but it held firm. Chet raised her other hand and clipped it into place, angled out from her body. His hand trailed down her arm and she squirmed and giggled. His smile broadened and he stepped away from her and searched through a bag on the floor.

Her body shook with excitement, every nerve sparking to attention. What was going to happen to her? Would she be pleased with the ceremony or would it be one of those that was necessary but unpleasant? She glanced at Chet as he scanned the room. It didn't matter; she would do it because she wanted to be his in every way.

Shawn stood chatting with Frey next to Chet. Several other similar scenes were in full swing about them. A werebear had a female hobbled in thick steel cuffs as she kneeled before him and sucked his cock. One of her hands circled his thick black penis; the other circled his bulging sack, pulling his balls down away from his body as her mouth worshipped the tip. Sliding him all the way in, she swallowed him until he was seated fully, then she sucked back out.

Nora's mouth watered. How incredibly erotic! The scene reawakened the images she had seen of her before Chet: her hands tied to the ring in his back as she kneeled before him, sucking his cock into her mouth. The flesh of her sex filled with moisture and her pulse soared.

The werebear stood before the woman, resting the tails of a long suede leather flogger on her back. The woman moved and he raised the flogger, smacking the tails hard across her back. Nora's pussy clenched with each stroke of the soft leather. The woman moaned in pure arousal and Nora squirmed, wetness leaking from between her thighs. One of her boyfriends in college used to play with her that way. Ages had passed since leather tails had licked her skin, and they never had in public, but the desire for such an experience tugged at her gut. She slicked her tongue across her parched lips as her chest rose and fell, struggling for breath.

"You wish to kneel, do you?"

Frey tested the fastening of her right arm, and Nora's attention turned back to him.

"Are you ready to give all of yourself to be a Dragna mate?"

She looked at him. His hard eyes, so much like Chet's, sparked with heat. The intense passion that blazed behind the liquid blue sucked the breath from her throat. Under all his sarcasm, he burned. Desire, passion, and the will to enjoy all pleasures flowed from him and through her.

"I am a Dragna mate, Frey." She twisted her shoulders, testing her range of motion.

"Are you?" His eyebrows rose. "Then you should have no qualms about being shared, about doing what makes you feel the most pleasure." His hand trailed over her bare shoulders down the center of her back. Tingles of warmth trickled down her spine and into the crack of her ass. Her skin dewed with evidence of the arousal his touch created. She glanced at Chet. This was what he wished. She would join with his brother because this was what it meant to be his, to be part of his family, and she'd wanted nothing more in all of her life.

Chet smiled, a sexy, seductive smile that unleashed her sensual being. A moan burst from deep within her and Frey trailed his hand around her waist to her stomach. His fingertip circled her bellybutton and then slid down to her crotch. Sliding a finger into her folds, he leaned forward. The heat of his energy blended with hers and she shivered; comfort, empathy, and desire poured from her for this man who had lost a woman he cared for deeply. His breath tickled her ear. "You're going to be exceptionally good for him, aren't you?"

Yes, she would be more than good. Being a Dragna mate meant you gave way to your sexual desires. That you did what your mate wished of you in exploring those desires. This was just the beginning of her experiences. She shivered with anticipation of all the things that she and Chet would share in their life together.

Frey's touch left her, and her body vibrated with the loss of his heat against her.

Chester watched as Frey caressed Nora. His chest tightened with pride and a strange tingling sensation pushed through his limbs. She was his and every move she made caressed him; he felt it almost as acutely as the feeling of the Royals. His blood pounded through him as she jerked against the restraints and Frey touched her. He would join with her again soon. He inhaled in an attempt to relax. Frey needed to be aroused by her;

it was how this worked. Frey's life came back to him by joining with the new Dragna's mate.

Then moving on to others . . .

It appeared Shawn would be his conquest tonight. Chet raised his eyebrows and frowned. Joining with a non-Dragna was against all the Royals' rules, but Frey did not care.

Frey walked to him and pulled his T-shirt over his head. "Ready, brother?" He kicked off his shoes and undid his jeans.

"Indeed. Let's get this part done with so that *I* can have her to myself for a bit." Chester glanced at Nora hanging in the middle of the room.

People watched her, watched them.

She would make him proud.

"Possessiveness? You are full of surprises today, Chet." Frey grinned, a smile that Chet had not seen from his brother since Ann's death. "I'm glad to see it, brother."

Chester unbuttoned his shirt and undid the buttons of his jeans, stripping down to nothing. He and his brother stood in the middle of the club in full Dragna glow. The light was enough to attract the most stubborn of moths to them. He glanced around. Most people in the room watched them, curious as to what would unfold.

Chet strode forward to Nora. He stood before her and lightly trailed his fingertips up the soft flesh of her sides. She jumped, her skin and muscles twitching. A smile crossed her lips and her eyes held his. Her pupils dilated wide with arousal and the smell of her spicy wet cunt made his mouth water.

Frey appeared behind her and grabbed her hair, pulling her head back and exposing her neck to Chester's sight. He licked his lips, staring admiringly at the exposed column of her throat. He needed to mark her delicate skin in a pattern any Dragna would be proud of. He would do it with his teeth.

He leaned forward, his tongue licking her spicy skin from

collarbone to ear. Her breath deepened and his cock twitched, aching to be touched by her hands, her mouth. He needed her hot skin; he needed her. In every Dragna's life one mate made them a better partner. Nora was that mate for him. He bit the flesh of her earlobe, breathing out warmed air from his lungs as he did.

Nora squirmed. As he dragged his teeth harshly down the warmed skin, she whimpered. The marks would stay . . . permanently etched on her skin in his blue-gold shimmer. Warmed by the fire of his breath, they would never leave her body, the marks saying to all she was his.

His hands pulled her lower body to his. The warm juices of her cunt touched his cock as he rotated his hips against her and he wanted nothing more than to sink into her.

He held himself still. Frey would have that first privilege tonight.

She gasped in delight as Frey's tongue traced the raised flesh Chet's mark had created on her neck, spreading her thighs farther and rocking her clit against Chet. The hot folds of her labia coated his skin with her increasing lust. Chet groaned and speared his brother with his gaze. *Get a move on, Frey.* Frey's eyes laughed back at him as he nodded his understanding.

Frey's tongue flicked in time to her pulse, hammering just below her skin; then in the reverse direction he marked her with his teeth. Nora cried out in pleasure and pain. The spicy smell of her pussy, dripping with arousal, filled Chet's nostrils and his mouth watered, wanting to taste her tartness.

Frey released his hold on her hair and dropped to the floor behind her, spreading her butt cheeks and spearing his tongue into her juicy lips.

Frey would get to do everything first tonight. Bugger it. Not if Chet could help it; he would make her come first. He dropped to his knees and drew a slick line down Nora's labia, flicking her clit with feathery touches. Nora groaned, her legs shaking. My Desna, she was so responsive to every caress. He could caress her however he wished and she would be in rapture.

Yes, oh yes. He would make her come, and hard. His tongue circled her bud and latched on to the hard flesh—sucking, then swirling her button again.

Frey's fingers kneaded Nora's smooth ivory buttocks and thighs as his tongue danced along her slit. The heat and moisture of his tongue mingled with Chet's and Nora's juices as the men elicited cry after pleasurable cry from Nora's lips.

Each subtle moan and full-out delightful scream made Chet's blood rush faster, blocking out everything but his oiled tongue lapping and swilling in Nora's gushing wetness. Her legs shook and jerked. She arched her hips toward him, reaching for the climax that he intended to provide her. Yes, lovely, come for me now. Come for me.

He swooshed his tongue over her clit and rapidly flicked the swollen nub of flesh. Nora screamed, her body thrashing against the restraints. Chet washed her labia with his tongue. Each hard pulse of her cunt spilled the thick oil of her cum onto his taste-buds. The tart, spicy taste of her juices set his cock standing upright. Perfect. She was perfect.

She settled, relaxing on the restraints. Chet pushed back from her body and stood. Frey did not. He thrust his fingers into her cunt. The sound of her wetness as his finger fucked her and her scent spilling into the air tightened Chet's chest. His eyes devoured Nora's every move. Her motions defined passion and sensuality. Her responsiveness would be the envy of most of the experienced Dragna mates.

Nora screamed, head tossed back, eyes closed, as her body jolted, splashing more of her cum onto the floor. Chet reached up and tilted her head forward. Nora's eyes, dreamy and immersed in pleasure, slid open. Frey stood up, grasped Nora's hips, and, with a harsh buck, slid his cock into her from behind.

Nora moaned, her eyes fluttering shut.

The transition was almost done. Soon he would fuck his lovely mate and never again would he let her leave his sight. Never would he ignore her as he had Jane. This seeing and being a part of her awakening, her discovery of her Dragna self, was important to him, to a healthy, long-lived relationship.

Frey groaned. His eyes closed. Chester knelt down in front of Nora's open legs. Frey's cock parted her labia wide. Glistening with her arousal, the head of his cock appeared, then thrust into her pussy, spreading her lips fully from behind. With each press of his cock, Nora's hips jerked, her body arching and pulling against the restraints. Chet would give her release.

Chet squatted down again. Reaching between Nora's legs, he caressed their joining, cupping Frey's sack and tickling Nora's entrance. They both quivered. He leaned in and touched the tip of his tongue to Nora's clit. Fluttering it against the swollen bud, he wrapped the button in his tongue's slickness. He circled her clit and pressed, timing the touches with Frey's penetration of her cunt.

"Oh! Oh! Ahhhhhh!" She broke.

Her body pulsed with her climax. Frey growled and his sack contracted as he ejaculated. He bit down on Nora's shoulder, drawing the new blood to heal his hurting heart. Nora screamed, her knees giving way as wetness dripped in a stream down her leg and onto the floor. Frey slid out of her and Nora hung languidly from her wrists.

Chet smiled at his brother, who bowed his head at him. Frey ran his fingertips across Nora's shoulders and into the sticky bite he had inflicted. Raising his fingers to his lips, he licked them and sighed. The color of his energy changed from the dull blue of mourning to his usual vibrant, passion-filled purple. He was healed . . . the pain would be gone now and he would see only the happy times he had spent with Ann. No sorrow.

Wrapping his arm about Nora's torso, Chet unhooked her

wrists from the bar above her head and lowered her to her knees on the floor. Her sated eyes gleamed to life as he pushed her back on the mat and wedged himself between her thighs. The heat of her sex drew his cock like a magnet to the entrance of her core. He hovered above her on his arms. She glowed everywhere. Her body was radiant, her passion and love a living, breathing thing that he would nurture.

"I am your mate, Chet. I am a part of you now. Of your family, of *our* family." She reached up and her silken touch caressed his face. The tender gesture warmed him, comforted him, and brought him home. She was his home.

"Indeed you are, my lovely." The tip of his cock touched her flesh and she quivered. Slowly he eased the head of his cock into the opening of her pussy. The slickness of her arousal and Frey's cum washed his hot skin like oil. He groaned.

Nora's hips rose to meet his probing tip and her velvet flesh slid down the length of his stiffness. The lingering moan that caught in her throat made him tremble uncontrollably. Every fiber of his being focused on her, on their joining, on spending his seed deep in her womb. Joining with her blew his mind. Her tightness. The way her body moved and shook beneath him. She was a goddess . . . Desna in sexual form.

He would worship her.

His chest tightened as he slid his cock out of her steaming flesh and rubbed the head along her swollen lips to her clit. She trembled, her stomach muscles contracting, pushing her clit and pussy up to him. He slid his cock back down to her opening and into her eager marrow.

His lips came down harshly on hers; teeth mashed together and tongues danced and mingled as he thrust his cock hard into her. Her body gave to him the sensations and emotions he needed. His mouth feasted on her breath, on her lips, as her pussy consumed him. He couldn't hold back; didn't want to. His body lit up in flames as, without restraint, he grunted, spilling his seed deep into her silken heart. The gushes filled her pussy and she convulsed beneath him.

"Oh, Chet." Her voice rasped in his ear as her nails clutched his back, digging into his flesh.

He held her small form tightly, his breath tickling her hair by her ear.

"Nora, my mate. You awaken feelings of hope, longing, and home in me. I will never leave you, my lovely."

A tear caressed his cheek and he lifted his head and gazed at her.

Her hand cupped his face. Eyes brimming with tears, she sighed. "Chet, I belong here with you. I feel it deep inside. I have since that first night. I just tried to ignore it. You are the other half of me."

His lips curved into a smile he could not suppress. "Yes lovely . . . Indeed I am."

Winter's Kiss

Morgan Hawke

Ten years ago...

"If I save you, will you be my bride?" The voice was a deep, velvety rumble.

Curled up tight against the trunk of a sweeping cedar in the middle of the forest, half buried under the snow, Kasi opened her eyes. "Huh?"

Huge sky-blue eyes burned like the hearts of flames in a huge black-and-white-striped feline face less than a hand's reach away. The face belonged to a gigantic cat nearly the size of a pony. The frost-white fur, banded with black, was practically invisible against the snow falling just beyond the cedar's sweeping branches.

Kasi stared, wide eyed. *A tiger?* She struggled upright, her thick red wool mittens sinking into the snow. Her pale pink nylon parka whispered with her efforts to sit up against the cedar's trunk. *I didn't know Japan had tigers.*

The white tiger sat down on his haunches with a huff and

loomed over her. "I asked you a question. It's only polite to answer."

Kasi blinked. The rumbling voice clearly didn't come from the tiger's mouth and yet she was sure it was the tiger that spoke. Well, she was pretty sure it was the tiger. A quick look around showed that no one else was near. She frowned up at him. "I, uh . . . What was the question?"

The tiger flicked an ear back and twitched his long tail. "If I save you, will you be my bride?"

"Your *bride* . . . ?" She frowned. What a strange tiger. "Shouldn't you be trying to eat me?"

The tiger's ears flicked forward. "Eat you?" His blue eyes closed briefly as he huffed, laying back his long whiskers . "I do not care for the taste of humans." The tiger hunched down and eased closer, settling his gigantic paws to either side of her knees. "Even if I did, you are much too small to make a whole meal." His enormous nose pressed against her snowsuit, sniffing loudly right over her heart. "I need a bride more than I need a quick snack."

Kasi rolled her eyes and folded her arms across her chest. "I'm too small to be a bride too. I'm only eleven."

The tiger lifted his head; his huge damp nose was only a finger's length from hers. "You will grow."

"I suppose." She couldn't stop looking at him. He was so pretty. His fur looked so soft. She eased her trembling hand from her mitten. "Why does a tiger need a bride?" She reached up.

The tiger's gaze shifted to her hand but he didn't move. "Does it matter?"

"I guess not, but . . ." Kasi sank her fingers into the thick fur behind his ear. It was so warm, and incredibly soft. The longer guard hairs were coarse and slightly stiff, like heavy cotton, but right under his ear it was like fine, fluffy silk. "Can't you just marry another tiger?" She scratched.

The tiger's eyes closed and he pressed against her fingers. "No." A loud liquid purr erupted from him.

Kasi smiled. *Wow . . .* That had to be the loudest purr she'd ever heard. She took off her other mitten and reached up to scratch the underside of his other ear.

The tiger's purr increased in strength and volume. He lifted his chin and angled his head until her fingers sank into the fur at his throat. "More."

Kasi obligingly scratched his throat and her smile broadened. *Big kitty.*

"Does this mean you agree to be my bride?" His voice seemed a bit hoarse, almost breathless.

Kasi shrugged. "Sure, but you'll have to wait until I'm older to get married."

"Agreed." The tiger pulled back from her hands to gaze into her eyes. "Will you kiss me to seal our bargain?"

Kasi blinked. A *kiss . . .* ? "Okay." She leaned forward and dropped a small smooch on his broad, damp nose.

The tiger blinked, then huffed. "No, I want a real kiss."

Kasi snorted and rolled her eyes. "I can't give a real kiss to a tiger."

His ears flicked forward, then one tipped back. "Ah . . ." He closed his eyes and his body undulated out of focus as though he were made of water. He slid back into focus, only this time he wasn't a tiger.

A boy in a white fur coat and tall black boots knelt over her. He stared down at her with huge sky-blue eyes under straight black brows from only a breath away. Delicately pointed ears parted long, frost-white hair that tumbled over the shoulders of his fur coat and spilled onto the snow. "How about now?" His voice wasn't nearly as deep as before.

Kasi frowned sourly. Pretty white hair or not, boys were pains in the butt. "I think I liked you better as a tiger."

He smiled, showing the points of small fangs. "I'm still a tiger, but this is me, too."

She lifted her hand and brushed her fingertips along the double set of midnight-blue stripes that marked his cheekbones and disappeared into his hairline. "Are these tattoos?"

He blinked and his smile faded. "You can see them?"

She snorted. "They're on your face; kind of hard to miss."

He rolled his eyes. "Never mind." He leaned closer, setting his forearm against the trunk of the cedar above her head. "I'm waiting for my proper kiss."

Kasi winced. She'd never kissed a boy before. "Do I *have* to?"

He nodded solemnly. "We're betrothed. We're supposed to kiss."

Kasi sighed. "Fine, whatever . . ." She leaned up to press her lips briefly to his, then leaned back. "Better?"

He looked away, frowning, and licked his lips. He nodded. "It will do." He sat back on his heels and grinned. "For now." He shivered briefly. "Oi, it's cold!"

Kasi smiled. "Is it? I don't feel it anymore." What she did feel was *sleepy*.

The boy stared at her, his blue eyes wide. "You don't feel it?" He curled his lip and tisked. "Idiot! When you don't feel the cold is when you die!" He shimmered out of focus and became a tiger once more, standing on all four paws right over her. "You will go home right now." The tiger's voice was achingly loud in her head.

Kasi leaned forward but couldn't find the energy to actually get up. She fell back against the tree. "I'm too tired."

The tiger's eyes narrowed and his long tail swished. "You *will* go home." He reached down and caught the fur-lined hood of her pink snowsuit with his monstrous teeth. He backed up, pulling her.

Kasi rocked forward onto her knees and was dragged up on her feet. "Hey!"

The tiger released her. "I will not lose my bride the same day I get her!" He stepped past her tree, turned around, and then lay down in the snow right next to her. "Get on. I will carry you home."

Kasi stared at the tiger's long, narrow back. "Get on . . . ?"

"Yes." The tiger flattened his ears and flicked his long tail. "Are your ears frozen as well as your common sense?"

Anger warmed Kasi's blood and she snapped fully awake. "My ears are just fine, thank you very much!" She leaned over the tiger's back and eased her leg over.

The tiger turned an ear back. "Oh, so it is only your sense that has frozen?"

Kasi gripped the tiger's fur tightly. "My sense is just fine too!"

"Is that so? Put your head against my neck, and hold on tight to the fur on my shoulders."

Kasi lay down along the tiger's back and grabbed two handfuls of white fur. "Okay."

"Good." The tiger lurched up onto his front paws, then up onto his rear paws. "So, it was sensible to run away during a blizzard?"

Kasi rocked hard but somehow stayed on. She was too angry to let go of his fur. "I wasn't running away! My dad's been transferred back to America and I . . ." And she didn't want to go back to America. She wanted to stay with *Obaachan*, her Japanese grandmother. She closed her eyes tight. Well, okay, so maybe she *was* running away. She sniffed. "I just wanted to . . . think."

The tiger moved out from under the tree and into the blinding white of the snowstorm. "Could you not have found a warmer place to think?"

The tiger's long strides rocked her from side to side. Kasi pressed her cheek into his fur. He was so warm. "I wanted to see the house. I . . . I meant to go back, but I couldn't see through the snow."

The tiger's ear twitched in her direction. "The house?"

"Yeah, the big house up on top of the mountain with the red pillars." Her hands tightened in the tiger's fur. The house that everybody said *wasn't* there. She had no idea how they missed it. It practically took up the whole top of the mountain.

The tiger stiffened under her, then strode forward. "You can see the house?"

Kasi scowled and twisted her hands in his fur. "I'm not making it up; it's really there!"

The tiger huffed. "Yes, it's there; calm down."

Kasi blinked. "You can see it too?"

The tiger shook his head. "Of course I can see it, but humans aren't supposed to be able to."

"Why not? Is it supposed to be invisible or something?"

"Or something." The tiger snorted. "Can you see other things that no one else sees?"

Kasi groaned. "Oh, I see stuff all the time. Dad says it's because my mom, my *real* mom, was an Irish fairy." She sighed. "Everybody else thinks I'm crazy." *Everyone except Grandma.*

The tiger tilted an ear back toward her. "Your mother was a *faa-ri*?"

"Uh-huh." She yawned into the tiger's fur. "She died when I was little." She yawned again.

"Do not fall asleep!"

Kasi groaned. "But I'm tired."

The tiger lengthened his stride. "Hang on tight. I will have you home very soon."

Kasi frowned. "You know where I live?"

The tiger huffed. "I know everyone and everything on my island, Kasi-chan."

1

Kasi Stewart jolted awake. She'd fallen asleep in broad day-light. Jet lag was obviously catching up with her; that and her poor sleeping habits of late.

She straightened from her slump on the deck bench of the chugging ferry and rubbed her eyes. *The damned snow tiger dream again.* It wasn't a bad dream, but ever since her twenty-first birthday it had gotten to the point where her childhood fantasy was the only dream she had anymore. Even the smallest of naps conjured visions of white fur and blue eyes.

She groaned. *Damn it, why can't I dream of something else? Anything else?* Booze didn't work; sleeping pills didn't either. Nothing stopped the tiger from walking into her dreams. At her wit's end, three weeks ago she'd finally called the one per-son who seemed to have all the answers to the strange things in her life, her Japanese grandmother.

"Come back to Japan, Kasi-chan. This is where it began. This is where it will end."

Kasi tugged her long, sleek, black ponytail free from the hood of her silver-gray parka and turned to look over the rail.

The sea was steel gray and choppy with foam-crested waves. The sky was a hard, bright blue. The rich, salty scent of the sea was almost . . . comforting. Her gaze was drawn to the forested island, with its lonely snow-covered mountain peak, the ferry was passing.

While the rest of the country was blooming with spring, Rishiri Island, at the very northern tip of Japan, was still wrapped in winter. Her destination was even farther north, to the tinier island of Shido. It was also crowned by a small mountain, but it wasn't on any map.

The ferry's steam whistle wailed, announcing that they were approaching the dock. The few other passengers began to gather on the deck.

Kasi unzipped her large square shoulder bag and checked her camera equipment out of sheer habit. Her very first camera had come all the way from Japan, accompanied by an amazingly well-timed phone-call from Grandma. *"If what you see is real, it will appear on film. If it is not, it will not."* She had chuckled dryly over the long-distance connection. *"Of course, this does not mean anyone will believe the pictures are real, but you will know. You will know."*

Kasi nodded. She did know. She had reams of film to prove it. She'd brought a whole album of her findings just to show her grandma. Her best pictures were of a violet and scarlet appaloosa mustang that the Native Americans called the Rain Horse; a giant Finnish reindeer with three sets of antlers known as Grandfather Winter, bringer of snowstorms; and a huge French wolf with scarlet stripes she had been told was a *loupe garou*, a werewolf.

No one else would ever believe her photos were actually real, but that was all right. Grandma knew.

Everything in her bag was in order. She'd brought only her favorite Nikon and the barest essentials for development. She didn't need much more than that for this trip. She wasn't going there as a professional photographer to capture wildlife on film. She was on a mission to retrieve her sanity, to understand the dream that refused to let her go.

The ferry's whistle blew again.

Kasi stood up and settled the strap to her heavy bag on her shoulder. Her gaze drifted back across the water to the island, barely visible through a haze of fog. She took a deep breath and released it in a whisper. "It's just a dream. There are no tigers in Japan."

"Oh, but there are tigers in Japan." The deep rumbling voice purred from right behind her. "But very few have the eyes to see them."

She stilled in alarm. She'd spoken in English. The masculine reply had also been in English. The fine hairs on her neck rose. The voice was frighteningly similar to the one haunting her dreams, only it was deeper and far more mature.

A tall, sleek, broad-shouldered man stepped from behind her, wearing a heavy black wool overcoat open over his off-white cable-knit sweater and well-worn black jeans. He moved to her left, toward the railing, and dropped a battered brown leather backpack at his feet.

The dark-haired, dark-eyed man lounged against the ferry's rail, resting on his elbows only inches from her. Long, straight black hair was pulled back in a loose tail that spilled down his back, very nearly to his waist. He turned to face her and regarded her with midnight-blue eyes. The elegant shape of his jaw, high cheekbones, and fine, straight nose gave his face an aristocratic air that was completely spoiled by the lush, sensual fullness of his smiling lips. "Things aren't always what they appear to be."

Kasi's breath hitched and her belly gave a little wet clench of interest. He was freaking gorgeous. She frowned slightly. His voice sounded familiar, but she didn't recognize him. Abruptly, her temples gave a slight throb and tingles erupted in the back of her skull. She winced. *What the . . . ?* The only time she felt that odd sensation was when she was about to see something strange, something weird, something . . . legendary.

The guy leaned closer. "Are you all right?"

She lifted a hand to wave him away and winced with the ache in her temples. "I'll be . . ." She froze, staring, and felt the world tilt a little to the left.

The dark eyes gazing at her with keen awareness under slanted black brows melted to blue-silver. A double set of midnight-blue stripes appeared on his cheekbones, disappearing into his hairline. His dark hair lightened from the temples outward to show black streaks threading through a frost-white mane. Delicate points tipped his ears and rose to part his white hair. His jawline and cheekbones refined, lending his face an exotic elegance and almost feline grace.

Whoa . . . Kasi couldn't stop staring at him. The graceful *Kirin* had been utterly breathtaking, but this creature was painfully beautiful, especially with all that snowy hair.

Snow-white hair . . . Her heart slammed in her chest. She knew that white hair, those ears, and those markings on his face. *Oh my god . . .*

His smile melted away. "What is it?"

Kasi couldn't quite find enough air. *It can't be him; that was a dream!* Was she still dreaming? She subtly pinched herself and flinched. The man's new appearance didn't change. He was really there. He was real. She decided to take Grandma's advice. *When in doubt, smile.* She pasted on a smile.

He frowned and turned toward her, leaving one hand on the railing, his body moving in a smooth roll of muscle. "You've gone pale. Are you going to faint?"

Kasi swallowed and eased away from him, her smile widening

to a grimace. *Don't panic, don't panic, don't panic*... She was used to seeing strange things, but from the far end of a telephoto lens, not close enough to touch—and be touched.

His nostrils flared briefly and his frown deepened. "You're afraid?"

Afraid? A nervous chuckle struggled to escape her throat. She was scared shitless. She'd gone on this vacation to avoid therapy, but right at that moment therapy and a bottle of prescription drugs wasn't looking so bad after all.

"Calm down." He lifted a hand tipped in curved, blunt claws rather than fingernails.

Her eyes focused on the long claws and froze. Her heart slammed so hard in her chest she was convinced it was about to break free. *Calm down?* How the hell was she supposed to calm down? He had freaking *claws!*

His gaze followed her gaze to his hand, then back to her face. "Crap . . . You can see me." It wasn't a question.

Kasi's gaze snapped to his sky-blue eyes. *See* him? Was he saying that no one else saw him this way? She released a small breath. Of course they didn't. No one ever saw what she saw.

He turned to face her and straightened, raising both hands, fingers spread, pale claws tipped in black and curved. "Don't scream."

Scream? Annoyance cut through her panic and her brows furrowed. She'd never screamed in her life. Yelled maybe, and cussed definitely, but she did *not* scream. And why the hell was she just standing there? She turned away from the rail, away from her walking, talking dream, away from him.

"Wait." He lunged in front of her, his outstretched arms blocking her flight, his coat flapping open in the sea wind. "There's no need to be frightened."

Kasi jerked back from him, her spine making hard contact with the ferry's railing. She stared up and up. He was a full head and shoulders taller than she was. Her bag slid from her shoulder and thumped onto the deck by her feet.

He moved closer and framed her with his arms, his hands gripping the rail on either side of her. The heat from his body washed over her. "I'm not going to hurt you. Talk to me."

Her eyes widened. Talk to him? And say what? *'Hello, tiger?'* She choked back a completely inappropriate chuckle. The warm aroma of his body, clean, fresh, and masculine, drifted to her, distracting her thoughts. He was so close. He was so beautiful. She'd never seen anyone, or anything, so utterly exquisite and yet so very masculine. The speed of her heart eased, though it continued to pound. Her belly fluttered and moisture pooled in her panties.

He smiled, revealing slightly oversized incisors. "You don't smell scared now."

Smell . . . ? Anger flashed through Kasi, freeing her tongue. Exotic or not, he was still a man, and he was much too close. "Back off."

He grinned, not bothering to hide his long teeth. "Oh, so you *can* talk?"

A small group of passengers wearing hooded parkas and carrying backpacks wandered nearby.

Kasi eyed them. She'd bet her entire bank account they saw nothing more than a man and a woman standing very close together, in fact, standing inappropriately close. Her gaze snapped back to his. "Oh, I can talk." She smiled. "I can yell too. Back off or I'll prove just how loud I can be."

His gaze narrowed but his smile didn't waver. "Are you threatening me?"

She bared her teeth in something that wasn't even close to a smile. "You bet your ass I am."

"Is that so?" His pink tongue flicked across his full bottom lip.

Her gaze followed the trail of his tongue despite her better judgment. He really did have the most kissable mouth, once you overlooked the fangs.

He snorted and his smile broadened. "Do it."

Kasi's gaze shot back up to his heated blue eyes. Do it? Anger surged through her. Did he think she wouldn't? Staring him straight in the eyes, she took a deep breath. What was the Japanese word for 'pervert'? Oh yeah, *'hentai.'* She opened her mouth and shouted. "Hen—!"

He swooped down and covered her open mouth with his, swallowing the other half of the word. His wet, slightly rough velvet tongue swept past her parted lips to brush against hers.

Kasi jolted with the invasion and stared eye to eye, shocked. *He kissed me?*

He stared right back, his eyes just as wide and, apparently, just as shocked. His tongue deliberately swept against hers slowly, more firmly, as though examining her flavor. His gaze narrowed.

She grabbed on to the upper arms of his coat-sleeves to shove him back. It was like shoving against a tree. His arms were as solid as knotted pine under his sleeves and rooted firmly to the rails to either side of her. A small moan of frustration escaped her.

He pressed closer, apparently taking her small sound for encouragement. His head tilted to the side, his lips shifting against hers to fully cover her mouth. His eyes drifted half-closed and his tongue stroked hers as though tasting something utterly delicious.

Kasi pressed her tongue against his, parrying his explorations out of sheer self-defense, and reassessed her predicament. He was kiss*ing* her, and he wasn't showing any signs of stopping. But worst of all, he was good at it. She hadn't been kissed this thoroughly, or enthusiastically, since . . . well, ever.

It didn't help matters that he tasted clean, like fresh water with a slight hint of tea.

His hands lifted to cup her head and hold her in place against his mouth. His claws slid into her hair to lightly score her scalp, leaving delicious tingles in their wake. Abruptly, he sucked, drawing her tongue into his mouth.

Shivers washed down Kasi's spine and her knees weakened. She stopped trying to shove at his arms and clutched at his coat-sleeves to keep from falling at his feet. Her tongue came in contact with one of his blunt upper fangs. Curious, she probed it with the tip of her tongue.

A rumble vibrated in his chest. It sounded like a purr.

Someone giggled.

Kasi's eyes snapped open. She didn't even remember closing them. Her gaze slid to the side.

A small, tittering crowd of about eight or so, possibly every passenger on the ferry, stood facing them, all pretending not to watch. Hands covered mouths; whispers and gazes slid between them and each other.

Kasi's cheeks heated. *Crap!* The island's town was really small. Not a whole lot of people even knew the island existed, which meant all of these people probably lived on the island or knew someone that did. It was only a matter of time before someone told Grandma she'd been kissing someone in public. *Crap! Crap! Crap!*

Kasi focused on the man kissing her and fury filled her veins. Public displays of affection were no big deal back home in America, but in Japan, it just wasn't done—especially not with men one didn't know. The bastard had just publicly labeled her as a slut. She slowly raised her fist and punched him against the side of his head, hard.

He flinched and broke the kiss. "Ow!" He grabbed her upper arms and his gaze narrowed. "What the hell did you do that for?"

Kasi narrowed her eyes at him and her voice rasped out in a low, angry whisper. "Who the hell do you think you are, grabbing and kissing people you don't know? Do you have any idea what you just did to my reputation?"

He smiled but his gaze remained narrowed. "But I do know you." He licked his reddened lips. "I'd know your taste anywhere."

The blood fled from her cheeks. "What?"

His smile returned and it was a touch smug. "Welcome back, Kasi-chan."

Kasi-chan? Kasi froze. *It's him . . .*

He winked and his gaze shifted to the people gathered behind them. His palms slid down her arms to clasp both her ice-cold hands, engulfing them in his warm palms. He turned to speak in semi-formal Japanese. "Please accept my most sincere apologies. It has been a small eternity since I have seen my betrothed." He turned to face Kasi and his smile broadened. "I was overcome . . . with joy."

"Your betrothed?" A young woman in a bright pink parka clasped her hands together and squealed. "Oh! Shiratora-*sama*, how romantic!"

Shiratora-*sama*? Kasi felt ice wash through her veins. This exotic man was a Shiratora, a member of the family that owned the whole island of Shido? *Oh my God . . .* She had to work to hide her wince. He was a Shiratora and she'd punched him in the head! Grandma was going to skin her alive for such disrespect to his family!

The entire small group approached and started bobbing and offering their congratulations.

Shiratora nodded and smiled at the small group, accepting their congratulations with casual ease.

Kasi blinked. Wait a minute, never mind that he was a Shiratora, he'd just told everyone that she was *marrying* him. Japan was one of the few countries where such announcements were practically legally binding. She pasted on a huge, fake smile, leaned close, and spoke in careful, but soft, English. "Your betrothed? Are you out of your mind?" She wriggled her fingers, attempting to slide her hands from his grasp.

"Hmm?" He turned to her, his fingers tightening around her hands, and his brows lifted. "But you *are* my betrothed."

The ferry's steam whistle blew twice, announcing that the ferry was about to dock. Their small audience wandered off, waving and smiling.

Kasi glared up at him and tugged at her captured hands. "I can't be your betrothed. I don't even know your name!"

"Ah . . ." He delivered a devastatingly warm smile. "I'm Shiratora. You may call me Yuki."

Kasi felt that smile all the way down to her toes. *Jeez, that smile is lethal, and not because of the fangs.* She swallowed hard. "Nice to meet you, Mister Shiratora." She kept her voice mild to hide the tremor that was trying to sneak in. "May I have my hands back, please?"

His smile thinned and hardened. "Call me Yuki."

Oh, you sneaky shit! Calling him by his first name gave him permission to use hers. Forget respect; she should have hit the pushy bastard harder. She ground her teeth. Why the hell was she even bothering to argue? He was already using her first name; hell, he was using her childhood name without her permission.

The ship's bell clanged, then a voice crackled over the loudspeaker in Japanese. "All passengers for Shido Island, please come to the forward deck to depart."

Kasi took a deep, calming breath. "Fine, Yuki. Now may I have my hands back?"

"It took you ten years to come back to me, Kasi-chan." He snorted. "Give me one good reason why I should release you?"

Kasi lifted her brows and smiled with all the sweetness she

could summon, which admittedly wasn't much. "I need to collect my camera bag." She rolled her eyes downward, leading his gaze to the large, battered bag at her feet.

Shiratora frowned down at her bag, then turned to his other side and frowned at his brown leather backpack just two steps away. "Shit."

Kasi smiled up at him and waited, breathing calmly and evenly, forcing her body to relax.

Shiratora scowled down at her. "You realize there's nowhere on that island I can't find you."

Kasi broadened her smile. "Then you have nothing to worry about." She tilted her head to the side. "Right?"

Shiratora snorted. His gaze narrowed and a predatory smile lifted the corners of his mouth. "You're a little troublemaker, I can tell."

Kasi lifted one brow. "Oh? Look who's talking?" Her voice was very dry.

Shiratora chuckled and released Kasi's hands.

Her smile firmly in place, Kasi took a deep breath and rubbed her wrists.

Shiratora turned and took a step to the side, toward his bag.

Watching him carefully, Kasi reached down to snag the shoulder strap to her bag.

He took a second step and reached down for his battered backpack.

Kasi bolted for the forward deck, running low and fast, her ponytail flying behind her, thoroughly grateful that she'd thought to wear her sneakers.

"Kasi!" The shout was loud and annoyed.

She practically flew past the man posted at the exit. Her heels thundered down the broad gangplank and she pounded across the gravel toward the small parking lot where Grandma had told her she'd be waiting. Screw her luggage; she'd come back for it later.

She spotted the small silver Subaru parked by the trees at curb and smiled grimly as she ran. Her heart pounded with excitement. He'd said he could find her, could he? Well, she was a trained professional when it came to hiding from predators. *Let's see him try.*

2

Naked and wet, Kasi stepped out of the surprisingly modern glassed-in shower stall as clean as soap and water could get her. Wafting steam hazed the air, softening the light gleaming on polished cedar walls. The shower stall was a new addition to her grandmother's old-fashioned bathing room, but the in-ground green and yellow tiled circular bath in the very back was exactly as she'd remembered from when she was little.

Grandmother was notoriously adamant about keeping her traditional Japanese farmhouse as traditional as she could.

She padded along the raised cedar walkway and eyed the knotted white plastic garbage bag sitting just off the walkway on the pebble floor. It contained the clothes she'd worn, including her coat. Those needed to go to the cleaners immediately.

She knelt on the tiles lining the bath's edge and shoved the huge, round cedar cover aside, revealing the sunken tub's steaming spring-fed water. The heavy scent of volcanic mineral water filled the room. She smiled. This was one treat she simply could not get in America. She snorted. *Not without paying a lot of money.*

She stepped down, sinking neck-deep into the damned-near-boiling vat of water, and groaned in sheer animal bliss. *Nirvana at last*... She leaned her head back against the tub's rim and stared up at the pearls of water dripping down on the frosted glass window overlooking the tub. A smile curved her lips. The shower had been refreshing, but there was absolutely nothing to compare to the muscle-relaxing properties of a proper Japanese bath.

Kasi resisted the urge to pick up the nearby neatly folded white towel to wipe off the sweat rolling down her face. A good soak and a hard sweat was precisely what she was after.

It was a trick she'd learned from one of her Native American guides while tracking wild horses. Sitting in a steam-filled sweatlodge the night before a hunt was more than just spiritually cleansing. A good long sweat in a steambath flushed out all of the body's natural oils, thoroughly erasing the human scent. A long hot soak did exactly the same thing. Animals tended to identify enemies by scent rather than sight, so the lack of a human scent allowed a crawling hunter to get very close to his intended prey.

However, in her case, she was the prey.

Kasi dunked under the hot water briefly. She rose and rubbed at her cheeks. Once her skin was literally squeaky clean, a generous application of the olive oil she carried in her bag would do to smother the scent her body naturally produced through sweat and from her more...intimate areas. Once she removed her identifying scent, all she had to do was stay out of sight.

She looked over at the knotted plastic garbage bag containing her clothes. The clothes she'd worn were the only things left with her natural scent on them. Once they came back from the cleaners there wouldn't be a trace of her left on the island.

She knew damned well she was being paranoid, but Shiratora's senses were obviously more acute than the average person's. He'd recognized her taste just from that little peck on the lips back when she was a kid. Assuming his sense of smell was pretty sharp too wasn't that far-fetched. However, she doubted he was anywhere as sensitive as the white tiger she'd dreamed about.

Unless he really *was* a tiger.

She ran her fingers through her wet hair and snorted. That part of her dream had to be pure fantasy. Admittedly, there were lots of strange creatures that no one believed in; she had a whole photo album full of them. Japan in particular was known for having *oni* goblins, *tengu* crow-people, *kitsune* foxes that were supposed to turn into people, and even elemental fairies. But a man that became a tiger? That couldn't possibly be real.

But what if she was wrong and Shiratora *could* turn into a tiger?

She shivered slightly and sank deeper into the water. God, she hoped not. Avoiding him would be very, very difficult. Tigers were superb trackers and patient stalkers, always waiting for the perfect moment to strike.

She grabbed one of the facecloths that had been left next to the towels and started scrubbing her skin. It was best not to leave anything to chance.

Kasi pulled on the dark blue winter-weight casual *yukata* robe that had been left for her, then tied the narrow gray *obi* sash snugly around her waist to keep it closed. Leaning back against the door on the left wall, she tugged on the *tabi* socks, fighting to get her big toe into the sleeve for it. She grimaced. The socks were going to get annoying fast. She hated anything sitting between her toes. She refused to wear thong sandals for exactly that reason.

Hopefully Grandma had been able to collect her abandoned

suitcase. She was not in the mood to spend her entire stay in layered *kimono* robes and toed socks. Lovely though they were, *kimonos* were worn far too tight to run in.

Kasi had absolutely no doubt she was going to need to be able to run, probably sometime soon.

Finally dressed, Kasi collected her camera bag and picked up the garbage bag with her clothes. It was time to go deal with Grandma and attempt to explain the 'Shiratora situation,' something she was not looking forward to doing. Gripping the inset door handle, she slid the door open and stepped up onto the waxed hardwood floor of the hallway that encircled Grandma's sprawling traditional house. The right wall was burnished cedar with painted paper sliding doors that led into the house's main rooms. The entire left-hand wall was lined with floor-to-ceiling sliding windows.

Kasi smiled at the magnificent view of the forested mountain and the light snow that was just starting to spiral downward. The hallway was chilly, but it felt refreshing after the thick heat of the bathing room.

The soft, feminine voice of her grandmother came from somewhere beyond the far right turn.

A deep male voice replied.

Kasi stilled and felt the small hairs on the back of her neck rise. It probably wasn't Shiratora, but she really didn't want to take the chance that she might be wrong. She bit down on her lip and slid the door to the bath closed behind her as quietly as possible. She needed to get out of that hallway; she was far too exposed.

She eased as close to the right wall as possible. The center of the antique floor tended to squeak. Stepping cautiously along the wall, she made her way to the closest door. She gripped the sliding *shoji* door's handhold and eased it open enough to peek into the small room. A low black lacquered table surrounded by six thick black floor pillows commanded the center of the room. A huge picture window masked by a reed blind took up the entire far wall. An elegantly painted silk screen blocked off the right corner of the room.

Kasi licked her lips and pushed the door open farther, just far enough to squeeze herself and her camera bag through. She tugged the garbage bag, squeezing it through the narrow opening. The plastic rustled softly.

The male voice stilled.

Kasi froze, her bag still halfway through the door. *He could not have heard that.*

Her grandmother's voice was soft but her words carried. "Is something wrong, Shiratora-sama?"

Panic washed through Kasi. *Crap, it's him!* She jerked hard on her bag, yanking it the rest of the way through the doorway. She shoved the door closed behind her, barely keeping the light door from clacking shut.

Light thumps announced that someone was coming down the hallway at a swift walk.

Crap! Crap! Crap! Kasi looked around. *Got to hide!* She dashed for the lonely wallscreen and looked behind it. A rather large TV occupied the screened corner. It was one of the older style RCAs framed by a wooden cabinet. She blinked. *Grandma has a TV?*

The heavy footsteps approached the door. "Are you quite sure your granddaughter isn't here, Grandmother?"

"Are you quite sure that you wouldn't like to tell me why you're so interested in my granddaughter, Shiratora-sama?"

Oh shit! Kasi's heart leaped in her chest. She shoved her bags in the corner behind the TV and sat down with her back to the side of the wooden cabinet, pulling her knees up tight against her chest. The scent of lemon wood polish drifted to her nose. She rolled her eyes. *I'm hiding behind a folding screen. The only folding screen in the room.* She shook her head. *Could I have found any place more obvious? God, I feel so stupid!*

The door to the room opened, clacking against the door-frame.

Kasi froze. She forced herself to breathe, taking in small, shallow breaths that not even she could hear. She closed her eyes and willed her muscles to relax. *Be calm, be still . . .*

Silence weighed heavily.

Kasi sat perfectly in place, holding still from years of practice tracking animals in the wild. She kept her breathing even and light. *Be calm, be still.*

Someone took a deep breath.

Startled, Kasi opened her eyes.

"Lemon polish and . . . salad oil?" Shiratora sounded slightly confused.

Kasi's heart thumped just a little harder, and her eyes widened. *He smelled the olive oil?* His sense of smell was that sensitive? Her brow furrowed. *He smells the oil, but doesn't smell me.* A slow smile worked its way across her lips. *He doesn't smell me! It worked!*

A low liquid growl rumbled.

A small sweat broke out at the small of Kasi's back. She fought the urge to swallow. If Shiratora's nose was that sensitive, it stood to reason that he might sense movement too.

"Shiratora-sama, are you growling?" Grandma sounded distinctly amused.

The growl cut off. "My apologies, *Obaa-chan.*" He cleared his throat. "I'm trying to find your granddaughter because I'm going to marry her."

Kasi blinked. *He . . . what?* He'd tossed the word 'betrothed' around, but she certainly hadn't thought he was actually serious.

"Oh?" The word came out soft and slightly breathless. Soft footsteps brushed against the tatami mat floor in the room and fabric rustled right in front of the silk screen. "Does *she* know you plan to marry her?"

Shiratora groaned. "Of course she knows."

Kasi scowled, but otherwise held perfectly still. *Don't you lie to my Grandma!*

"Mmm . . ." Grandmother cleared her throat from very close to Kasi. "I take it that she hasn't exactly agreed to marry you?" Humor drifted back into Grandma's voice.

Kasi smiled very slightly. *Sic him, Grandma!*

Shiratora huffed. "She agreed before she ever left Japan."

"Indeed?" Grandma's soft words held just the slightest hint of doubt.

"She agreed to marry me the night I brought her back during that snowstorm." Shiratora spoke firmly.

Kasi frowned slightly. She could feel the floorboards shifting slightly under her knees, as though someone heavy were walking from one side of the room to the other, but she didn't hear any footsteps.

"I see . . ." Grandma sighed. "Shiratora-sama, are you . . . prowling?"

The floor stopped shifting.

Grandma chuckled. "You're more than welcome to sit down and join me."

There was a soft grunt. "I'm . . . Thank you, but no. I'm rather pressed for time."

"Well, then . . ." Fabric whispered, indicating that Grandma had shifted slightly. "Considering your news, I assume that you are here to ask for my blessing to court her favor?"

Kasi blinked. *Court my favor . . . ?* God, how old-fashioned could Grandma get?

"Shiratora-sama, are you . . . sniffing my parlor?" Grandma sounded distinctly amused.

Shiratora coughed softly. "I came here hoping to find your granddaughter."

"Then you don't want my blessing?" Grandma sounded very disappointed.

"What?" Shiratora choked. "I mean, of course I do!"

"Oh? Then when were you planning on asking for it?"

Kasi absolutely positively refused to slap her own forehead. *Grandma, what are you thinking?*

Shiratora took a deep breath. "May I have your blessing to marry your granddaughter, *Obaa-chan*?"

Kasi's mouth almost dropped open. He did *not* just ask her grandmother for her hand in marriage.

"Will you love her?"

Shiratora took a deep breath. "I will provide well for her."

"That wasn't quite the answer I was looking for." Grandma's voice was gentle, yet hinted at amusement.

Kasi clenched her teeth. *I can provide for myself, thank you very much!*

Shiratora released a heavy sigh. "I like her." It was spoken like a question, or rather, an offering. "She's . . . interesting."

Kasi frowned. *Interesting?* She couldn't decide if she should be flattered or insulted.

Grandma released a small chuckle. "I suppose that's a good place to begin."

"I need her." His voice was soft, yet stark.

Huh? Kasi blinked. Why did he sound so serious? She was dying to peek out to see the expression on Shiratora's face, but she was afraid that making even the slightest movement would give her away. She wasn't a hundred percent sure that Grandma would be able to keep him from literally carrying her off.

Shiratora took a soft breath and the floor shifted subtly. He was probably pacing again. "She sees me. She can see the house."

Grandma huffed. "Of course. She *is* my granddaughter."

"Most definitely." Shiratora groaned. "She certainly has your stubborn streak."

Grandma chuckled. "I'll take that as a compliment."

A gruff chuckle whispered through the room. "Good; it was actually meant as one."

Compliment, my ass! Kasi bit down on her tongue to keep from turning her head and sticking it out in his direction.

Grandma took a deep breath. "If you can gain my grand-daughter's agreement to marry you, then I will give my blessing, Shiratora-sama."

Kasi's mouth fell open. *Grandma, are you out of your mind?*

The floor stopped shifting. "She will marry me." Shiratora's deep voice held firm conviction.

"Shiratora-sama, I am not the one you need to convince." There was a lofty and somewhat serious lilt to her words.

"You're not going to tell me where she went." It wasn't a question.

Grandma shifted slightly. "Ah . . ." It sounded suspiciously like a soft flirting coo. "I wouldn't dream of ruining all your fun."

"I will find her." Shiratora's voice deepened to a low, rumbling growl. "There's nowhere on this island that she can hide."

A smug smile lifted the corners of Kasi's mouth. *Oh, really?*

Grandma spoke softly. "I think my granddaughter just might surprise you."

Warmth flooded Kasi's heart and she closed her eyes. *I love you, Grandma.*

Shiratora sighed heavily. "Thank you for seeing me, *Obaa-chan.*"

"Oh, you're leaving, Shiratora-sama?" Grandma rose and stepped away from the silk screen, her retreating footsteps barely whispering on the tatami matting. "Are you sure you wouldn't like to stay for a cup of tea?"

"No, thank you." Shiratora's voice softened, as though he'd turned away. "I still have yet to . . . unpack."

Grandmother's footsteps moved farther away. "You have been away from the island for quite some time."

"I wanted to see a bit of the world." Shiratora's voice retreated.

"And did you?"

"It was . . . interesting."

A soft clack announced that the room's door had closed.

Kasi sat perfectly still behind the silk screen, listening to the retreating footfalls, not quite sure what to think. Deep silence settled around her.

Very quietly, Kasi rose to her feet and collected her bags from behind the TV. Hefting both bags, she crept across the small room to the closed door. Shiratora thought she would marry him because of something she'd said when she was eleven? Seriously? He was insane!

Or desperate.

She slid the door open as silently as she could and peeked up the deserted hallway, frowning. It couldn't be desperation. How could a man that good looking, with enough money to own an entire island, possibly be desperate to find a woman to marry? Women had to be flocking to him.

It just didn't make any sense. Out of all the beautiful women in the world, why would he want to marry her?

And why the hell was Grandma encouraging him?

3

She dreamed of snow. . .

"Where are you?" The voice was deep, feral, and edged with a growl. The tiger sounded annoyed.

As usual, Kasi sat with her knees folded and her back against the trunk of the huge cedar tree, its long sweeping bows heavily laden with snow. She rolled her eyes. "I'm right where I always am; stuck in a dream with you."

"Is that so?" The tiger's deep voice sounded closer.

"Yeah." She thumbed a stray lock of her long black hair behind one ear and looked around. "I haven't dreamed of anything else but you in years." The tiger was nowhere in sight. She frowned slightly. *That's different.*

The tiger's purr rumbled. It sounded like he was very close. "I'm . . . pleased."

She smiled and swept her gloved hands down her silver-gray parka and then her black jeans, brushing off snow. "Why am I not surprised?" She suddenly realized what else was different. She wasn't a child in this dream.

A bell rang. The deep tone was muffled and distant as though it called out from miles away. The singular note faded completely, only to be followed by another deep, sonorous tone, and then another. It was a lonely sound.

It was a persistent sound.

Kasi started awake, staring up at a distant, shadowed ceiling, vaguely wondering why her bed was so hard. She blinked and rubbed at her eyes, shifting restlessly under the heavy comforter. *Oh, yeah . . .* The bed was hard because it was a thick Japanese futon spread out on the floor. Grandma did not believe in Western furniture. Kasi smiled. *Except for her TV.*

The bell rang out in the distance.

Kasi frowned. *What's with the bell?* She turned to her right and looked up at the window. Not a trace of light. It was still fully dark outside. She rolled up onto her side to squint at the glowing hands of her battery-powered travel alarm. It was just after four in morning. She flopped onto her back, her head hitting the tiny pillow, and groaned. What kind of maniac was ringing bells at four in the freaking morning?

A soft knock sounded on the light sliding door to her room. "Kasi-chan?" The voice was soft but perfectly recognizable.

Kasi sighed and sat up, shoving the comforter down to her waist. "Yes, Grandma?" She tugged at the soft blue sleeping robe that was twisted all the way around her, trying to get the thing back where it belonged. Apparently she'd turned in her sleep, a lot.

The door slid open, shedding soft light from the hallway into the room. Grandma peered in, her salt-and-pepper hair pulled up on top of her head in a somewhat disheveled bun. She squinted into the shadows. "Kasi-chan?"

Kasi finally got the robe somewhat straightened. "Sorry, Grandma; I'm not used to sleeping in a *yukata.*" A yawn came out of nowhere. She covered her mouth with one hand while fingering the tangles from her hair with the other. "Whoever is ringing that bell needs to be shot."

Grandma blinked, then smiled. "Well, they don't use the message bell very often."

"God, I hope not." Kasi dropped her hand from her hair and frowned at her grandmother. "Was there something you wanted?"

Grandma tugged at the collar of the heavy amber-and-orange flowered *kimono* she wore over her white sleeping *yukata*. "I was just checking to make sure you were . . ." She cleared her throat softly and her gaze shifted off to the side very briefly. ". . . to see if you were sleeping comfortably." She looked back at Kasi and smiled.

Kasi rolled her eyes. "I was sleeping just fine until that bell woke me up." She'd still dreamt of the tiger, though it had been different. She froze, staring at her grandmother. The tiger dream *had* been different. The dream had changed.

Grandma's brows lifted. "Kasi-chan?"

Kasi blinked. "Hmm?" She shook her head. "It's nothing."

"Well, since we're both up . . ." Grandma slid the door open all the way. "Why don't we have some tea?"

Kasi stared. "Tea?" *At four in the morning?*

Grandma smiled. "Don't you want to have tea with your favorite grandmother?"

Kasi smiled and rolled her eyes. "Let me pull on a warmer kimono."

Walking down the long hall from the kitchen at her grandmother's side, Kasi smiled down at the steaming mug of tea held in her hands. The hallway was chilly. The heavy midnight-blue *kimono* embroidered with pale pink petals kept her nice and warm, but the kneesocks from her suitcase were her true source of happiness. She hadn't been sure how much longer she would have been able to stand wearing those toe socks.

Kasi turned to smile down at her grandmother. She wasn't quite sure how old the petite woman actually was. Other than smile lines framing her eyes, silver threading her upswept blue-black hair, and a softness to her gently rounded face, she appeared quite young. Grandma hadn't changed one bit in ten years. Kasi leaned to the side to nudge her shoulder. "How is it that you stay so young looking?"

Grandma chuckled and tucked her chin, dodging Kasi's gaze. "Old family secret."

Kasi grinned. "You'll tell me, right?"

Grandma waved a small hand. "Eventually."

Kasi sighed in sheer happiness and wrapped an arm around her grandmother in a quick hug. Sharing a cup of tea had been a good idea, even at four in the morning. She had missed her grandma terribly.

Grandma looked up at her with a sly smile and a definite gleam in her eye. "By the way, Kasi-chan, using olive oil to mask your scent from Shiratora-sama was very clever."

Kasi bit down on her bottom lip and felt her cheeks warm. "It was a guess. I wasn't sure if his sense of smell was quite that sensitive."

"Good guess. His senses are very keen." Grandma lifted her chin. "He had no idea that you were even in the room with us."

She turned to her grandmother and lifted a brow. "You knew?"

Grandma shook her head. "Not until dinner when I noticed that you smelled strongly of . . . salad oil." She grinned and winked. "As I said before, that was very clever."

Kasi's cheeks warmed with a touch of pride. "It allows me to get closer to the animals I photograph, especially the predators."

Grandma lifted a hand to cover her laugh. "Especially the predators?"

Kasi rolled her eyes and groaned, then looked down at her tea. "Since we are speaking of predators . . ." She glanced at her grandmother. "When I saw Shiratora on the ferry, he looked completely human, with black hair, but then he . . . changed."

She frowned, remembering long silver hair framing a strangely elegant face wearing a sensual, if fanged, smile. A shiver spilled down her spine. *And claws; let's not forget the claws.*

Grandma stopped in the hallway and eyed Kasi thoughtfully. "Then you can see his true aspect under the illusion?"

Kasi tilted her head and raised her brow. "White hair, pointed ears, fangs?"

Grandma nodded and continued walking. "So, you *can* see him."

Kasi wasn't quite sure what to think. She'd seen lots of strange and unusual creatures, but this was the first time she'd met one that walked and talked like a real person. "Is he . . . human?"

Grandma shrugged. "There's human in him. His people have been intermarrying with humans for quite a while now, but he's not *completely* human, no."

Kasi stared at her grandmother, wide eyed. "Grandma, what exactly *is* he?"

Grandma sighed. "He's from an elder race, a people that were here long before the first humans arrived on the islands."

"Can he really turn into a tiger?" Kasi winced and looked away. *Idiot!* People didn't turn into animals. "Never mind, it was a silly question."

Grandma raised a hand and shook her head. "No, no, it's not a silly question."

Kasi stared down at her. "It's not? Then he can be a tiger, for real?"

Grandma took a deep breath, clearly considering what she was about to say. She sighed and tucked her chin. "It's not so much that he is a man that can become a tiger, more that he is a tiger that can become a man."

Kasi frowned in thought. *A tiger that can become a man?* "You mean the way *Kitsune* foxes put a leaf or a human skull on their heads to look like humans?"

Grandma smiled. "Not quite. *Kitsune* are a lesser power and truly foxes, so they actually have to work at appearing human. Only a truly old *Kitsune* can hold a human form for very long. Shiratora-sama's people move between aspects far more easily, though one form is usually dominant over the other."

Kasi nodded thoughtfully. "So, Shiratora's human aspect is dominant."

Grandma tucked her chin and sighed softly. "I'm afraid not, though clearly he wishes it to be so."

Kasi's brows lifted. "The tiger is his dominant form?"

"Neither, actually. Until he secures a human bride or a tiger mate, he will shift back and forth between them, and the longer he waits, the less . . . control he has over his appearance."

"You mean he could switch without meaning to?"

"I mean he would assume a form that lies between the two, making him far too frightening to gain either a mate or a bride, and he would remain that way."

Kasi's mouth fell open. "Really?" The image of a massive white tiger that stood on two legs like a man filled her imagination. "And then what?"

Grandma sighed. "He would be forced to go into isolation, hiding completely from the world, which would be a great pity." She turned to regard Kasi. "Shiratora-sama has lived among humans for quite some time and has become something of a social creature. I'm afraid that being forced to leave all human contact behind might shatter his spirit."

"Shatter his spirit?" Kasi shivered slightly and clutched at the neck of her *kimono*. "In what way?"

Grandma turned away to grip the inset handle of the sliding door to the main sitting room of the farmhouse. "Kasi-chan, loneliness can make anyone quite bitter, and bitterness can very easily become hate." She turned to look at her granddaughter. "Should Shiratora-sama give in to bitterness and hate, it's quite possible that, being what he is, he could become a danger to us all."

Kasi frowned at her tea, thinking of the tiger that had purred under her fingers in her dreams and the man that had kissed her so gently. "He wouldn't, not him."

Grandma's brows lifted. "No?"

"No." Kasi shook her head firmly. "He's bossy and he can be a pain, but he's not hateful. He would never hurt anybody if he could avoid it."

Grandma smiled. "I'm glad you feel that way." She pushed open the sliding door and froze. "Oh, dear."

"What?" Kasi looked past her into the room.

All of the furniture—the lacquered tables, the heavy sitting cushions, the silk folding screens, even the vases with their flower arrangements—had been shoved up against the walls. Occupying the center of the room were three large black trunks, practically covered in gleaming gold scrollwork, with their lids propped open. Heavy silks in every conceivable color spilled out of each of them. Sitting among the silks, spilling from the center trunk, was a long, unrolled ricepaper scroll decorated in red ribbons and covered in heavy ornate brushwork.

Standing shoulder to shoulder with her petite grandmother, Kasi stared, the mug of tea forgotten in her hands. "Grandma?"

Grandma strode into the room and stepped to the right to set her mug of tea down on a small table. She walked over to the center trunk and picked up the decorated scroll. She examined the writing and tisked. "I see we are going with tradition."

Kasi followed her into the room and set her tea mug down on the long, low table that had been pushed off to the right. "What is all this?"

Grandma nibbled on her bottom lip, then looked up from the scroll to peer at the contents of the trunks. "I would say *kimonos*, bedding, and wall hangings."

Kasi pointed at the scroll her grandmother was reading. "What's that?"

Grandmother frowned at the writing on the scroll. "From the way this is worded, I'd say this is your marriage contract."

Kasi felt the blood leave her cheeks. "My *what?*"

Grandma waved a hand absently toward the three trunks. "And this is your bridal trousseau, courtesy of Shiratora-sama."

Kasi's knees wobbled under her. She decided right then and there that she needed to sit down, so she did, collapsing in an ungraceful sprawl right there on the *tatami* matting. "Holy . . . cow." One did not curse in front of Grandma. "He's this serious? He really wants to marry me?"

Grandma rolled up the scroll in her hands and eyed the three trunks. "I would venture to say that Shiratora-sama is definitely serious in his pursuit of your hand in marriage."

Kasi shook her head. *Unbelievable . . .* "So, when did all this arrive?"

Grandma looked down at the contents of the center trunk. "I suspect that they were delivered about the same time that the message bell began to ring."

Kasi frowned up at her grandmother. "The bell that woke us up?"

Grandma nodded and brushed a finger down a length of scarlet silk spilling from the trunk. "That particular rhythm alerts those that serve the family that a message is about to be delivered."

Kasi waved a hand at the trunks. "Then you didn't know this was here?"

Grandma shook her head briefly. "I'm just as surprised as you."

Kasi stared at the three massive trunks, then turned to look behind her at the small sliding door. "How did all this get in here? I didn't hear a thing."

"*Shikigami* would be my guess." Grandma looked about, clearly searching for something.

"Shiki—what?"

"*Shikigami,* paper servants." Grandma stepped past the trunks and moved toward a small table that had been pushed back into the far right-hand corner of the room against the tall floor-to-ceiling windows of the back wall. Three elaborately folded black paper *origami* birds sat side by side on the small table. "Ah, here they are."

Kasi pushed up onto her feet and walked closer to get a better look at the tiny paper birds. "Here what are?"

"The *shikigami.*" Grandma stepped away from the table and moved to the left, along the back wall. At the far corner, she caught the edge of the long blinds and pushed them back to uncover a siding glass door. "A few of the local *tengu* are quite skilled at making them."

Kasi stared at her grandmother. "We have *tengu,* crow-people, on the island?"

"Of course. A number of them have served the Shiratora family since the beginning." She released the lock on the glass door and pushed, sliding it all the way open. A chilling winter wind swirled into the room. "Stand back, Kasi-chan. Don't get in their way."

The wind brushed the three paper birds, making them tip precariously. Blue light erupted around each one, engulfing the tiny paper forms and expanding. The light winked out and three perfectly normal crows looked up at Kasi, tilting their heads in evident curiosity.

Kasi backed away from the table, bumping into the last trunk. *Oh my God . . .* While she knew that odd creatures walked the world unnoticed, this was something else entirely. "Magic?"

Grandma chuckled from the far side of the open door.

"Well, of course it's magic, dear. Paper doesn't turn into live birds without it."

The three crows turned sharply to look over at Grandma.

Grandma bowed. "Please thank your master for this delivery."

Collectively, the crows bobbed their heads and cawed. With a flutter of black wings and loud caws, the three burst into flight. They circled the whole room, then dove out the open door and into the night.

Grandma shoved the sliding glass door closed, then turned to smile at her granddaughter. "Well, now, that was exciting. Don't you think?"

"I think . . ." Kasi turned and walked back over to her abandoned tea mug and stared down at it. Not one thought was in her head. "I think I need another cup of tea." She lifted the mug and wandered out the open door and into the hallway.

Standing in the small alcove for the kitchen's back door in her freshly cleaned parka over her warmest clothes, Kasi stomped into her hiking boots. "The Jeep has gas?"

"A full tank." Still in her *kimono* and sleeping robes, Grandma held a cardboard box of canned goods, the car keys dangling from her thumb. She bit down on her lower lip, clearly upset. "Kasi-chan? Are you sure you want to leave right now? It's the middle of the night and it's still snowing! The snow will be much deeper on the mountain."

Kasi slung her camera bag over her shoulder and hefted her suitcase. She took a deep breath and faced her grandmother. "I need to think, Grandma. I really, really need to think before I . . ." She stilled. Before she what? Married the most incredible man she'd ever laid eyes on? Before she gave up her whole life and career to someone she barely knew.

Traditional Japanese men rarely allowed their wives to

work. Having a wife that worked implied that the husband could not provide for her. It implied that he was lacking.

Tiger-people or not, Shiratora's family was wealthy, well-connected, and extremely traditional, if that pile of *kimonos* in the living room was anything to go by. There was no way in hell she'd be allowed to continue to work. Her career as a world-traveling professional photographer would be over.

Kasi's jaw tightened. She wasn't about to give up her hard-won career without a fight. "I need to go before the snow gets too deep to drive in." She slid open the back door and faced the snow-covered yard and the shed beyond. She turned back to her grandmother. "The keys to the cabin are in the box?"

Grandma held up the box. "They're on the keychain. You remember how to get to the cabin?"

Kasi took the box with her free hand and nodded. "Take the second left off the main road, keep driving, no turns. The road ends at the cabin."

Grandma clutched at her robes. "Kasi-chan?"

Kasi leaned forward and dropped a kiss on her grandmother's cheek. "I've driven in far worse weather. If I can survive Tibet, I can handle a little snow in Japan." She stepped back through the door and into the snow.

Grandma nodded, but she was quite obviously not happy. "May the mountain spirits protect you."

Kasi smiled sourly. "I was under the impression that it was the mountain spirit I was avoiding."

Grandma tossed her head and waved her hand. "Impudent child!"

Kasi turned and slogged through the ankle-deep snow, heading for the shed Grandma used as a garage.

4

The Jeep crawled slowly but doggedly up the night-shadowed mountain road, accompanied by the rhythmic thumping of the windshield wipers and the jangling of the tire chains. The headlights blazed, white and brilliant, against the heavily falling snow.

Kasi's gloved hands ached from her death grip on the steering wheel. She had been driving for over an hour and still hadn't spotted the cabin, or anything else for that matter. Her entire world consisted of falling snow, the road under her tire chains, and the downward-arching, snow-weighted branches of the surrounding trees. She'd already had to dodge more than one oversized fallen limb. The only signs of the low stone wall that bordered the narrow mountain road were snow-covered humps to either side.

She thumped her palms against the steering wheel in annoyance. "Damn it, I didn't miss the turn! I know I didn't, so why aren't I there yet? Did I pass it?" Looking for any kind of landmark, she squinted, trying to see through the snow-smeared windshield.

Something large and dark appeared on the left side of the road, almost in front of her.

Kasi's heart leaped into her throat. *What the hell is that?* A fallen branch? A deer? A dog? A person? She couldn't tell. She turned the steering wheel to the right to avoid it while pumping the breaks slowly to slow the Jeep down.

The Jeep slowed and began to slide.

The dark obstruction moved farther onto the road, toward the Jeep. Eyes reflected bright red in the headlights.

Kasi gasped in a breath. "Shit!" Whatever it was, it was big and alive, and she was definitely about to plow straight into it. She shouted in sheer frustration. "What the hell are you doing?" She twisted the steering wheel hard while slamming down on the brakes. "Stupid suicidal animal!"

The Jeep went into a slow, almost gentle spin, and didn't stop.

"Shit! Shit! *Shit!*" Kasi turned the steering wheel into the skid in an attempt to straighten the sliding vehicle, but everything outside her windows was a white blur. She couldn't even tell which way she was supposed to be pointing.

The Jeep slammed into something and the front end rose.

Kasi yelped in alarm. Reflexively, she slammed the Jeep in reverse. What the hell had she hit, the animal in the road? *Can't be, this is much too big.*

The Jeep's tires spun, but the vehicle stayed exactly where it was. Slowly, the Jeep tipped forward, and forward, until it pointed nose down. Tree branches pressed against the windshield, but the front tires were clearly hanging in mid-air.

Frozen in absolute terror, Kasi realized what she'd hit: the low wall that acted as the guardrail on the narrow mountain road. With her blood rushing loudly in her ears, she wondered how far away the ground was.

Gently, the Jeep slid forward.

Kasi gripped the steering wheel and felt her stomach lurch. "Please, God, please, please, please don't make this a cliff!"

The front tires made contact with something solid.

Relief and hope washed through Kasi in a numbing rush. Her breath rushed out of her. "It's not a cliff. Thank you, God!"

The Jeep continued its forward slide.

She reassessed her situation. No, it wasn't a cliff, but it was a really steep incline in the middle of a forest of massive cedar trees, all with windshield-height, low-hanging branches. She was dead meat if she stayed in that Jeep. Completely panicked, she grabbed for the door handle and her fastened seatbelt. She needed to get out, now!

The back tires hit hard and the entire back end rocked up. Kasi was tossed upward, her head barely missing the ceiling, and then slammed back down into her seat. The Jeep plunged, rolling downward at breathtaking speed.

Ice-cold fear washed through Kasi's veins. Out of sheer instinct, she threw herself to the side, pressing belly-down against the bench seat, and grabbed on to the other door handle. She did not want to go flying through the windshield when the Jeep finally crashed into a tree.

The Jeep slammed to a crunching, glass-shattering stop, throwing Kasi forward hard, her still-fastened seatbelt bruising her side and her hips. Bits of safety glass sprayed all around her. Silence fell.

Her head buried in her arms, Kasi blinked. *I'm not dead?* She pushed up slowly to get a look at her situation. Trees were jammed tightly on both sides of the Jeep, bowing both front doors inward. The four side windows had all shattered. Oddly, the windshield was completely intact. The Jeep's headlights were a bright haze on the other side of the snow-coated windshield.

It seemed that instead of nose-diving straight into a tree, the Jeep had somehow wedged itself between the trunks of several huge cedars.

Sitting up fully, she stared at the surrounding trees and the serenely falling snow. *Holy shit, I'm alive!* She turned the key. The Jeep's engine started. Her mouth fell open and she sat back in amazement. She eyed the bowed-in doors, courtesy of the trees pressing up against them. The engine might be okay, but the Jeep was jammed in tight. There was no way she'd be able to drive out of this.

She sighed and reached for the cell phone in her pocket. The engine ran but the Jeep was still totaled. Grandma was going to kill her. Flipping the small phone open, she stared at the lit screen.

No signal.

"Crap!" She closed the phone and jammed it back in her pocket. *Now what?* She licked her dry lips. As long as the engine ran, the headlights would stay on. As long as the lights were on. it was possible that someone would find her. She flipped on the flashers. Blinking yellow lights stained the surrounding snow.

Kasi rolled her eyes. "As *if* someone is going to find me in this mess?" She turned and stuck her head out the driver-side window. Broken branches, mangled brush, and dirty snow marked the path the plunging vehicle had taken. She smiled sourly. She wasn't even close to being lost. All she had to do was follow that trail back up to the road and go downhill from there.

She took a deep breath and considered her options. *Stay here and wait, or climb back up to the road and walk back?*

The walk back wouldn't actually be that big a deal. She'd marched through far rougher terrain for days on end. Technically, it would barely be a hike for her.

But it was still fully dark, snowing, and clearly below freezing. If she tried to walk back right then she could very well freeze to death before she got there. With daylight, the temperature wouldn't climb that much higher, but sunlight tended to warm dark clothes and she would also be far easier to spot if someone drove by.

Kasi sighed and unfastened her seatbelt. It would be smarter to just wait until morning to hike back. By staying in the Jeep her odds of surviving the night were much better. The engine was running, so she had some heat, even though the windows were gone. The wind was somewhat blocked by the windshield, and she was under a roof, so the snow wasn't falling directly onto her.

Kasi yawned. *Besides, I could use the sleep.* She turned and tugged the lap blanket off the back of the Jeep's seat and tucked it around her legs. After pulling her parka hood up over her head, she reclined on her side. Tucking her gloved hands into her parka sleeves, she curled up on the Jeep's bench. With the Jeep's heat and the engine purring, it was actually quite comfy.

Kasi shivered hard and awoke suddenly. Something was wrong. She frowned, listening to the wind and the soft whisper of snowfall. She didn't hear any movement near the car. She didn't hear anything at all. The winter silence was unbroken. So what had awakened her? Her eyes widened. *The silence. . .* The Jeep's engine had stopped and the heat with it.

She turned her head and looked out the window. It was still snowing. The sky was a dark, hazy, luminescent gray. She had no idea what time it was. The Jeep was an older model without a dashboard clock, and she hadn't bothered to wear her watch. *Damn it!* She huddled on the seat of the Jeep, trying to decide if she should get out and build a fire.

A small scratching noise came from the door by her feet.

Hmm? Kasi looked back toward her feet.

A crow perched in the open window. It tilted its head to the side and peered at her with one eye.

Kasi smiled in sour humor. "If you happen to be a *shikigami,* or a *tengu,* would you mind letting my grandmother know that her granddaughter has wrecked the Jeep? I could really use a tow truck to get me out of here." She shivered. "Preferably before I freeze to death?"

The crow hunched and mantled its wings, then cawed.

Kasi nodded as gravely as she could while being curled up on the front seat of a Jeep. "Thank you."

The crow launched into the air, cawing into the distance.

Kasi couldn't help but giggle just a tiny bit. *I'm hoping a bird will bring me a tow truck.* She rolled her eyes, and set her head back down on her arm. *Okay, it's official. My mind has gone right off the deep end.*

A yawn stretched her jaw wide. She watched her breath steam past her lips. It was right damned cold. She should probably get out of the Jeep and build a fire to keep warm.

She groaned and curled up tighter on the bench, hoarding what little warmth she had left. She really should build a fire, but she didn't relish the idea of slogging out in the freezing snow and getting her feet all wet scrounging for firewood. With her luck, dawn would arrive just as soon as she got the fire going and she would have to put the fire back out so she could start hiking back to the road. An awful lot of work for such a short period of time.

Maybe it was best if she just waited. Dawn couldn't be that far away.

Somewhere very far away, she could vaguely hear someone snarling out obscenities in a deep, rumbling voice. Apparently, they were seriously pissed off. Not that she cared. She was warm and comfy right where she was and just couldn't see the reason to be bothered about it.

Metal shrieked nastily in the distance, and her soft bed shuddered.

Her brows knit in annoyance. The sound and the shaking were almost enough to rouse her from her comfortable slumber.

Something hot was pressed against her cheek. A familiar voice growled next to her ear. "Practically frozen solid... Damn it, woman! Why is it you always want to sleep in the snow?"

She smiled in her sleep. "Hello, tiger."

Silence fell in a thick blanket. Crows squawked in the background.

"Yes, yes, I got it." Metal screamed. "No, we don't need your big brother. I got it, okay?" There was a wrenching howl and a heavy clunk. Her bed shuddered hard. "No big deal, see?"

She felt something warm and infinitely soft wrap around her. Warmth burned against her skin. She let out a soft moan of protest. "Hot . . ."

The crows cawed louder.

"The house is too far away. We need something a lot closer."

The crows fell silent. One cawed.

"That'll do. We'll go there. Collect her belongings and meet me there."

The crows started up again.

"No. Thank you, but no. I'll handle this myself."

The voices faded into the warmth that was rocking her into a fathomless sleep.

Sprawled out on her belly, she felt a delicious, yet unexplainably heavy warmth pressed against her back and across her thighs. She pushed to roll onto her side, away from the warmth.

A weight, very much like an arm, tightened around her hips.

Confused, she opened her eyes.

From barely a kiss's distance away, sleepy silvery-blue eyes stared back at her from a far-too-familiar masculine face; it was framed by a cascade of silver hair that blended into the white blankets drawn up to the man's shoulders.

Her thoughts stilled and then focused. She was in a bed and

he was right on the other side of her pillow. She was sharing blankets with *Shiratora*.

Her breath stilled utterly and every hair on her body rose. Icy panic washed down her spine. *No way . . . !*

Shiratora's dark brows lowered, his eyes narrowing to the bright blue of a blowtorch. "Don't scream."

Her panic crashed to a halt and hot indignation took its place. She clenched her jaw. "I don't scream."

His lips curved into a relaxed smile and his brows lifted, banking the heat in his flame-blue eyes with cooling silver. "Good."

Liquid heat pooled in her core and her nipples tightened. Alarmed, Kasi shoved away from him, desperate to get out from under his arm and put some distance between them. "Where am I?"

He rolled his eyes and lifted his arm to rake his clawed fingers through his long, snowy hair. "*We* are in a cabin."

She smiled sourly. "Gee, I hadn't noticed."

His smile gleamed with pointed teeth. "Be nice and I'll let you have the rest of your clothes."

My clothes . . . ? Kasi jerked upright and looked down at herself in alarm. She was wearing the black T-shirt she'd worn under her sweater, and an uncomfortable pull around her chest proved that she was still wearing her bra. The sheets caressed the bare skin of her thighs. Apparently, she was not wearing her jeans, but she could feel her knee socks and her panties. She hadn't been stripped to the skin. A strange mixture of relief and regret washed through her.

He chuckled, low and deep. "Disappointed that I didn't ravish you?"

She turned back to him, scowling. "You wish, you . . ." The rest of her words dried in her mouth.

The blankets that had pooled to her waist had slid down to his hips in the process, revealing him to her wide eyes. He was shirtless and his bare, muscular back was etched with jagged blue lines that radiated out from his spine to disappear under the blankets. He rolled over onto his back, revealing a broad chest and strong belly defined by layers of sleek, wiry muscle. Jagged blue lines curved up from his back to arch across his upper pectorals, practically framing his erect nipples.

She swallowed hard. She'd never seen a body with such finely defined musculature. She'd never seen anyone so obviously built like a predator. Her core throbbed and a spat of moisture slicked her thighs.

His eyes closed briefly and his nostrils flared. His gaze focused hotly on her and his smile broadened enough to reveal the curve of a long fang. "Like what you see, do you?"

Anger and alarm in equal parts burned through her. *Damn his nose. Damn her body's reaction to him.* She tore her gaze from his body and dug her fingers through her long hair, flipping it over her shoulder. "So, how did *we* get here?" Her gaze slid back to him.

He lifted his muscular arm to tuck it under his neck and shrugged. "I brought you."

She had to drag her gaze from the stretch and flex of muscles in his torso up to his face. "What?"

A dark brow lifted, and then he snorted in obvious amusement. "I brought you here from your wrecked vehicle. This was the closest cabin."

She frowned. "How did you find me?"

He smiled. "A friend told me."

Her brow lifted. "Unless your friend is a crow . . ."

He tilted his head and shrugged. "Well, it just so happens . . ."

Kasi blinked. "The crow really was a *tengu?*"

He nodded solemnly. "I just happened to be at your grandmother's when he arrived to deliver his news of your . . . accident." His eyes narrowed. "Care to tell me why you've been running away from me?"

Kasi scowled and crossed her arms under her breasts. "I wasn't running away!"

"Oh no? What else would you call taking off in the middle of the night during a snowstorm?" He leaned up on his side, the blanket sliding downward to expose his navel and a stripe curving over the muscles defining his hip. "For the second time, I might add." He set his chin on his upraised palm.

Kasi's eyes widened and a shiver spilled through her body. She might be somewhat clothed, but it was entirely possible that Shiratora wasn't. She twisted all the way around, presenting her back to him.

Where the hell were the rest of her clothes? She eased her legs over the side of the bed, setting her stockingfeet on the braided rag rug on the floor. She looked about the small room, noting a small dresser against the wall facing the foot of the bed and the staircase before her. There was no sign of clothing anywhere.

A soft but deep growl vibrated the bed. "I'm waiting for an answer."

Kasi started and suddenly felt the urge to growl herself. "I wasn't running away. I just wanted to think."

"You wanted to think." His tone was very dry. "Gee, where have I heard that one before?"

Her hands fisted in the sheets at her sides. "Why do you want to marry me so badly?"

Warm fingers closed around her wrist and tugged.

Kasi tipped back and sprawled across the blankets, her free palm landing on Shiratora's bared hip. His skin was hot under her palm.

His gaze locked on hers. "Because I do." He lifted her captive hand to his lips and his tongue snaked out. Hot, wet velvet stroked across her knuckles. "Olive oil." He smiled. "Extra virgin." He licked his lips and nodded. "Very, very clever."

Her captive hand trembled in his grasp. He knew. Desperate

to drag his attention away from the fact that she'd been in the same room with him when he'd spoken to her grandmother, she grabbed on to his other implication. "I am not a virgin." She wasn't exactly widely experienced either, but he didn't need to know that.

His smile broadened. "Neither am I." He released her wrist. "There's a shower room at the bottom of the stairs." He flopped back onto the bed and sighed, his eyes closing.

She pulled away and sat up on the edge of the bed, frowning while wiping at the dampness on her knuckles. "You want me to take a shower?"

He turned his head to look at her. "Let's just say I prefer your natural scent."

Kasi lifted her brow. "Are you ordering me to bathe?"

He chuckled, low and deep, but his gaze was hard and narrow. "Consider it a strong suggestion." He lifted a brow. "Unless you'd prefer me to bathe you?" He licked his lips.

Kasi scowled. "No, thank you." She rose and sedately walked across the room to the small wooden staircase that led downward. *Pushy bastard!*

5

At the bottom of the narrow staircase that led from the loft, Kasi brushed her palm along the left wall of the staircase and found the light switch. She was determined to find her clothes and leave that bossy, arrogant prick behind, even if she had to walk all the way down the damned mountain to do it.

Light bloomed from the standing lamp in the far right corner. Just two steps away on the left wall was a closed door. The entire back wall was heavily curtained. On the far right was a plush gray loveseat, draped with a huge black wool throw, set before a river stone fireplace that took up the bulk of the wall. The cedar planks of the floor were spread with thick rag rugs.

She stepped farther into the main room and stopped at a heavy cedar table with four sturdy chairs that sat just behind the couch. Behind the staircase was a tiny corner kitchenette. The counter held a coffeemaker by the small sink, and next to it was a mini-stove. The small refrigerator was set under the narrow stairs to the bedroom loft above. Two windows framed the front door set in a small alcove.

It was all very nice, and quite cozy by Western standards, but she was not in the mood to admire it.

Kasi's gaze narrowed. Her suitcase and camera bag were nowhere in sight. Maybe he'd left them in his vehicle?

She strode toward the front door and looked out the window on the right. Thick snow fell beyond the glass. The blizzard was still going in full force. The snow directly outside was unmarred even by fading footprints. She frowned. There was no sign of a vehicle; not even tire tracks.

How the hell had she gotten here?

She turned around and eyed the curtains along the back wall. Maybe he'd parked his car out back? She strode across the length of the cabin and grabbed the edge of the gray wool curtains covering the sliding glass doors. With a quick tug, she shoved them to one side. The sliding rings jingled on the curtain rod.

A small roofed porch ended in canopied stairs and a walkway that descended to a slate-flagged patio with a tiny, steaming pool framed by natural boulders. The pool and patio were partially shielded from the falling snow by a slanted, shingled roof.

Kasi's mouth fell open. *A natural hot spring?* She opened the curtains all the way. Beyond the patio and its steaming pool was a rising forest of cedar and beyond that, the peaks of the mountain in all its snow-covered majesty. The snow was clean and untouched as far as the eye could see, completely devoid of any sign of a car, a truck, an SUV, or even a snowmobile.

Kasi turned and eyed the narrow staircase to the loft. Shiratora had hidden his transportation and her clothes. He was one sharp bastard.

And he'd ordered her to bathe.

She sighed heavily and stepped into the small bathroom by the staircase.

* * *

Damp from her shower, Kasi stood at the edge of the outdoor hot spring, staring down at the steaming pool of pale effervescent water. The flag stones at the edge of the pool were smooth and surprisingly warm under her bare feet. That water had to be really hot to keep the stones that warm. It also looked pretty deep.

She set a thick white towel down on a jutting stone and freed the tie to the thick white bathrobe she'd found on the back of the bathroom door.

Shiratora had wanted her to bathe, so she was damned well going to.

She let the terrycloth slide from her bare shoulders. Completely nude, she folded the robe casually and dropped it by the towel. Warm steam washed across her skin, quickly followed by an icy breeze. Chills raced across her skin and her nipples tightened. She closed her arms across her breasts. The pool's water might be hot, but the air was seriously cold.

She double-checked the chopstick holding her long black hair in a loose knot on top of her head, then stepped down the smooth stone steps and waded into the pool. Hot, silky water closed around her legs with just enough bite to encourage tingling shivers. "Oh, damn . . ." She stepped all the way down to the soft, sandy bottom, submerging herself to the tops of her breasts. Heat closed around her and dug warm fingers into her aching muscles. She moaned in sheer animal response. Grandma's bath was wonderful, but this was a gift from the gods.

She moved to the very edge of the pool's shielding roof and found a submerged stone to sit on, then leaned back against the wall of the pool. Soaking in volcanically heated water with her back to the cottage, she sighed and watched the snow fall among the cedars only a few steps away.

"Enjoying yourself?" The masculine voice was a deep, rumbling purr, and it was right next to Kasi's ear.

A cold, hard wave of shock spilled through her, quickly followed by a warm, delicious coil of heat. *Shiratora...* She stilled. "I was." Her voice was calm and even, in total contrast with her heart, which was trying to beat its way out of her chest. Panicking was always a bad idea, especially around predators. Very slowly, she moved away from the edge of the pool and turned around.

Shiratora crouched on the edge of the pool with one clawed hand gripping the edge, the other resting on his upraised knee. A generous amount of pale, muscular thigh peeked out from the part in his shimmering white *yukata*. His long silver hair spilled down around his shoulders, brushing the stones at his feet. His bare toes ended in neatly filed claws like those on the tips of his fingers.

Kasi swallowed. It was painfully obvious that he wasn't wearing anything at all under that robe. She forced her gaze up from the display of his muscular thighs to meet the amusement dancing in his blue eyes. "When do I get my clothes back?"

A small smile playing on his lips, he eased down to sit on the pool's edge. He dunked his feet in the water and folded his hands in his lap. His brows lifted. "When will you fulfill your promise to be my bride?"

Kasi narrowed her eyes at him. "In all these years, you never found a woman to be your bride?"

His brow lifted. "I found you."

She rolled her eyes. "We were kids!" She shook her head, trying to make sense out of his stubbornness. "You never found anyone else?"

Shiratora looked down and stirred the water with his foot. "I don't want anyone else."

She released a growl of frustration. This was getting her absolutely nowhere. He was dead set on marrying her. She took a deep breath. "You won't change your mind?"

"Of course not!" He actually sounded offended.

She shook her head. This wasn't making any kind of sense.

"There is no way I'll believe that you've been in love with me for the past ten years."

Shiratora scowled. "We were separated all that time. I don't know you well enough to love you."

She flinched, but only a tiny bit. *Well, that was certainly truthful.* "Then why do you want to marry me?"

He rolled his eyes and scraped his hand through his hair. "Because I have to! I chose you."

She tilted her head, her brow furrowing. This was getting weirder by the second. "Then you don't want to marry me?"

Shiratora spoke through his clenched teeth. "Damn it, woman, you're missing the point!"

She stared. *She* was missing the point? She lifted her hands in exasperation. "Then what the hell *is* the point? Most people get married for love or money. You don't love me, and you have tons of money, so why me?"

Shiratora took a slow, deep breath, quite clearly grasping for patience. "Did your grandmother tell you anything about what I am?"

"Yes . . . some. She said that you're a tiger that walks as a man. You can move between either forms."

His flame-blue eyes focused on her. "Correct. I may look human, but I am not."

Kasi shrugged. "You look human enough to me."

He blinked, then looked away and smiled. "There are . . . differences."

Kasi cleared her throat and spoke very dryly. "Gee, I hadn't noticed, fang-boy."

He smiled sourly, then shook his head. "There are differences beyond appearance." He lifted a finger. "The main difference being that humans are ruled by their emotions. They do things because they're driven by love, hate, anger, fear, and so on." He set his palm over his heart. "My people are ruled by their instincts, their drive to survive."

Kasi nodded thoughtfully. Grandma had said that he was more tiger than man, so that actually made sense.

He took a deep breath and focused on her. "My instincts chose you."

Her brow lifted. "When I was eleven?"

He sighed heavily. "Yes."

Kasi raked her fingers through her hair. That was the part that didn't make sense. "How can someone decide on their marriage partner before either one is old enough to actually . . . marry?"

His shoulders slumped and he chuckled. "Honestly, I don't know." He shrugged. "But that's what happened." He sighed and his smile faded. "If we hadn't been separated, we would have had the time to get to know each other."

She blinked, wondering what it might have been like to grow up alongside him. High school certainly would have been far more interesting. She shook her head and sighed. "So now what do we do?"

Shiratora shrugged. "We marry." His gaze heated and his smile turned positively predatory. "And we make up for lost time."

Kasi lifted her chin. She'd been wondering when his arrogance would reappear. "So, your instincts picked me and that's it? No one else will do? No ifs, ands, or buts, just—game over?"

His gaze narrowed to slits and he spoke through his clenched teeth. "Correct."

She lifted one brow. "And it doesn't bother you that you didn't have a choice?"

Shiratora snorted and leaned back to fold his arms across his chest. "I'm perfectly happy with my choice, thank you very much."

She leveled a glare at him. "What about my choice?"

He leaned toward her, returning her glare with one hand

gripping the rim of the pool and the other fisted on his hip. "You made your choice. You agreed to be my bride."

She held his gaze. "I can't talk you out of it?"

His predatory smile returned with fangs. "No."

She turned her back on him and clenched her teeth. *Stubborn, pushy, obnoxious, jerk!* "Arguing with you is like arguing with a wall!"

"Then stop arguing." Fabric rustled suspiciously. There was a soft splash.

Kasi closed her eyes. *Dear God, please tell me he's not in the water with me.* A small wave pushed against her back. She stilled. A coil of heat formed deep in her belly. He was right behind her, and she knew he was naked, just as she was naked. The hairs on the back of her neck rose and her heart thumped hard.

His low whisper caressed her ear. "Is there a reason you don't want to be my bride?"

Her belly clenched with hunger and in spite of the water's relaxing heat, her nipples tightened. She had to suck in a breath. *Damn his sexy voice!* She grabbed for her scattering thoughts. "I won't give up my career as a photographer to be a wife."

"I never said you had to." He sounded a little confused.

She stilled. He was willing to flout tradition? "What will your family say about your wife having a job?" She turned around to see his reaction.

Shiratora smiled from less than a handspan away. The water barely reached his nipples. "That's not even a concern."

Kasi sucked in a sharp breath. He was so tall, and so close she could actually smell his masculine aroma. Too close, and too gorgeous . . . She backed away and it wasn't easy. Her knees felt like rubber. The pool's rim pressing against her neck forced her to stop. *What was I saying? Oh, yeah . . .* "Your family doesn't care what society will think?"

All expression evaporated from his face, leaving it stark and painfully blank. "Believe me, they are far from caring about what human society thinks."

Her throat tightened. Were they dead? "You're not the only one left of your family?"

Shiratora looked away. "I have . . . family in Siberia and Tibet, but I am the only one left in Japan."

She frowned. "Why didn't your family stay in Japan?"

He sighed and scraped a hand through his long hair. "As you know, when we reach a . . . certain maturity we seek a bride, a mate."

Kasi rolled her eyes. "Yeah, I gathered that."

He eased closer, the water barely rippling around him, his silver hair fanning out in the water around him. "Are you aware that it is our mates that govern whether the tiger or this more civilized form is in dominance?"

She bit down on her bottom lip. Her heart thundered in her chest, but she couldn't quite make herself move away. "Grandma mentioned something like that, yeah."

He stopped less than a handspan away and looked down at her. "I am the only one that has found a human bride."

Kasi stared up at him, a little confused. "The only one?" That couldn't be right.

Shiratora smiled sadly. "Humans have always had difficulty accepting something or someone different from them. Tigers are more . . . forgiving of the unusual. However, Japan does not welcome tigers."

Anger sparked, and she scowled. "You're not *that* strange or unusual. So you lead with your nose and can go furry. Big deal!" She rolled her eyes. "It's not like you eat people or anything." She had her reasons for thinking twice about marrying him, but . . .

Wait a minute, hadn't he just said that he wouldn't make her quit her job? She looked up at him. Maybe she was being a little too hasty about refusing him. Would it hurt to actually consider his offer seriously?

He chuckled, deep and low. "You really are perfect for me." His warm, damp palms closed on her shoulders.

Kasi jumped just a little but didn't move away. She didn't want to move away. Something was humming in the region of her belly and throbbing way down low. She knew arousal when she felt it, but something else was sparking in her, too, something that felt like . . . connection. "Who, me?"

"Yes, you." Shiratora leaned closer, his cheek brushing against hers, his voice whispering directly into her ear. "I don't need to hide my nature from you. You accept it. You're shy, but not afraid. You don't scream." He chuckled. "And I like you."

Kasi blinked. *And* he liked her, as though it was an afterthought, as though it didn't actually matter. She turned to ask him more about that, and instead her parted lips met his.

6

Lip to lip in the steaming backyard hot spring, Shiratora's blue eyes widened, then his tongue flicked out, brushing against Kasi's bottom lip in a quick caress.

Out of sheer reflex, Kasi chased after that fleeting touch, her tongue meeting his. The hairs rose on her body and she flushed with heat and expectancy.

His body went rigid, his fingers tightening on her shoulders, his blunt claws digging in just a little. His tongue swept boldly across her upper lip, then his front teeth closed on her bottom lip in a tender bite. A low rumble vibrated low in his chest, making the water ripple slightly around them.

She felt dizzy and her thoughts disintegrated. She couldn't quite hear the sound he was making, but she could feel it traveling all the way down to settle deep in her belly. A soft sigh that was almost a whimper escaped her.

He groaned, his eyes closing. He turned his head and sealed their mouths together, his tongue sweeping in to pursue hers. Hot, moist, slightly rough velvet stroked her tongue, encouraging her to stroke, to taste, to explore.

She shivered. He tasted of fresh, clean water and lightning. Her tongue encountered a fang. She explored the curved length.

The rumble increased in volume to very nearly a purr. It sounded like approval. It sounded like hunger.

Her knees buckled, simply refusing to work. She grabbed onto his arms to keep from going underwater while desperately trying to keep her lips and tongue in contact with his.

His palm slid down her arm, his claws leaving delicious shivers in their wake. He closed his arm around her waist, supporting her, pulling her against his hard, muscular body. The heat of his erection pressed against her belly. His other hand rose, delving into her hair to capture the back of her neck. He cupped the back of her head. His thumb claw brushed the back of one ear.

She moaned into his mouth and arched against him, restless. He was so warm against her belly, against her breasts. Her hands slid up his arms and encountered the hard muscles of his broad shoulders. The fine silk of his damp hair slid over her hands, thick strands sliding through her fingers. The desire to feel it against her skin was overwhelming.

He pulled back just a little, his mouth leaving hers. His lips brushed against her cheek, then drifted lower to explore the line of her jaw. His long teeth nipped lightly, delicately, swiftly followed by the brush of his tongue. He tilted his head and opened his mouth against the left side of her throat to stroke it with a wet tongue, exploring her, tasting her.

She sighed and lifted her chin to encourage him. She was rewarded with the graze of teeth along the long tendon, followed by the wet swirls of his tongue. She groaned deep in her throat. She'd never felt anything like this. *Shiratora might be an arrogant jerk, but, God, he sure knows what to do with his mouth!*

Against the small of her back, his clawed fingers spread open, the pads exploring the curve of her spine in a slow, languorous caress.

She slid her hands from his shoulders downward, pressing against his chest. Her fingers lightly explored the shapes and hollows of all those fascinating muscles. Her thumb encountered the small hard nub of his nipple and stilled, feeling his heart thumping steadily under her palm.

He groaned against the side of her throat and gave her a tender bite, massaging the tendon captured in his teeth.

She gasped and shivered under the points of his fangs, the soft caress of his lips, and the swirl of his wicked tongue. Her thumb brushed across his nipple in a delicate pluck.

He shuddered and sucked in a breath.

She smiled. *Oh, liked that, did you?* She thumbed his nipple again.

He exhaled sharply and pulled back. He looked down at her. With his lips slightly parted, he took small, quick breaths, almost panting. His flame-blue eyes focused on hers, hungry. His hand slid from her hair to rest on her shoulder, his thumb claw sliding back and forth over her collarbone.

She swallowed but did not remove her hand.

He closed his eyes. "Please, Kasi-chan, let me have you. Be my bride." His voice was hoarse and a little breathless. He opened his eyes. "I swear I will do everything in my power to make you happy."

Kasi licked her lips. "Will you love me?" As soon as the words were out of her mouth she wanted to call them back. Her cheeks heated.

He smiled just a little. "I'd like to. Will you let me try?"

Somehow his words hurt. Tears pricked at her eyes. She blinked to hold them at bay. Did she really want to spend her life with a storybook fantasy come to life? She smiled. "Will you turn into a tiger every now and again for me?"

He bowed his head and pressed his brow to hers, releasing a rough chuckle. "I do remember you saying something about liking me better that way."

She lifted her palm and pressed it to the stripes on his cheek. "Actually this way isn't too bad."

He trembled under her fingers. "Kasi-chan?"

Kasi took a deep breath. "I will be your bride, Shiratora."

His breath stilled. He stared into her eyes, a trace of shock and hope flaring in the depths of his blue gaze. He lunged, enclosing her in a tight embrace, and lifted her up against him, belly to belly, chest to breast. His mouth swooped in and devoured hers in a kiss that bruised her lips and sucked the breath from her lungs. His tongue swept across hers as though he'd never tasted anything finer in his life. A moan escaped his throat.

Kasi closed her arms about his neck, her fingers burrowing into all that soft silver hair, and kissed him back. He might not love her yet, but she strongly suspected that she'd fallen in love with him when he'd kissed her on the ferry. She smiled against his lips. However, he didn't need to know that.

His hand slid downward to grasp the backs of her thighs. He tugged, encouraging her to wrap her legs around his hips. Supporting her, he turned with her held snugly against him and started walking, the hot water swirling around them.

Kasi had no idea where he was going with her, and, frankly, she didn't give a damn. She was more interested in the fact that something long and firm was pressing against her belly, shifting against her with every step. A soft moan escaped her.

The erotic pressure was so distracting she barely noticed when Shiratora released her legs and set her down on the stone steps that led from the pool. He pulled away, finally releasing her from his kiss.

Her knees wobbled under her, refusing to hold her up. "Whoa!" She grabbed on to his shoulders to keep from falling.

Shiratora chuckled and caught her around the waist. "I have you." He ducked low to press his shoulder into her belly, then stood, tipping her over his shoulder.

Kasi yelped in surprise and yanked up her head. Her chopstick slid from her coiled hair, unfurling the dark, damp mass. "Hey!" She shoved her hair out of her face. "What are you doing?"

Shiratora continued up the steps and headed for the house, both of them dripping wet and stark naked. "What does it look like? I'm carrying my bride to bed!"

Kasi kicked out. "I can walk, you barbarian!"

"Oh, really?" He chuckled and strode onto the covered porch to open the sliding glass door. "Didn't look that way to me."

Kasi groaned, then her gaze focused on Shiratora's truly fine butt. *Like marble . . .* Only it moved, the muscles flexing in a truly fascinating display. She simply could not resist reaching down and touching it. The skin was smooth under her palm. She squeezed. It was firm too. *Wow . . .*

Shiratora grunted and stopped. "Woman, did you just grope my ass?"

Kasi felt her cheek fill with volcanic heat. "Um, yes?" She lifted her head and discovered that in her contemplation of Shiratora's butt, she'd completely missed that they not only had entered the cabin, but also were about halfway up the stairs to the bedroom.

Shiratora snorted and continued up the stairs. "And you called *me* a pervert?"

Kasi's mouth fell open. "Hey!" She shook her head. "Are you saying that your bride shouldn't admire your ass?"

Shiratora chuckled. "I wouldn't dream of telling my bride that she shouldn't admire any part of me." He turned, stepping into the bedroom. "But I'd rather have more than just one part admired."

Kasi grinned. "Well, you do have pretty hair, too."

He stopped cold and choked. "*Pretty* hair?"

Kasi ran her fingers through his silver mane. "Oh, yes, silky and smooth. Tell me, what salon products do you use to keep it so shiny and tangle free?"

A growl rolled from Shiratora, vibrating all the way through her belly. "Revenge shall be mine."

Kasi dissolved into giggles.

Shiratora tugged hard on her legs and bucked, flinging Kasi over his shoulder.

Kasi shrieked in surprise. She landed in a sprawl among the pillows and mussed blankets of the bed with a soft thump. She pushed up onto her elbows, her knees spread wide. "Oh, you . . . !" She suddenly found herself face to face with her first full-frontal view of the man she'd just agreed to marry. The words dried in her mouth.

Three steps away, Shiratora stood with his feet apart and his hands on his hips. Water droplets gleamed on his muscular form and on the deeply blushing head of his fully erect shaft that very nearly touched his navel. It rose from a nest of silky white curls that guarded the soft roundness of his scrotum. He smirked. "See something you like?"

Kasi blinked and focused on Shiratora's smug expression. Her cheeks burned. "Well, it's nice to know that the carpet matches the drapes." She smiled as wide as she could.

Shiratora blinked, then grinned, showing long teeth. He shook a finger at her. "You are in so much trouble, woman." He lunged toward the bed.

Kasi squealed and tried to get out of the way. "Me? What did I do?"

Kneeling on the bed, Shiratora pounced and grabbed her by both ankles, dragging her across the blankets toward him. "What did you do?" He tugged until her legs were positioned to either side of his knees, then fell over her, framing her shoulders with his hands. His long frost-colored mane draped over his left shoulder and spilled across the blankets. He smiled down at her. "You grew up to become entirely too desirable for your own good."

Kasi stared up at him, her heart pounding in her throat. She licked her lips. "I did?"

His gaze locked on her mouth. "You did." Slowly he descended to rest on one elbow, his chest brushing against her breasts. "And for that . . ." He lifted his other hand and brushed his fingertips against the bow of her upper lip. His voice dropped to a husky whisper. "You shall be thoroughly chastened." He caressed her trembling lower lip, exploring her and leaving tingling warmth behind.

She felt a distinct warm pulse, deep and low in her core, and gasped.

The tips of his claws brushed across her cheekbone and slid down to brush her collarbone, then farther down to her breast. He spread his hand, cupping the soft flesh and then squeezing it gently. Her nipple rose under his palm. His claws plucked at the rosy flesh.

A wave of erotic fire lanced from her nipple downward, triggering a deliciously hard clench in her core. Kasi bit down on her bottom lip to hold back a moan.

Shiratora's head slid to the side and his warm lips closed on her nipple, enclosing it in the scorching heat of his mouth. His tongue flicked and then his teeth closed on her.

A bolt of electric heat stabbed downward and pulsed in her clit, inducing a gush of warm wetness to slick her thighs. She arched up with a gasp and sank her hands into the fine silk of his hair. Her palms slid across his shoulders and down his back, probing the muscles moving under his skin.

He released her nipple, only to turn his head and capture her other nipple. He nipped lightly, delivering sharp, tiny pains that enflamed the ravenous ache within her.

Kasi moaned and dug her fingers into his back, digging her

heels into the mattress below her to press her hips upward and against his rigid flesh.

He groaned and leaned up, pulling his lips from her breast with a wet smack.

She shuddered and groaned at the loss of his mouth, and let him slide from under her hands, his hair gliding between her fingers.

He leaned back, sitting up, and opened his hands, extending his fingers, baring his claws. His gaze was hungry and intent. Gently, he raked his claws down her breasts and across her belly to her hips, leaving pale pink lines of warmth in their wake.

She trembled and grabbed for the blankets to either side of her, her breath escaping in pants from her parted lips.

His claws raked farther downward to lightly mark her inner thighs, encouraging her to spread them wider. He leaned down and pressed his open mouth over her belly. With tongue and teeth he nibbled and sucked the softness of her rounded belly. His fangs grazed over the bone of her hip.

She couldn't stop herself from writhing up against his mouth, against his teeth, any more than she could stop the wet ache that throbbed in her core.

His hands closed on her hips to still her movements and his tongue slid into the crease of her leg. He lapped and nipped the softness of her inner thigh. He drove his tongue into the wet, aching emptiness at her very center.

Kasi choked out a gasping cry, yanking on the blankets she'd fisted, her back arching and her hips shuddering under his palms. She lifted her head.

Shiratora's hot blue gaze caught hers. A slight smirk curled his lips. He extended his tongue and swept it upward in one long, rough, velvet lick, from the very bottom of her pussy all the way up to her burning clit.

The heat of his tongue seared her. Kasi released a cry that was very nearly a shout.

He lapped at the tiny point of her clit with determined ferocity.

Bolts of erotic fire burned with every stroke of his tongue; anticipation coalesced and tightened in her belly. A small cry escaped her throat and her toes curled, hard.

He began to nibble at her with teeth, tongue, and fangs, then slid a long finger carefully within her. He pressed something utterly delicious deep within her, then flicked lightly.

She bucked in automatic response to the light flicks of his fingers and the matching strokes of his tongue.

His chest began to vibrate in the softest of purrs, the sound transferring straight into her most intimate flesh.

The heat of his mouth, the wriggle of his finger, and his deep, low sounds tormenting her flesh compounded into sheer, agonizing pleasure. She bucked harder, twisting, fighting the hands that held her down, fighting the driving insanity caused by his purr and his lapping tongue and nipping teeth.

His cruel lapping and ruthless nibbling did not let up. His merciless tongue pursued her and cornered her. His delicate purr forced her to submit to the fiendish torment of pleasure.

She screamed in anguished delight and tore at the bed sheets, desperate for release, completely unable to form a single word, or even a thought, but she could see him smile.

Despite his working teeth and tongue, Shiratora smiled broadly, clearly reveling in sheer, sadistic glee and earning the title her grandmother had given him: *tai-youkai*, arch-demon.

7

Shiratora lifted his head, releasing her burning flesh from his torturing mouth, and pulled his writhing finger out of her. He swept his long silver hair over his shoulder with his free hand while licking his fingers and palm with obvious relish. "Delicious." His voice came out in a deep bass vibrato that thrummed low in her belly.

Her thoughts scattered and her body trembling from the excruciating pleasure he'd delivered with his sinful mouth, she could do little more than gasp for breath.

Gently he cupped her thigh, lifting her leg and easing her over onto her belly. He rose behind her and over her. His palms sank into the blankets at her sides while his knees spread her thighs wide. He leaned down and his tongue traced across the light sweat that had gathered along her spine. His hands closed around her upper arms and he pulled. "Come."

Kasi was drawn back to sit in Shiratora's lap, her legs straddling his thighs. Her back met with the broad, hot expanse of his chest. The hot, rigid length of his erection pressed against her butt.

She lifted her arms, reaching up to sink her hands into the frosted silk of his mane. Smooth, like water, it spilled down her arms and over her breasts. She turned her head and rubbed her cheek against the long fall of living snow. It smelled of cedar, lightning, and him.

He lowered his head and rubbed his cheek against hers. His hands cupped her breasts, claws pressing into her pale skin. He squeezed, kneading the soft flesh in his hands. His thumb claws plucked at her swollen nipples.

She jolted and a soft whimper escaped her throat. A fresh spat of moisture slicked her over-sensitized flesh. Urgent hunger clenched in her core, pulsing and aching.

His lips pressed against the left side of her throat. The rough velvet of his tongue stroked upward and his long teeth closed on the tendon in a tender bite. A low, purring rumble vibrated from deep in his chest.

The sound resonated all the way through her and straight down to her clit. She writhed on his lap, arching into his working hands, fisting her hands in his hair, and rubbing against the erection nestled in the seam of her butt. Soft moans escaped her lips. She was beyond words, beyond thinking. All she could do was feel, and *burn*.

His breathy chuckle brushed her ear. He set his clawed hand against the back of her neck. "Lean forward." He pushed against the back of her neck, urging her downward onto her hands. His scorching palm pressed against her belly, encouraging her up onto her knees. A hot, hard, intimidating length brushed against the curve of her butt.

She panted, trembling on her hands and knees. The musk of his masculine arousal wrapped her in a thick blanket of lust's perfume. Her heart thundered in her ears and heady, agonizing anticipation rushed through her body to pool deep and low in her belly. Lush urgency coiled tight. She wanted, she hungered, she *needed* . . .

He rose behind her and the mattress shifted under her. His smooth, warm thighs pressed against the inside of hers, spreading her wide. The hot, damp crown of his shaft nudged against her covetous nethermouth, sliding among her wet intimate folds with clear intent. His soft pants scorched across her back. "Take me."

She surged back against him, pressing him into her snug opening. The broad head entered and stretched her flesh with unexpected and enticing delight. Savage, carnal hunger seized her. She needed him; she needed him in her. She moaned and greedily pressed back. His scalding length followed.

He cupped her ass with his hands and squeezed, keeping her from sheathing him all at once. His deeply indrawn breath was released in a hoarse, growling whisper. "Easy, don't rush."

Her body stretched to envelop him in her hungry depths, squeezing him intimately. The pleasurable ache of being filled forced a moan from her throat.

He groaned, low and deep. "You feel like a hot, wet fist around me." He dropped along her back and reached up to catch her nipple in his claws. He tugged gently, then more insistently.

Sharp spikes of exquisite and ruthless pleasure stabbed straight down to her throbbing clit. She ground back against him, her hips moving in a circle, making his shaft move within her, making her body adjust and accommodate, taking him deeper, pressing him against something exquisite in her depths. Her breath left her in a rush of moaning delight.

He growled and rubbed his chest against her spine, his hot damp skin sliding sensuously against hers. His mouth closed on her right shoulder, his fangs scoring her without breaking the skin.

She groaned and writhed, begging him to move, to thrust into her, to fuck her.

He opened his hand against her belly and pressed inward.

He pulled back and surged in hard, obeying her request, striking that exquisite spot deep inside her.

Pleasure seared her. She cried out in utter joy.

He rocked back and surged in, his palm pushing up into the muscles of her abdomen with his thrust.

A luscious wave of intensely carnal heat bloomed in her belly, robbing her of breath. Desperate to feel it again, she rocked forward, sliding his shaft partway from her wet depths. She shoved back, driving him into her.

He groaned and met her with his thrust, pressing his hand into her belly

The pressure of his palm intensified the pleasure that washed through her. A soft cry escaped her lips. *More... I have to have more.* She rocked forward and slammed back.

He groaned and pushed to meet her with a punishing thrust that hammered straight into that delicious spot deep within her.

She gasped out a cry of carnal bliss.

He bit down on her shoulder, his fangs not quite breaking her skin. He squeezed her captured breast, his blunted claws digging into her flesh while pinching her nipple. His other hand cupped her ass, urging her to greater speed.

She rocked forward and hammered back onto him with rapturous and frenzied appetite.

The sounds of damp flesh striking damp flesh and her small gasping cries filled the small room. Her climax rose in a smoldering wave of delirious pleasure that boiled into a froth of tempestuous foment. She moaned in desperate urgency.

The feel of ozone skittered across her skin, accompanied by the scent of frost, snow, and sleeping cedar—the aromas of deep winter—washing across her senses. It gathered around them, pressing inward, enclosing them. Every hair on her body rose. "What ... ?"

Shiratora groaned, released her shoulder from his teeth, and licked his lips. "My *youki*, my soul, my self. All that I am." His fingers, spread on her belly, dug in, his claws scoring her flesh. His breath burned against her cheek. "Let me in. Open and let me in. Let me live in you."

Something bloomed in her belly, a hidden essence she'd never even known was there. It pulsed with the rush of her blood, with the beat of her heart. Kasi gasped in agonized delight. "Is that . . . mine?"

He released a small breathless chuckle. "Yes, that is your *ki,* your human soul."

The wintry essence in the air coalesced tight around her body, burning like frost against her skin. It sank into her, submerging to ignite within her blood, racing straight for her heart. The essence enclosed and sank in, then bloomed outward with drugging euphoria. She gasped and moaned, drowning under a wave of intense pleasure unlike anything she'd felt before.

"Oh, yes . . ." He ground his cock deep into her. "That's what I need." His hand rubbed firmly, possessively, against her belly. His hips pumped his cock in, and in, and in, fucking her with strong and utterly exquisite strokes. "Come to me, and be mine."

His whisper burned across her mind and echoed in her soul.

Release crashed in a ruthless wave of body-shaking ecstasy. The essence coiled within her heart ignited, setting her blood on fire, then exploded in a brutal, white-hot firestorm that was too intense for her skin to hold. Blinded by the ferocious and incandescent wave, she arched up from under him, rising to her knees, and screamed.

He rose with her and held her tight against him with one arm around her chest, her breast clutched tightly in one clawed hand. His other hand splayed open on her belly. His mouth closed on her shoulder and his teeth sank in deep.

The winter fire spilled out of her in a second release of luscious, euphoric delight that eclipsed her original climax in sheer physical gratification. She writhed, impaled in his lap, her hands reaching up to grip his frost-white hair.

Locking her in his upright embrace, he ground his cock up into her and his hand moved on her belly, his claws digging in.

She moaned and arched her head back, writhing in a raw, carnal pleasure unmatched by anything she'd ever felt.

His lifted his head from her shoulder and groaned. Abruptly he pulled his cock free from her body. Gripping her arms, he pressed her down among the blankets and turned her over onto her back. Straddling her on his knees, he grasped his cock with one hand, pumping it hard.

Rolling in the last waves of pleasure, she looked up at him.

He stared down at her with his fangs bared. His eyes were solid blue orbs of fire. The stripes on his face and on his body were the same incandescent blue. He screamed, a sound feral and raw, rattling the windows. "Mine, *mine!* My mate!" Hot streams of cum spilled onto her belly.

He was utterly breathtaking.

Kasi awoke deep in the night, with the hard warmth of Shiratora pressed against her back, spooned into his embrace. *Yuki, his name is Yuki . . .* She stared out the dark window, took a deep breath, and let it out. "So now what do I do?"

A soft kiss was pressed to her brow. "We go back to your grandmother's and get officially, legally married, and then you move in with me."

She frowned. She should be upset about his high-handed assumptions, but she just couldn't work up the ire. She wanted him too much. "What about my job? It's in America."

He shrugged behind her. "This is the Internet age. I'm sure something can be arranged."

"But I'll have to go on photo shoots."

His lips brushed against her ear. "Would you mind if I came with you?"

She stilled, fighting down the sudden excitement that burned in her heart. "Can you? Don't you have legal and financial responsibilities?"

He chuckled. "This is the Internet age. I'm sure something can be arranged."

She turned over to look at him. "You'd have to be assigned as my assistant."

He snorted and smiled sourly. "As long as I get to keep you by my side, you can assign me as your pet, for all I care." He lifted a clawed finger and pushed a lock of her hair behind her ear. "Being an assistant to a wildlife photographer sounds . . . interesting."

"That reminds me." She lifted a brow at him. "What do you do when you're not playing Lord of an island? Grandma said you spent a lot of time overseas."

He looked away and plucked at the blankets. "I climb mountains."

"Really?" She blinked. He was a mountain climber? That was certainly different. "How did you get into that?"

He lifted his hand to splay his fingers, showing his claws. "It's a natural inclination, I suppose."

She smiled. "Sounds interesting."

He grinned, showing his long teeth, and rolled over to lie on top of her. "It is."

She reached up to run her fingers through his frosty silk hair. Her fingertips brushed the stripes marking his cheekbones. "You'll have to tell me all about the mountains you've climbed."

He leaned down and pressed a soft kiss to her lips. "You'll have to tell me all about the places you've visited to photograph wild animals." He pressed another kiss to her lips. His tongue brushed against her bottom lip. "But not now."

She closed her arms around his neck and leaned forward to rub her cheek against his. "Not now?"

A rumbling purr vibrated in his chest. "We have better things to do right now."

She licked her lips and tried to ignore the fluttering deep in her belly. "Like what?"

He leaned back smiled. "Like take a bath. We stink."

She swatted his shoulder lightly. "And whose fault is that?"

He kissed her brow. "Yours."

Her mouth fell open. "Mine!"

He lifted his chin and nodded sternly. "I told you before; you're much too desirable for your own good."

She snorted and rolled her eyes. "Look who's talking!"

He grinned, showing fangs. "Ah, so you find me desirable?"

Kasi leveled a glare at him. "Yeah, when you're not being an arrogant bully."

He frowned at her, his brows lowering over his bright blue gaze, but a smile danced at the corner of his lips. "I'm a lord. I'm supposed to be arrogant!"

Kasi rolled her eyes. "Oh boy, I can just tell how this marriage is going to go."

All trace of a smile left Shiratora's lips. "Oh?" His hands closed tight around her. "How about telling me?"

"Certainly." Kasi smiled up at the tiger who walked as a man. "Our marriage will be very interesting."

Turn the page for a sneak peek at
Dawn Thompson's latest novel
LORD OF THE DEEP!
Available now!

1

Meg saw the seals from her window, their silvery coats rippling as they thrashed out of the sea and collected along the shore. She'd seen them sunning themselves on the rocks by day and had watched them frolic in the dusky darkness from that dingy salt-streaked window in her loft chamber many times since her exile to the island, but not like tonight, with their slick coats gleaming in the moonlight. Full and round, the summer moon left a silvery trail in the dark water that pointed like an arrow toward the creatures frolicking along the strand, lighting them as bright as day. Meg's breath caught in her throat. Behind, the high-curling combers crashing on the shore took on the ghostly shape of prancing white horses, pure illusion that disappeared the instant their churning hooves touched sand. In the foaming surf left behind, the seals began to shed their skins, revealing their perfect male and female nakedness. Meg gasped. It was magical.

Her heartbeat began to quicken. She inched nearer to the window until her hot breath fogged the glass. The nights were still cool beside the sea—too cool for cavorting naked in the moonlight. And where had the seals gone? These were humans, dark-haired, graceful men and women with skin like alabaster, moving with the undulant motion of the sea they'd sprung from in all their unabashed glory. They seemed to be gathering the skins they'd shed, bringing them higher toward the berm and out of the backwash.

Mesmerized, Meg stared as the mating began.

One among the men was clearly their leader. His dark wet hair, crimped like tangled strands of seaweed, waved nearly to his broad shoulders. Meg's eyes followed the moonbeam that illuminated him, followed the shadows that collected along the knife—the straight indentation of his spine defined the dimples above his buttocks and the crease that separated those firm round cheeks. The woman in his arms had twined herself around him like a climbing vine, her head bent back beneath his gaze, her long dark hair spread about her like a living veil.

All around them others had paired off, coupling, engaging in a ritualistic orgy of the senses beneath the rising moon, but Meg's eyes were riveted to their leader. Who could they be? Certainly not locals. No one on the island looked like these, like *him*, much less behaved in such a fashion. She would have noticed.

Meg wiped the condensation away from the windowpane with a trembling hand. What she was seeing sent white-hot fingers of liquid fire racing through her belly and thighs, and riveting chills loose along her spine. It was well past midnight, and the peat fire in the kitchen hearth below had dwindled to embers. Oddly, it wasn't the physical cold that griped her then, hardening her nipples beneath the thin lawn night smock and undermining her balance so severely she gripped the window ledge. Her skin was on fire beneath the gown. It was her finest. She'd worked the delicate blackwork embroidery on it herself.

It would have seen her to the marriage bed if circumstances had been different—if she hadn't been openly accused of being a witch on the mainland and been banished to the Isle of Mists for protection, for honing her inherent skills, and for mentoring by the shamans. But none of that mattered now while the raging heat was building at the epicenter of her sex—calling her hand there to soothe and calm engorged flesh through the butter-soft lawn . . . at least that is how it started.

She inched the gown up along her leg and thigh and walked her fingertips through the silky golden hair curling between them, gliding her fingers along the barrier of her virgin skin, slick and wet with arousal. She glanced below. But for her termagant aunt, who had long since retired, she was alone in the thatched roof cottage. It would be a sennight before her uncle returned from the mainland, where he'd gone to buy new nets and eel pots, and to collect the herbs her aunt needed for her simples and tisanes. Nothing but beach grass grew on the Isle of Mists.

Meg glanced about. Who was there to see? No one, and she loosened the drawstring that closed the smock and freed her aching breasts to the cool dampness that clung stubbornly to the upper regions of the dreary little cottage, foul weather and fair.

Eyes riveted to the strand, Meg watched the leader of the strange congregation roll his woman's nipples between his fingers. They were turned sideways, and she could see his thick, curved sex reaching toward her middle. Still wet from the sea they'd come from, their skin shone in the moonlight, gleaming as the skins they'd shed had gleamed. They were standing ankle deep in the crashing surf that spun yards of gossamer spindrift into the night. Meg stifled a moan as she watched the woman's hand grip the leader's sex, gliding back and forth along the rigid shaft from thick base to hooded tip. Something pinged deep inside her watching him respond . . . something urgent and unstoppable.

Her breath had fogged the pane again, and she wiped it away in a wider swath this time. Her breasts were nearly touching it. Only the narrow windowsill kept them from pressing up against the glass, but who could see her in the darkened loft? No one, and she began rolling one tall hardened nipple between her thumb and forefinger, then sweeping the pebbled areola in slow concentric circles, teasing but not touching the aching bud, just as the creature on the beach had done to the woman in his arms.

Excruciating ecstasy.

While the others were mating fiercely all along the strand, the leader had driven his woman to her knees in the lacy surf. The tide was rising, and the water surged around him at midcalf, breaking over the woman, creaming over her naked skin, over the seaweed and sand she knelt on as she took his turgid member into her mouth to the root.

Meg licked her lips expectantly in anticipation of such magnificence entering her mouth, responding to the caress of her tongue. She closed her eyes, imagining the feel and smell and taste of him, like sea salt bursting over her palate. This was one of the gifts that had branded her a witch.

When Meg opened her eyes again, her posture clenched. Had he turned? Yes! He seemed to be looking straight at her. It was almost as if he'd read her thoughts, as if he knew she was there all the while and had staged the torrid exhibition for her eyes alone to view. She couldn't see his face—it was steeped in shadow—but yes, there was triumph in his stance and victory in the posturing that took back his sex from the woman's mouth. His eyes were riveting as he dropped to his knees, spread the woman's legs wide to the rushing surf, and entered her in one slow, tantalizing thrust, like a sword being sheathed to the hilt, as the waves surged and crashed and swirled around them.

Still his shadowy gaze relentlessly held Meg's. For all her extraordinary powers of perception, she could not plumb the depths of that look as he took the woman to the rhythm of the waves lapping at them, laving them to the meter of his thrusts, like some giant beast with a thousand tongues. She watched the mystical surf horses trample them, watched the woman beneath him shudder to a rigid climax as the rising tide washed over her—watched the sand ebb away beneath the beautiful creature's buttocks as the sea sucked it back from the shore. All the while he watched her. It was as if she were the woman beneath him, writhing with pleasure in the frothy sea.

Captivated, Meg met the leader's silver-eyed gaze. She could almost feel the undulations as he hammered his thick, hard shaft into the woman, reaching his own climax. Meg groaned in spite of herself as he threw back his head and cried out when he came.

She should move away from the window . . . But why? He couldn't see what she was doing to herself in the deep darkness of the cottage loft . . . Could he? All at once it didn't matter. A hot lava flow of sweet sensation riddled her sex with pinpricks of exquisite agony. It was almost as if *he* were stroking her nipples and palpating the swollen nub at the top of her weeping vulva as she rubbed herself, slowly at first, then fiercely, until the thickening bud hardened like stone. She probed herself deeper. She could almost stretch the barrier skin and slip her finger inside, riding the silk of her wetness—as wet as the surging combers lapping relentlessly at the lovers on the beach. A firestorm of spasmodic contractions took her then, freeing the moan in her throat. It felt as if her bones were melting. Shutting her eyes, she shed the last remnants of modest restraint and leaned into her release.

The voyeuristic element of the experience heightened the orgasm, and it was some time before her hands gripped the windowsill again instead of tender flesh, and her gaze fell upon the strand below once more. But the silvery expanse of rock-bound shoreline edged in seaweed stretching north and south as far as the eye could see was vacant. The strange revelers were gone!

Meg tugged the night shift back over her flushed breasts, though they ached for more stroking, and let the hem of the gown slide down her legs, hiding the palpitating flesh of her sex. Her whole body throbbed like a pulse beat, and she seized the thrumming mound between her thighs savagely through the gown in a vain attempt to quiet its tremors and made a clean sweep through the condensation on the window again. Nothing moved outside but the combers crashing on the strand. But for the echo of the surf sighing into the night, reverberating through her sex to the rhythm of fresh longing, all else was still.

No. She hadn't imagined it. The naked revelers mating on the beach had been real—as real as the seals that frequented the coast. Selkies? Could the shape-shifter legends be true? She'd heard little else since she came to the island.

Meg didn't stop to collect her mantle. Maybe the cool night air would cure the fever in her flesh. Hoisting up the hem of her night smock, she climbed down the loft ladder, tiptoed through the kitchen without making a sound, and stepped out onto the damp drifted sand that always seemed to collect about the doorsill. Nothing moved but the prancing white horses in the surf that drove it landward. Waterhorses? She'd heard that legend, too: innocent looking creatures that lured any who would mount them to a watery death. Real or imaginary, it didn't matter. The people she'd just seen there having sex were real enough, and she meant to prove it.

The hard, damp sand was cold beneath her bare feet as she padded over the shallow dune toward the shoreline. The phantom horses had disappeared from the waves crashing on the strand, as had every trace that anyone had walked that way recently. There wasn't a footprint in sight, and the sealskins Meg had watched them drag to higher ground were nowhere to be seen, either.

Having reached the ragged edge of the surf, Meg turned and looked back at the cottage beyond, paying particular attention to her loft window. Yes, it was close, but there was no way anyone could have seen her watching from her darkened chamber. Then why was she so uneasy? It wasn't the first time she'd touched herself in the dark, and it wouldn't be the last, but it had been the best, and there was something very intimate about it. The man who had aroused her seemed somehow familiar, and yet she knew they'd never met. Still, he had turned toward that window and flaunted himself as if he knew she had been watching, exhibiting his magnificent erection in what appeared to be a sex act staged solely for her benefit. Moist heat rushed at her loins, ripping through her belly and thighs with the memory.

Meg scooped up some of the icy water and bathed the aching flesh between her thighs. She plowed through the lacy surf where the lovers had performed—to the very spot where the mysterious selkie leader had spent his seed—and tried to order the mixed emotions riddling her. Absorbed in thought, she failed to feel the vibration beneath her feet until the horse was nearly upon her. It reared back on its hind legs, forefeet pawing the air, its long tail sweeping the sand, a *real* horse this time, no illusion. Meg cried out as recognition struck. There was a rider on its back. He was naked and aroused. It was *him*, with neither bridle nor reins to control the beast, and nothing but a silvery sealskin underneath him.

He seemed quite comfortable in the altogether, as if it was the most natural thing in the world to sit a horse bareback, naked in the moonlight. She gasped and gasped again. The horse had become quite docile, attempting to nuzzle her with its sleek white nose as it pranced to a standstill. She didn't want to look at the man on its back, but she couldn't help herself. He was a beguiling presence. As mesmerizing as he was from a distance, he was a hundred times more so at close range. Now she could see what the shadows had denied her earlier. His eyes, the color of mercury, were dark and penetrating, and slightly slanted. Somehow, she knew they would be. And his hair, while waving at a length to tease his shoulders in front, was longer in back and worn in a queue, tied with what appeared to be a piece of beach grass. How had she not noticed that before? But how could she have when he'd made such a display of himself face forward? Besides, her focus was hardly upon his hair.

Her attention shifted to the horse. At first she'd thought its mane and tail were black, but upon close inspection, she saw that they were white as snow, so tangled with seaweed they appeared black at first glance. But wait . . . what had she heard about white horses whose mane and tail collected seaweed? A waterhorse! The phantom creature of legend that seduced its victims to mount and be carried off to drown in the sea . . . But that was preposterous. Nevertheless, when its master reached out his hand toward her, she spun on her heels and raced back toward the cottage.

His laughter followed her, throaty and deep. Like an echo from the depths of the sea itself, it crashed over her just as the waves crashed over the shore. The sound pierced through her like a lightning bolt. The prancing waterhorse beneath him whinnied and clamped ferocious-looking teeth into the hem of her night shift, giving a tug that brought her to ground. She landed hard on her bottom, and the selkie laughed again as she cried out. Plucking her up as easily as if she were a broom straw, he settled her in front of him astride.

"You cannot escape me, Megaleen," he crooned in her ear. "You have summoned me, and I have come. You have no idea what it is that you have conjured—what delicious agonies you have unleashed by invoking me." His breath was moist and warm; it smelled of salt and the mysteries of the Otherworldly sea that had spawned him. "Hold on!" he charged, turning the horse toward the strand.

"Hold onto what?" Meg shrilled. "He has no bridle—no reins!"

Again his sultry voice resonating in her ear sent shivers of pleasure thrumming through her body. "Take hold of his mane," he whispered.

His voice alone was a seduction. He was holding her about the middle. Her shift had been hiked up around her waist when he settled her astride, and she could feel the thick bulk of his shaft throbbing against her buttocks, riding up and down along the cleft between the cheeks of her ass. The damp sealskin that stretched over the animal's back like a saddle blanket underneath her felt cool against Meg's naked thighs, but it could not quench the fever in her skin or douse the flames gnawing at the very core of her sex. The friction the waterhorse's motion created forced the wet sealskin fur deeper into her fissure, triggering another orgasm. Her breath caught as it riddled her body with waves of achy heat. She rubbed against the seal pelt, undulating to the rhythm of the horse's gait until every last wave had ebbed away, like ripples in a stream when a pebble breaks the water's surface.

In one motion, the selkie raised the night shift over her head and tossed it into the water. Reaching for it as he tore it away, Meg lost her balance. His strong hands spanning her waist prevented her from falling. Their touch seared her like firebrands, raising the fine hairs at the nape of her neck. The horse had plunged into the surf. It was heading toward the open sea, parting the unreal phantom horses galloping toward shore.

Salt spray pelted her skin, hardening her nipples. Spindrift dressed her hair with tiny spangles. The horse had plunged in past the breakers to the withers. Terrified, Meg screamed as the animal broke through the waves and sank to its muscular neck.

"Hold on!" he commanded.

"I cannot," Meg cried. "His mane . . . It is slippery with seaweed."

All at once, he lifted her into the air and set her down facing him, gathering her against his hard muscular body, his engorged sex heaving against her belly. How strong he was! "Then hold onto me," he said.

"W-who are you?" Meg murmured.

"I am called Simeon . . . amongst other things," he replied. "But that hardly signifies . . ." Heat crackled in his voice. Something pinged in her sex at the sound of it.

He swooped down, looming over her. For a split second, she thought he was going to kiss her. She could almost taste the salt on his lips, in his mouth, on the tongue she glimpsed parting his teeth . . . But no. Fisting his hand in the back of her waist-length sun-painted hair, he blew his steamy breath into her nostrils as the horse's head disappeared beneath the surface of the sea.

Meg's last conscious thought before sinking beneath the waves in the selkie's arms was that she was being seduced to her death; another orgasm testified to that. Weren't you supposed to come before you die? Wasn't it supposed to be an orgasm like no other, like the orgasm riddling her now?

The scent that ghosted through her nostrils as she drew her last breath of air was his scent, salty, laced with the mysteries of the deep, threaded through with the sweet musky aroma of ambergris.